DAY DRINKERS

KITTY TURNER

DAILY HOUSE

Copyright © 2025 by Daily House, LLC

All rights reserved.

No part of this book may be reproduced in any form or by any electronic or mechanical means, including information storage and retrieval systems, without written permission from the publisher, except for the use of brief quotations in a book review.

Day Drinkers

Publisher: Daily House

Author: Kitty Turner

First Edition

Copyrighted Material

Library of Congress Control Number 2025918841

ISBN 978-1-7336687-8-1 (Paperback)

ISBN 978-1-7336687-7-4 (Ebook)

This is a work of fiction. All of the characters, organizations, and events portrayed in this novel are either products of the author's imagination or are used fictitiously.

In loving memory of my sister, Elizabeth Walther, and with deep gratitude to her beloved husband, John Noh, for his enduring support.

PART I

1

THE COMMITTEE

Boon held court under a blue FEMA tarp stretched taut by furring strips screwed between two ramshackle sheds. The equatorial sun shone through the plastic roof and flooded the poor excuse for a chandlery with the color of tropical seawater. Greybeards and the occasional sea-hardened woman sat in a circle of mismatched chairs, cast off from luxury vacation rentals and salvaged from the island dump. Boon and only Boon sat behind the workbench, scrutinizing the crowd from his behemoth leather office chair, creaking and patched with a crisscross of duct tape. His orange Croc-covered feet were beacons propped up amid a scatter of carburetors, boat zincs, and wayward projects abandoned in the shop for a day, a week, or forever.

At Boon Dock Marine, the coffee was free, but Heinekens from the jumbo Igloo cooler required a deposit in the 'honor' jar, and Boon ensured all remained honorable like a hawk. The industrious ones, those who still had their knees and backs intact, worked for Boon—a bottom paint job here or an outboard repair there. These youths, beers beaded with condensation in hand, waited next to Boon's open-air desk for assignments, which came infrequently and were executed haphazardly. Most of the harbor's liveaboards, those either passing through or permanently moored in Sargasso Cove, spent their lazy days earning a few dollars from pickup labor and tending the low flame of a perfect buzz.

Staticky Cowboi Rivers songs romanticizing American life played from the worn speakers of a decades-old radio set sitting on a shelf above Boon's head. The multiple Grammy-winning country singer got plenty of airplay and cred around Boon Dock Marine, perhaps more than his due, because of his status as an honorary islander and Boon's friend. Cowboi owned property all over St. Columba, most notably an exclusive resort on a mysterious private island that was swimming distance from the west side.

"I heard Rivers' wife divorced him because he's into jailbait," said one of the sailors.

This conjecture about Cowboi's illicit love life was the first thing Gemma heard as she ducked under the tarp to fill her mug from the crusty Mr. Coffee, its hotplate caked with the sediment of a hundred overflowed pots. Her gold name tag glinted from the lapel of a navy blue blazer, accessorized with yellow flip-flops and a matching vinyl roll-top dry bag. The uniform gave away that she was among the legitimately employed, a rarity around Sargasso Cove.

"Biggest mistake of Cowboi's life—marrying that Hollywood bitch. She's got a mouth as big as a barn door. That's where those rumors come from, and I won't listen to them around here," Boon said with irritation.

As Gemma's eyes adjusted to the blue-tinted shade, she greeted the crowd with the customary "mornin'." Her gaze rested on Boon, who nodded in her direction. The color of Boon's hair could be described as dull blond, if someone were forced to describe its nondescript, salt-stiffened hue. It hung in long clumps around a face that years of island living had etched with a nautical map of broken capillaries and wrinkles, framing blue eyes that could change as fast as the skies from clear to stormy. Boon was substantial in the way that someone becomes when they've thoroughly claimed a space, his faded t-shirt bearing the silhouette of some long-forgotten regatta stretching across a torso that had rounded with age.

Gemma knew from experience that Boon shut down any loose talk about his hero before it could gain momentum. On this island, Cowboi was more legend than man, and legends bred stories. Out of courtesy, Gemma shifted the subject to something of more importance than the alleged sexual activities of a music star.

"Any news on Vaughn?" she asked.

Boon flashed her an indecipherable look.

Some days, especially after post-work drinks, Gemma gossiped and joked with the best of the Heineken crew.

But today, she stood somber, speculating about the disappearance of one of their own. Vaughn, a Boon Dock regular, hadn't shown up at the tarp-covered hangout for over a week. Vaughn had been known to sleep off a particularly nasty hangover for a few days, but he'd never been missing for this long without a word.

"I saw him getting on the airport ferry. It was Vaughn, I swear," Crab said.

If you could have a first mate on land, then Crab would be Boon's. Crab reminded Gemma of a Slim Jim wearing a Greek fisherman's cap. His desiccated arms and legs were permanently tanned and salted. In the leather of his face, pale eyes burned with the fever of a consistent .08 blood alcohol level. Crab, a friendly soul, was always happy and ready to motor out to the lobster traps to feed the crowd from a big steel pot he tended over a propane barbecue. He had the jovial nature and skills of a man born to boats.

"Cheese and bread, Crab, you must have spent your day in a bottle again if you saw Vaughn. That drunk is drowned and rolling at the bottom of the bay, as sure as I am sitting here in front of you." Boon pursed his lips and scowled at his friend with disdain.

Crab and Boon were always at each other's throats in a brotherly way. To Boon's dismay, Crab plucked a pepperoni off a piece of day-old pizza, greasy and gathering flies, and flung it at Boon's head like a frisbee. Slightly off target, it pucked off the back of Boon's hand and landed in the bottom-paint-poisoned dust beyond the glowing blue light of the shack. A one-eyed Siamese streaked out from between the dirt foundation and the plank floor to snap up the meaty prize.

Gemma would have to wait until after work to find out if Crab had truly discovered anything new about Vaughn's disappearance. Her commute across the island took thirty minutes on a good day, and today was not so good. A hangover of the alone-drinking variety parched her palate and sucked the energy from her legs.

BLUE and white flashed at the crest of the hill on the far side of the bay. It was the bus, and that meant Gemma had ten minutes to make it to the crossroads before she missed her ride to town. She downed the rest of her coffee, threw the straps of her dry bag over her shoulders, and ran. Her pack thumped heavily in the middle of her back as she crossed a stretch of potholed asphalt that passed for Boon Dock's parking lot. Up a dirt path, she cut across the brown, neglected Bermuda grass of the playing field behind the abandoned school and made it to the bus stop with no time to spare. With a flick of her wrist, she tied her long, thin dreadlocks into a bun with a cheap nautical-print scarf and mounted the steps. Air conditioning wrapped her in a cold shroud as she climbed through the inward-folding doors and slipped into the vacancy of a plastic seat near a window.

She wiped away the slick of sweat from her forehead and upper lip. Shivers rippled through her body. Her cashew breasts overflowed from the cups of her bra, visible through the wet fabric, but she knew her blouse would dry before the end of the line on the other side of the island. It always did.

Gemma often caught people studying her, trying to place her, wondering if she was one of them or just someone passing through. Her dark amber skin made her an eternal question mark to locals who cataloged everyone by family ties. She pulled a tube of berry-colored gloss from her bag, dabbed a dollop on her lips, and brushed the rest across her high cheekbones, enhancing a natural glow that turned heads whether she wanted attention or not. With a practiced indifference to the stares, she crossed her long legs and settled in for the ride. The island's complexion was as mixed as her own, yet there was always a silent question of belonging, of who was 'authentic.'

At twenty-six, she'd grown accustomed to the scrutiny, both here and where she grew up in Vermont, her mother being mostly Italian and her father hailing from a large family that had been brought to St. Columba as slaves in the 17th century. Her history intertwined with the island's own complicated past, but she spent her formative years surrounded by ice skating ponds and friendly hippies—a world far removed from the heat and the vibrant pulse of the islands.

As the bus followed the mangrove-covered coast around Sargasso Cove, Gemma gazed at the floating constellations of boats on the other side of the pane. She tapped the glass. Her heart gave a loving flutter when she spotted *Luna*, the small, battered sailboat on which she lived, bobbing gently on the waves. It was the only place that truly felt like hers—a tiny space she held in this world of contradictions. Her touch against the window cleared a button of condensation as she traced a circle with her finger around the scruffy little boat. *Luna* turned on its chain to face her like a happy puppy watching her leave—a trick of the wind.

Potholed streets relaxed into snaking curves. The ride through the outskirts of Sargasso was familiar now, the buildings tired and sagging. This was the island she was trying to reclaim as her own, a place where her father's blood ran deep, but her mother's foreignness made her a stranger. Vines whip-cracked against the side of the bus. Clusters of coconut palms sprouted in tangled ravines, their heads bowed in the slow conversation of plants. Everything here had its own story to tell.

2

YACHT HEAVEN

Gemma's bus lurched to a stop at the locals' market. Past the terminal, proud aunties in long cotton calico skirts and tall head wraps avoided confused-looking tourists who anxiously studied the maps issued by their cruise lines or hotels. These island visitors hung back with stiff postures and whispered to each other in various languages. Occasionally, a brave soul stepped out of the security of their tour group to purchase a mango or a bag of limes with the pride of a pioneer.

Skunky, pungent marijuana smoke blended with the mouthwatering aroma of grilling fish and fried sweet plantains. A weave of staccato speech and good-natured haggling mixed with snatches of reggae and soca emanating from a dozen radios. On blankets sat neat rows and mounds of nuts, spices, furry roots, and fruity-smelling green and orange orbs of all shapes and sizes. There were herbs, yams, wild celery, and tomatoes to buy.

Outside the black iron fences that enclosed Yacht Heaven Mall, folks napped on benches or sat under EZ-UPs erected to protect their market wares from the tropical sun. But inside the gates, the patchwork of chaos gave way to a neat grid of walking paths lined by fragrant blooms cascading from flower boxes and hanging baskets. Shops yawned in prefabricated newness. Bistros alternated with perfumeries, high-end specialty food stores, and souvenir shops. Under the shade of a monolithic cruise ship terminal, a stoned-eyed man leaning against a sign reading "The Luxury of Ownership" waved at Gemma.

"Smells like you had a good night, Cruz," Gemma said.

Gemma was a kettle calling a pot black, but Cruz's hangovers were an easy target and the subject of routine jokes. Her own habits didn't escape her awareness, but there was a camaraderie in acknowledging each other's vices. She knew Cruz closed his days at the Last Resort Bar because she joined him there at least three nights a week.

At thirty-five, Cruz possessed movie-star good looks—deep mahogany skin, close-cropped hair, and a smile that flashed like sun on the water. His broad shoulders and athletic build suggested discipline beneath the casual island persona he projected. While others deteriorated in this climate of perpetual leisure, Cruz maintained an alertness that seemed at odds with his rolling laughter and generous nature. He moved with a fluidity that could be mistaken for island rhythm but occasionally revealed itself as something more purposeful.

Gemma didn't stop to talk with Cruz more than she needed—her boss was a stickler for punctuality. Instead, after their customary greeting, she passed him and stepped into the stylish fractional real estate showroom. On the bench just inside the door, she kicked off her flip-flops, extracted a pair of low walking heels from her bag, and slipped them on. Chilled wines in buckets and pitchers of iced tea rested on the sideboard, along with neat stacks of glossy brochures. Someone, probably Cruz, had already set out the plates of cheese and fruit that were designed to lure tourists in from the rippling heat outside.

The contrast between the island's raw energy and this ruthlessly controlled space was always jarring. Here, everything was curated to sell a dream that had little to do with the real St. Columba. Large framed photos of the resort's glistening swimming pools and beachside restaurants hung elegantly above the buffet, each image perfectly staged to capture the illusion of paradise. Palm trees crowded every frame, while models posing as guests lounged with cocktails in hand, smiling against a backdrop of distant turquoise water and clear blue skies.

The photos created an illusion of effortless tranquility, masking the island's true complexity—a fantasy that timeshare buyers readily embraced, unaware of the lives and histories that lay beyond the resort walls. A world within a world, polished and detached, where reality was rewritten into picture-perfect scenes.

Sawyer, a short, piggy man with a tussle of salt-and-pepper hair, looked up from his paperwork spread across a tall table at the back of the room. Perched on a barstool, his feet dangled comically inches from the ground. Gemma grabbed the stool next to him as he launched into his daily briefing.

"Good, you're here. We got a new promo today. Corporate wants to squeeze every dollar out of the last busy month of the year. You get $200 extra for each qualified purchase for the next thirty days. Fire, right?"

Gemma rolled her eyes at her middle-aged white boss's insistence on using the latest slang. Money was the motivator, but the grind of selling a sham to gullible tourists was wearing on her. Gemma studied the new prospect sheet that Sawyer slid to her across the table. He pointed to a block of boilerplate sentences and rested his finger on a checkbox.

"This one's important. A combined annual salary of $250,000. Your singles probably won't qualify, so shoot for couples. Understand?"

Almost every tourist couple that stepped onto the Yacht Heaven mall met this salary requirement, and almost everyone who lived in the flats didn't. The class divisions on St. Columba ran in swaths as clean-cut as stripes on a flag. Gemma felt that divide more acutely than most, torn between a stateside upbringing and the inescapable history of her father's people.

Her mixed heritage placed her in a perpetual state of limbo—too American for the locals, too island for the mainlanders. When she walked through the market and the mall, she could feel the weight of both worlds pressing down on her shoulders. Her salon-groomed dreadlocks framing her pretty face sometimes felt like a costume when she spoke to customers with the practiced cadence of her New England upbringing. It was just one of many masks she wore—slipping into a lazy country twang when hanging out with the Heineken crew at Boon Dock Marine, then awkwardly attempting island patois when visiting her grandmother at Mariposa's End.

"You with me?" Sawyer asked, interrupting her reverie.

"Sorry, boss. Got it. What else?" Gemma asked, snapping back into the chilled reality of the showroom.

"They must be on a cruise," Sawyer said.

"Shit, Sawyer, seriously? Cruisers are impossible! They're all geriatric and only interested in restaurant coupons and free island tours. Plus, they're lonely and talk my ears off for hours."

Sawyer barreled on. "I guess that's why the head office dreamed up this genius promo—right? We're parked at a damn cruise ship dock, and our numbers are crap in that demo. July 31st is the last cruise to dock here until November 25th. We've got one month before Yacht Heaven is a ghost town, so here's the deal: warm them up before they even sniff the presentation room. That's the only way you're getting a bonus. You know the drill. The old-timers always stop—use it. Ask about their grandkids. Better yet, lay it on thick with your island-girl-sailor fairytale bullshit. Adventure, high seas, all that crap. Those dust farts eat you up like tapioca pudding. Your close rate's solid because you're exotic. So lean into it, sweetheart."

Exotic. The word grated on her every time. It was what the tourists saw when they looked at her, their imaginations stirred by her good looks and her sailing lifestyle. But to her, it was just another layer of the mask she wore every day, catering to the fantasies of people who didn't know what it was like to be caught between two worlds. Regardless, her real advantage was simple—she was a damn good salesperson.

"Cruz!" Sawyer bellowed out the door before Gemma could protest further.

Cruz's face appeared in the shadow of the door. "Yes, boss."

"You and Gemma, stop wasting my air conditioning. I see you lurking in the slipstream. According to the schedule, a Carnival Cruise is docking as we speak. It's a big one, so go hustle your asses!"

Gemma sighed inwardly. The grind was relentless, but what choice did she have? She wasn't part of the wealthy crowd that owned the tourist industry. Her father's family had hundreds of years of history here and thousands of acres of land, but how they used this wealth, she didn't understand. They seemed to sit on massive swaths of prime beachfront real estate without using it for much more than grazing goats and sheep.

She followed Cruz into the humid morning, the sharp tang of his rum-laced breath trailing in the breeze. Ahead of them, a towering ship rose like a rainbow-colored colossus, ten stories of party decks stacked high above the turquoise water. The enormous vessel loomed over the docks, as if a whole city block had casually pulled up to the curb of St. Columba.

Wide-eyed and buzzing with excitement, the disembarking passengers gazed around as if this were a theme park meticulously crafted for their entertainment. Cameras clicked as they captured images, and the soft murmur of awe mixed with the shouts of guides and vendors jostling for attention. Gemma could almost feel the disconnect, the surreal sense that they were watching a spectacle rather than stepping into a real place with its own heartbeat. She glanced at Cruz, who seemed unbothered, accustomed to this invasion that came in as surely as the tides.

"Showtime," said Cruz, his rallying cry. Cruz was always on the hunt for the wealthiest tourists, his sharp eye trained to spot logos. He ranked his marks by what they wore—Coach, Rolex, Louis Vuitton, and Gucci; knock-offs were just as good as the real deal. Fake or not, designer labels showed an obsession with status—and status was the key ingredient for Cruz's timeshare pitch. To succeed, the swarming salespeople needed to deconstruct this stream of vacationers and sun-seekers into their triggers and insecurities within seconds. Timeshare agents worked in packs, separating out the weak for the kill. Hesitate, and the rival companies would pick the opportunities off on all sides.

"The couple with the Nikon," Cruz shouted, "I'm going to crush it today."

Gemma pointed excitedly. "That woman has a dog in her purse. Dibs!"

At lunch, Gemma sorted through her growing stack of lead sheets. Her first capture, the semi-elderly woman with the dog—pulled taut and sculpted with fillers and surgery—oozed vanity, a flaw that Gemma recognized and pried wide open. A spa day and the seaside buffet with a jumbie show had been incentive enough for the woman to drag her reluctant boy toy—at least fifteen years her junior, with bleached teeth and a permanent tan—to a ninety-minute sales presentation at the resort. Gemma could picture it vividly: the boyfriend, bored out of his mind within the first ten minutes, would inevitably duck out to the poolside bar, leaving his sugar mama alone to face the barrage of PowerPoints and contracts designed to wear down resistance.

Normally, wealthy women like this were pure gold in the timeshare game, reliable for their impulsive spending and desire to impress and placate. But Cruz had been right in his assessment; this particular sale, promising as it seemed, didn't meet the specific criteria for today's special bonus. This prospect had flown in on the morning island hopper from Grenada, not sailed in on the Carnival megaship.

By late afternoon, the crowds from the cruise ship began to thin. Gemma leaned against a column, nibbling a pâté she had purchased from a food cart outside the gates. The fried dough was filled with a rich and savory mixture of spiced chicken seasoned with green onions, thyme, and the subtle heat of Scotch bonnet. As she took a bite, the pastry's crisp outer layer crumbled, giving way to a tender, buttery softness, the filling bursting with warmth and the earthy taste of Caribbean spices. It was a comfort that grounded her, however briefly. The inexpensive snack reminded her of childhood and the stuffed mini-calzones her mother would bring home from the restaurant where she worked.

Gemma's phone buzzed with a text from Sawyer: "Numbers are down. I can see you limin' in the shade. Get your ass back to work."

The unrelenting sun had moved well past its zenith, granting some relief from the griddle-hot pavement. Gemma sighed, stuffed the phone into her blazer pocket, and readied herself to step back into the fray, but a commotion from the market beyond the gates caught her attention. She turned to see a cluster of locals from Sargasso gesturing wildly, their animated shouts rising above the usual din. Among them, she spotted Crab, his fisherman's cap bobbing as he seemed to organize the group.

What was he doing on this side of the island? Intrigued, she walked along the waterfront and out the gate to the public market stalls to talk to him. Fishmongers called out, announcing fresh-off-the-boat catches. Red snapper, tuna, and dorado glistened on ice, available for anyone to buy for a small fortune. The much cheaper fish lay hidden under the tables—old wife and barracuda—eaten by locals and only available by request. This was her father's world, but it was alien to her in so many ways. Only now was she learning the language of these foods. Even the simplest things, like buying ingredients for dinner, made her feel like a visitor in her own skin.

When she reached the group from Sargasso Cove, Crab spotted Gemma and immediately waved her over.

"We got a call from the Port Authority 'bout an hour ago," Crab explained, his cap tilted askew in his agitation. "They found Vaughn's dinghy just bobbin' around, completely empty, adrift near the ferry dock!" he said. "We all piled into whatever vehicles we could find and caravanned over from the Cove. Now we're organizing a search party. We could use all the hands we can get."

Several other Sargasso regulars nodded grimly behind him. Gemma's heart quickened. Vaughn's disappearance had been the troubling undercurrent of her day, lurking beneath her sales pitches. Now it seemed the mystery was deepening into something potentially darker. She thought of his ramshackle boat, sitting neglected at its mooring, and of his recent erratic behavior that everyone at Boon Dock had noticed but few had mentioned.

"I'll help," Gemma said without hesitation, already unbuttoning her blazer. The fatigue that had been weighing on her limbs all afternoon melted away, replaced by a surge of adrenaline and purpose. "Just tell me where you need me to go."

Somewhere on the bay, she hoped they'd find Vaughn safe. But a nagging dread gnawed at her, whispering that it might be too late.

Gemma called Sawyer. "They spotted Vaughn's dinghy. I'm taking off early to help with the search," she said, her words quick and precise. There was a brief pause on the line, and then Sawyer responded with a low sigh of resignation.

"All right, but stop by the office on your way out. Your pay's ready," he replied.

Back at the timeshare office, Sawyer handed her an envelope with little more than a nod. She nodded back, tucking the cash into her bag. She slipped back into the mall, her mind already focused on finding Vaughn, or what was left of him.

3

SAHARA DUST

Searching the sea for Vaughn was elusive in the shifting light. Flashes revealed facets of jade green on the crests of wavelets. Silver in motion, pale purple in patches, the ocean's heart remained a mystery. Red dust from the Sahara tinged the sky, painting the sunset in apocalyptic fire. As the season waned, the tourists who crowded this island in winter would vanish. The heat of the African summer baking an immense desert four thousand miles away sent billions of tiny particles soaring into the atmosphere and migrating across the Atlantic to the Caribbean—an effect both heralding and fueling the oncoming hurricanes.

The hypnotic beat of the ocean, combined with the whispers of Africa, lulled Gemma into a trance. The rhythmic pulse stirred memories of childhood episodes that had always terrified her mother. As a child, these twilight states would overcome her whenever she encountered rhythmic sounds or flashing lights. Only recently had Gemma learned that these fits were more than medical.

At six years old, just months after her mother had uprooted them from the Caribbean and brought her to Vermont following her father's tragic death, Gemma experienced a seizure on the park's merry-go-round. The memory stayed vivid: the dizzying whirl of bright autumn leaves and a shadowy figure—her father, arms reaching toward her, mouthing something urgent. The next thing she knew, she was flat on the ground, a ring of anxious faces hovering above. When she told Mom that Dad had commanded her to return home and claim her birthright and protect the family's land, the reaction was swift. From that day on, her mother sharply resisted any mention of Gemma's island family and avoided activities that might trigger these spells, though she couldn't prevent them entirely.

Even as a toddler back on St. Columba, Gemma's small body would go rigid, her eyes rolling back. At her mother's insistence, island doctors ran expensive tests that drained her parents' meager savings but found nothing physically wrong with Gemma's developing brain. No epilepsy, no tumor, nothing to explain the way she sometimes froze, staring into empty corners as if watching invisible visitors. Her father quietly understood what these episodes meant, but her mother refused to accept that such things were normal in the August family, especially among the women.

What her mother refused to acknowledge was that

these episodes were doorways—moments when the veil between worlds thinned, allowing glimpses of what Gemma's grandmother would later explain as messages from ancestors and spirits tied to their family's past, present, and future. The seizures weren't the cause of her visions; they were the physical manifestation of a gift Gemma's body hadn't yet learned to contain.

When Gemma turned back to the boardwalk that lined the seaside edge of the mall, the sun had already dropped an hour lower in the sky. She scanned the beachfront for Crab and the rest of the search party, but the sand lay still and gray under the failing light. She squinted into the shadows toward the dinghy rental shack a hundred yards away. There, she saw flickers of movement. Was the dusk playing tricks on her eyes? She gasped. The shadowy but unmistakable figure of Vaughn sat on the bench where workers gathered during the day. Despite the distance, his gaze seemed to burn into her. His back hunched, and his arms hung limply at his sides. Was he hurt?

"Vaughn!" she called.

Her flip-flops slapped against the uneven planks of the old boardwalk steps and onto the damp, packed sand. Gemma kept her eyes glued to Vaughn's shape at the end of the line of empty shops. In the closing distance, his form began to lose focus. The plastic thong of her shoe broke free from the rubber sole. She stumbled, causing her to break her line of sight. When she recovered, Vaughn was gone. She fixed her flip-flop by popping the tab back through the sole and walked the remaining

Sahara Dust | 25

length of the beach to search the palm grove around the dinghy rental shack. Nothing. Not even footprints.

She pulled out her phone and called Crab.

"What happened to you, darling?" Crab asked. "There was no sign of Vaughn, and then you went missing. The search team called it a night, and I assumed you had jumped on the bus back to Sargasso, but no one saw you come through Boon's or Paradise Burger."

"I'm still in Taino Bay. I thought I saw Vaughn by the dinghy shack," she began, but she reconsidered describing the apparition. She had learned that her visions frightened most people. Shaken, Gemma continued, "But it was nothing. A trick of the light." Crab would think she was crazy if she told him she saw ghosts.

Gemma hung up and ducked into The Last Resort for a drink to steady her nerves before the bus ride home. The dive bar had been around for decades and was popular with both tourists and locals. The weathered wooden sign above the entrance swayed over the propped-open door, its paint chipped but still legible after years of exposure to sun and salt. Inside, ceiling fans spun lazily overhead, barely disturbing the humid, rum-scented air that clung to everything like an invisible film.

The Resort's Oceania-inspired decor had little to do with the Caribbean. Bamboo-framed mirrors reflected the glow of puffer fish lamps, while plastic hula dancers and carved tiki gods watched over patrons from dusty shelves. Fishing nets draped from the ceiling were adorned with glass floats and plastic seashells that had never seen the ocean. This kitsch design, inspired by Hollywood movies rather than any authentic culture, could be found in vacation bars worldwide, from Cancun to Phuket. The real St. Columba was something else entirely: the smell of diesel, the sound of dominoes slapping on makeshift tables, the taste of her grandmother's goat curry.

Gemma found Cruz perched on his usual stool and slid onto the one beside him to compare sales numbers. It was their ritual—this post-shift decompression—and most of Gemma's leads this week had closed, leaving her with a hefty payday. She looked forward to boasting about it.

Cruz had already ordered his rum on the rocks, the ice barely melted, while the bartender automatically slid Gemma's Dark and Stormy across the worn bar top without her having to ask. The familiarity of it all—the sticky menus, the overhead fans ticking in the gloom, and the way Cruz cupped his hand around the cool of his glass—had become as much a part of her island routine as checking *Luna*'s mooring lines each morning.

Cruz took a long sip, giving Gemma a sidelong glance. "So, what's your secret? You've been killing it this week."

Gemma grinned, pulling her backpack closer to the bar. "People can't resist the picture I paint of an escape from their affluenza."

He laughed. "Maybe I should start pitching the 'adventure lifestyle' angle myself."

"It works. Plus, I need to save up. Not starving, like I did last summer, is a great motivator," Gemma replied, patting her pack. "But I'd better call it a night."

"Smart move," Cruz said, raising his glass. "No point in

sticking around too long. This place is full of desperation with ears."

Gemma smiled, grabbing her things. "Exactly. Catch you tomorrow."

On the ride home, Gemma rested her head against the bus window. The air-conditioned chilled glass pressed against her temple. Snatches of low conversations drifted from the other seats, two older women murmuring to each other in voices too soft to follow. Outside, dense jungle flanked the narrow, climbing road. The engine hummed beneath her feet. Palm fronds waved in the streetlights, and shadowy boughs brushed the side of the bus with a soft whisper.

As the bus crested the summit of Mount Calabash, tree-shrouded mountain villas slowly gave way to a sprawl of cement houses clustered along the hillside. The contrast was stark—luxury on one side of the island, while below, the homes wore their perpetual incompleteness like badges of resilience. Rebar jutted from half-built second stories in crowns of thorns, rusted and reaching toward the sky. Boon had explained to Gemma that in the Caribbean, it was common to leave houses unfinished for years; property taxes didn't have to be paid until construction was declared complete. So local families left skeletal frames and open-ended plans, building only as money or necessity allowed.

Down the path from the crossroads, Gemma made her usual detour to Paradise Burger for a roadie before heading toward the shipping container that housed Boon Dock Marine's office. Glowing white in the moonlight, the twenty-six-foot shoebox was featureless except for the air conditioning unit, protruding like a wart from one end. Next to the converted shipping container, an ancient air compressor let out a loud hiss like an angry tomcat. Just looking at the racks of tanks Boon rented to unsuspecting tourists gave her the chills. Gemma knew they were a decade out of date and probably had never been inspected.

Boon might still be inside, she thought.

She knocked on the closed double-wide cargo doors with one hand while she held her half-finished Bushwacker in the other—a sort of milkshake made from three kinds of alcohol, with a shot of whipped cream on top. Treacle vapors rose from her nightcap. The bolt slid open with a scrape and a clunk, and Boon peered out.

What passed for marina services in Sargasso Cove—mooring fees, storage lockers, and outdoor showers—only cost $500 a month, but Gemma, like many others, still struggled to pay expenses during the empty months of summer.

"Gemma, hey. It's late. I'm heading home soon. Can whatever it is wait until tomorrow?"

"Can I pay my mooring fees through November? I don't want to hold onto all this money."

"Really? You got four months in advance?" Boon asked.

Boon pushed open the door and stepped aside, motioning for Gemma to come in. She followed him to an old steel desk stacked with yellowing papers at the back of the rust- and oil-smelling room.

A tall stack of cash could always motivate Boon.

Sahara Dust | 29

4
LOW SEASON

The familiar scent of corroded metal inside Boon's converted shipping container reminded Gemma that the routine of securing her boat for hurricane season was fast approaching. Most of the other sailors dry-docked their vessels or navigated to safer hurricane holes in July or August. She was one of the rare liveaboards who stayed on her boat year-round.

From November to July, she thrived, like most in the resort community. During this time, St. Columba's population swelled fourfold, with tourists eager to part with their dollars. Hotels overflowed, and restaurant lines stretched down the street. But from July to November, most of the transient workforce would scatter to distant shores—Thailand and Croatia for affordable living, or India and Indonesia in search of community. The popular destinations changed year by year.

Gemma, however, rode out the squalls aboard *Luna*, listening to the persistent creak and groan of her vessel's hull as it strained against its mooring lines during tropical storms. She had developed a sixth sense for approaching downpours, often waking throughout the night to bail out her trailing dinghy before the torrential rains sank it under the waves from the sheer weight of the water that filled it.

Standing in the breeze of the fan on Boon's deck, Gemma reflected on the winding path that had brought her back to St. Columba. Unlike most of the people who lived in the anchorage, Gemma had been born on St. Columba, although the vibrant tapestry of her early childhood remained frustratingly out of reach. She could barely recall the sensation of sailing Sunfish, the tiny racing boats, with her mom or the rough texture of mango tree bark beneath her small palms and soles as she climbed with neighborhood children. The faces of her homeschool group—a collection of local kids whose parents preferred self-led education to the Western-influenced schools—were merely shadowy outlines in her mind.

Trauma had erased these precious early memories, leaving only faint impressions where vivid recollections should have been. An American tourist, speeding down the narrow island roads with a blood alcohol level three times the legal limit, struck her father's motorbike, killing him instantly. Overwhelmed by grief and unable to confront the constant reminder of her husband's memory around every corner of the island, her mother hastily packed their belongings and fled back to Vermont, taking six-year-old Gemma away from everything and everyone she had known.

Gemma's first solid memory was of the accident scene at the crossroads. While the gawking crowd saw only her father's body lying on the hard-packed dirt, she witnessed something more—his shimmering double, confused and desperate to reach her. When she grasped for his translucent hand, her fingers closed on empty air. No warmth. No substance. Just the memory of an insubstantial touch that would haunt her for years.

Against her mother's fierce objections, Gemma returned to St. Columba after finishing two years of community college. She was determined to reconnect with her paternal family and uncover the father she'd barely known.

Her search led her to Mariposa's End, a remote settlement where her grandmother Mari lived alongside many other relatives. Here, generations of Gemma's ancestors had once sought refuge from colonial oppression, weaving together a cultural fabric marked by resilience and quiet defiance.

Mari revealed what Gemma had long suspected— their bloodline carried an ancient connection to the healing arts and prophecy. As the matriarch shared stories of their heritage, Gemma began to understand that she might inherit far more than just history. She might possess Mari's gifts of both leadership and magic.

At The End, as locals called it, Gemma hoped to unravel the complex cultural tapestry that had been denied to her—a heritage woven with the threads of unbreakable community bonds. The elders spoke in a melodic patois that still sounded foreign to her ears, their stories punctuated by knowing glances and meaningful silences.

The breeze from the oscillating fan in Boon's office brought Gemma back to the present moment. She took out a wad of cash from her pack and laid out twenty hundred-dollar bills on the only square of steel that wasn't covered in ragged sailing magazines and purchase orders. Boon counted the money under a caged trouble light hanging from its orange cord. He always counted, even though Gemma had never shorted him once. Boon wasn't a trusting man.

"Alright! Paid through November. Hey, I know it got tough for you last year, food-wise and all that. Tell you what. With Vaughn missing, some work has opened up. If you're interested. It pays well."

"Oh, really! Sure, I'm interested!" Gemma said.

The mention of work reminded her of just how desperate things had gotten last summer. Pitching timeshares to the slow trickle of budget travelers in low season had been dismal. She had been lucky to earn fifty dollars a week. Cruz owned a rental condo and made enough year-round from the income to live decently well without any sales, but Gemma did not have that same luxury. The only option for seasonal workers like her was to take shifts in the telemarketing boiler room. However, during the off-season, the commission-only phone job paid close to nothing, and that was being generous.

Boon's job offer might save Gemma from the indignity of snatching unfinished meals from restaurant tables before the busboys cleared them away. Servers understood, perhaps better than anyone, that this was a feast-or-famine economy. They did not judge, and it rarely came to stealing food, but Gemma had to be honest. She had been hungry enough to dumpster dive last year, and she would likely find herself in that position again this year—unless—

"What's the work?"

"Well, it's not strictly legal, but it's not illegal either," Boon said.

Gemma's heart sank. Of course, Boon's offer was shady. She had no reason to expect more.

"I'm not going to mule drugs up my butt, Boon. No way."

Boon laughed at the mental image Gemma had conjured but continued without uttering the rude comment that was clearly on the tip of his tongue.

"It's nothing like that. It's actually kind of glamorous. You'll be a sort of tour guide for Cowboi's private island. Here's the gig. You take my Sea Ray over to the airport and pick up—"

"Pick up! Boon! This is drugs. I knew it."

"Chill out. Listen. It's not drugs. If you're gonna keep interrupting me, I'll offer the job to someone else."

A blush of embarrassment warmed Gemma's cheeks. Showing weakness and emotion was ruinous in her tough-talking, hard-drinking sailor community. Being a woman and island-born made things even more difficult.

Low Season | 35

She needed to be twice as funny, tough, and irreverent to simply fit in. Some days, she wondered why she tried so hard to be included.

Cheap rent was one reason she found Boon Dock appealing, and the sailing crowd was nearly identical to the lake resort community that had formed around the Vermont mountain inn where her mother worked as a waitress. But the chief attraction of living on a sailboat, at least in theory, was Gemma's freedom to weigh anchor whenever she wanted. However, in practice, she hadn't ventured past the neighboring islands in her little sloop, and she rarely had time for even that.

"Okay. Sorry. I'll listen. What's the job?" Gemma said. She forced calm into her voice.

"So, you're going to do pickups. Three or four girls will fly in at a time. They are actresses and fashion models. You know, young, dumb— Anyway, just check them in through customs. Get their luggage at the baggage claim. Then you get the girls to Easter Cay. Just drop them at the dock, and Cowboi's staff will take it from there. It's easy. See? It's not drugs, and it's not illegal."

"Vaughn did this work for you before?" Gemma asked, suspicious of the whole deal.

"Yeah, but he's missing, so Cowboi asked me to recruit someone new."

Gemma felt uneasy. True, picking up girls and dropping them off wasn't strictly against the law. A taxi driver did the same. But she had heard rumors. Namely, Easter Cay was Cowboi Rivers' private brothel for the rich and famous, and the girls he kept there were underage and basically captives. Before tonight, she had avoided speculation or even having an opinion about what was happening on the mysterious island that twinkled off the west end. None of her business.

Gemma hadn't accepted Boon's offer, but she hadn't turned it down either. Instead, she asked Boon if she could sleep on it. She walked to the dinghy dock with the last of her Bushwacker melting in the bottom of her red Solo cup and swung her body into her inflatable boat. She woke the engine with one smooth, long pull of the starter cord, cast off the painter line, goosed the throttle, and wove her way through the anchorage to her floating home.

While climbing down the companionway into the cabin of *Luna*, she flipped on the lights from the main panel. The sun's energy had been collecting during the day. Now, its captured radiance lit the brightwork of polished nooks and shelves inside her home. Maritime bronze accents and quirky carvings glinted in the incandescence. Across from the galley was her navigation station—a small desk cluttered with charts, pencils, books, a clock, and an antique compass.

She needed another drink to ponder Boon's offer—a can of pineapple juice and the handle of cheap rum she kept for emergencies would have to do. With a moon-nailed finger, she picked off the sticky price tag from the glass jug of Paradise: three dollars and forty-eight cents. On St. Columba, water was the only thing less expensive than rum, and if you bought bottled water, that wasn't even true.

Back topside with her drink, a gentle whoosh emanated from the dark shore. The harbor song of clinking halyards, sundowners being enjoyed, and low laughter was melancholy tonight. Why couldn't Boon have offered her honest work—varnishing, winterizing, or caretaking? Nothing was stopping her from snapping up those low-season jobs, and really, she should just go to the job board at the mail exchange and look. She knew prime jobs were there for the asking. However, Boon's under-the-table offer paid a lot more than painting bar tables or working the telemarketing phones at Taino Bay.

The rum didn't help with her decision. Instead, it burned Gemma's throat and upset her stomach. Unlike the mellow buzz of her Bushwacker and the drinks at The Last Resort, this rotgut firewater stoked the electricity of her anger and stubborn pride. Airport pickups had been Vaughn's job. Now he was gone. Her thoughts tangled, short and scattered, refusing to form any kind of clear path. And yet, she knew that finding clarity might only lead her to a dangerous truth.

GEMMA WOKE IN HER HOT, stuffy cabin without remembering how she got down to her bunk. A swollen ankle spoke of a stumble or fall. Anxiety crawled across her skin, and the smell of rotten fruit and partly metabolized rum swirled around her head. Dried pineapple juice had spilled across the white of her work shirt.

Shit—if Gemma didn't jump in her dinghy immediately, she would be late for work. She stripped off her soiled clothes, threw on some sweats, and stuffed a fresh change of clothes in her dry bag. Onshore, the gravel drain of the outdoor shower bit into the soles of her feet. The rainwater from the cistern was cold, but the temperature in St. Columba never dropped below 80 degrees, so a heater was unnecessary. Her vision warped, and phantom figures intruded on the edge of her sight as last night's rum purged from her body in a stream of sweet-smelling urine between her feet.

Hangovers were common among everyone she knew in Sargasso Cove, but she was young, and the self-inflicted symptoms usually faded by noon. Today, however, she could tell that the suffering would linger, perhaps even into tomorrow or the next day. By her calculations, she had four drinks onshore and nearly a fifth of rum at home. Nothing could conceal her bleary eyes or the swelling that riddled her body.

The bus ride faded into a queasy blur. Just beyond Sawyer's line of sight, Cruz lingered as usual, savoring the cool breeze drifting from the open door of the sales office. Leaning casually against the wall, a smirk tugged at his lips as Gemma approached. She winced against the glare of the morning sun.

"Look what the cat dragged in," Cruz quipped.

It was Cruz's turn to get a dig in about her obvious, merciless hangover. Cruz didn't waste the chance, arching a brow when she grimaced. His teasing was a familiar beat in their friendship that, in its way, softened the sharp edge of her headache and the uneasy remnants of last night's choices. At least the trials of hard and fast living were a shared experience.

"Yeah, well, I had a lot to think about. Boon offered me a job, and it pays a thousand dollars a day," Gemma said defensively.

"What about that offer needed to be chased down with a distillery?" Cruz laughed. When an alcoholic like Cruz had this much on her, she had to question her own bad habits.

"Plenty. Boon wants me to take girls over to that weird Cowboi Rivers resort between here and St. Lucy. I'd be like his personal water taxi captain."

Cruz let out a low whistle. A strange expression crossed his face. "Easter Cay? Hmm. That's wild. You know you need a net worth of at least fifty million just to set foot on the sand there, right? I've heard some stories—big money, no rules."

"Yeah, I know that, and you're not helping," Gemma muttered. "Anyway, that's not the point. I thought selling timeshares was rock bottom, but getting mixed up in that freaky scene? Way worse. Isn't it?"

Cruz leaned back, stretching his arms behind his head, feigning indifference. "I don't know, Gemma. Hookers have been around since forever. World's oldest profession and all that."

She shot him a look. "Yeah, if you like jailbait."

Gemma found it irritating that Cruz never seemed to commit to one opinion or another. Whenever she voiced a stance, Cruz would maddeningly take an opposite position.

Cruz smiled. "Maybe there's an opportunity in this for you. Cowboi grants favors, I hear. He could be your fairy godfather."

She rolled her eyes. "What kind of favors are we talking about?"

Cruz said smoothly, "I'm just saying, you don't have to be at the bottom of the food chain anymore. To Cowboi, money is practically meaningless."

What unnerved Gemma most about Cruz was how often their discussions drifted into these morally gray areas. He made it sound almost rational to abandon the rules altogether, pushing her to take control of her fate by any means necessary. More than once, she found herself wondering whether he was steering her toward something darker, grooming her in the way she had heard Cowboi groomed his charges.

"You know, I had to steal half-eaten burgers off restaurant tables last summer. I'm tempted."

"Well, there you go. Take the job. Like you said, you're just a taxi for a superstar."

The conversation reminded her of how life on St. Columba seemed to operate by its own set of rules. Since her arrival, she had embraced a certain laxity, slipping into habits dictated by the island's code. Nights blurred into dawns as she partied hard with Cruz and Sawyer, hustling tourists with charm and half-truths, and indulging in fleeting connections with whoever caught her eye.

Low Season | 41

There was a predictable script to it all: strangers bragging at the bar about their adventures or wealth, the charged moments of connection that followed, and the passionate, consequence-free nights that dissolved into a casual goodbye with the morning light. It wasn't just her—it was the culture among the workers and college students who cycled through St. Columba. They arrived like waves, drawn by the promise of easy money and sun-soaked freedom, and left just as quickly, their lives intersecting in fast, reckless bursts.

The turquoise waters, the rhythmic thrum of steel drums, and the warm nights spiced with sea salt and nutmeg seemed to encourage this way of living. Everything felt temporary, like nothing mattered beyond the next sunset. Even the tourists seemed to lose themselves in it, stepping outside their real lives to play at a fantasy that didn't follow them home. No commitments, no consequences—just the immediacy of the moment bringing people together and pulling them apart.

Lost in thought about what pleasures and torments this life offered, Gemma felt her pulse hitch, a familiar glitch in her body's rhythm that sent a ripple of unease through her chest and nausea through her stomach. Her fingers tingled, and a wave of vertigo swept up her body, as if the ground beneath her were tilting, trying to throw her off balance. She reached out instinctively for Cruz to steady her but grabbed empty air. A strange sound rang in her ears, like the chime of a bell.

Gemma recognized this creeping sensation all too well. It was how her seizures always began. Her vision tunneled as her thoughts unraveled into a rush of disjointed images. When she woke, her back rested on the sun-hot cement of the mall walk. She blinked up at the sky. Sawyer and Cruz loomed over her, their faces pinched with worry. Shit. She blinked at the ring of Yacht Heaven pedestrians standing a few paces back, their curiosity tempered by unease.

"Gemma! Are you okay?" Sawyer held out a glass of water. She didn't know if he would throw it in her face or offer her a sip.

"I'm fine." Gemma sat up. Little pearls of blood welled up from a strawberry on her knee. She must have scraped it when she fell. She rubbed the side of her head.

"I'm so sorry, Sawyer. I must be really dehydrated."

"It's okay," Sawyer said, handing her the glass. "Believe me, you're not the first sales associate to drop like a sack of potatoes."

He gave her a quick once-over, his tone shifting to something softer, more paternal. "Tell you what—you take the day off. Corporate sent over some free passes to the yoga studio up the hill. They want us to check it out, see if it's worth adding to the tour incentives. Consider it a special assignment."

Gemma took the glass, her hand trembling slightly as she sipped. "Yoga?"

Sawyer grinned, patting her on the back. "You need some clean living, girl. Go stretch, breathe, or whatever it is they do up there." He reached down to help her to her feet.

She had made a spectacle of herself, but instead of

Low Season | 43

yelling, Sawyer offered her kindness. Keeping his agents selling was his job; even if his gift might have been self-serving, maybe something healthier in her life would give her the clarity she needed to make the right decision. She had never done yoga before, but Sawyer and Cruz were right: rum wasn't the solution.

5

ROYAL ASANA

Clutching the yoga coupon Sawyer had given her, Gemma made her way toward the address on a hill past the local market. At a shady, flat spot on the climb, she turned back to the beach, observing the humanity churning in the heat below, where overfed tourists frolicked in the waves or baked themselves cancerous on candy-colored towels. Even from this height, she could smell the coconut sunscreen and the smoke from the barbecue grills.

She continued to walk when a hand-painted sign for Royal Asana beckoned from a grove of trees, leading Gemma off the pavement into the wildness of the open-air studio. The hum from a gas-powered generator harmonized with a chorus of insects. Ferns, frangipani, oleander, and palm trees dripped quietly in the sun-dappled shade around a raised platform of polished tropical hardwood. Near an outdoor kitchen, a vegetable patch vibrated with color and variety, where Malabar spinach, moringa, and passion fruit vines thrived.

A man with a physique as hard and polished as cast bronze sat bare-chested in loose linen pants on the wooden floor, shaded by a pergola. He exuded the aura of a desert prince surrounded by his entourage. Gemma kicked off her flip-flops and climbed the steps, feeling the smooth varnish under her feet. As she entered, the heat, traffic, and fumes from her walk up the hill dissolved into a sandalwood-scented sanctuary.

"Namaste. I'm Nihir." A radiance illuminated his face. "Have you practiced yoga before? Do you have any injuries?" His voice transmitted peace.

Injuries, she thought; do hangovers and moral decay count? But Gemma simply offered her name in return. The weak sound of her own voice embarrassed her. Normally, she possessed an authoritative alto, a confidence she cultivated as a tool to sell real estate. She regained control of her breath and admitted this was her first time.

"Welcome, Gemma." Nihir gestured toward the mats. "Please take a mat from the stack there and place it at the front, where I can offer guidance."

He aligned his seat on the floor, his voice carrying the measured cadence of someone accustomed to teaching. "We begin each practice in stillness—a few moments of meditation to arrive fully. Then we'll move through a sequence of asana, the physical postures. I move at a steady pace, and you'll hear Sanskrit terms that may sound foreign at first." His smile was patient and knowing.

"Don't be concerned if you feel lost. Simply do what you can, and when you need rest, return to this position."

He demonstrated a kneeling position with his forehead folded to the mat, then rose up to sit back on his heels. "Child's Pose. Consider it your refuge. And this is Easy Pose." Nihir rearranged his legs into a simple cross-legged position.

Easy for you. The smug thought gave Gemma a moment's reprieve from her awkward feelings. *Check your attitude, girl,* she corrected and sat on her purple mat, mirroring Nihir's position. Her hands trembled as she placed them on her knees. Despite the cool breeze, sweat beaded on her forehead and gathered in the palms of her hands.

She closed her eyes and focused on breathing in cool air and exhaling warmth. At first, it felt like a band was squeezing around her chest. Since that morning, anxiety and dehydration from her hangover had disconnected her from her body and her surroundings. She had to remind herself that this was a safe space with supportive people.

Nihir's voice flowed like warm honey. "Close your eyes. Become aware of your body—feel its weight, its connection to the earth beneath you. Now broaden your awareness. Observe your thoughts, emotions, memories—all these elements that form your constructed identity. Notice the quiet spaces between thoughts. Gently expand these spaces. Breathe into them. Allow yourself to sense how these spaces grow, becoming more vast with each breath."

By Gemma's calculation, they sat for exactly an

eternity. She had followed the instructions, but panic seized her as soon as Nihir's voice gave way to silence. *What space?* Her mind was a hurricane—chairs, roofs, and uprooted trees whipped around inside her head, smashing into each other. Her heart pounded in her ears, and her breath came in short bursts.

Why was she here? She felt hideous. Peace was the last thing her body and mind would give her. When Nihir's voice returned, Gemma's eyes popped open, and she gasped. She looked around. The others had sprung to their feet and stood like soldiers at the tops of their mats.

"Gemma, are you all right? Join us," Nihir said. Gemma stood like the others. Nihir's voice was soft and encouraging, and his focus had shifted to her.

"Okay, let us begin. Surya Namaskara," Nihir continued.

The other students moved with effortless precision, gliding through push-ups, arches, and jackknives like a synchronized dance, while she stumbled, heavy—a lumbering bear among hummingbirds. Her muscles burned, her breath ragged, as she strained to keep up. Just when she thought she'd caught onto the pattern, the sequence shifted again; the movements twisted into something even more elusive. Desperation prickled at her as she scrambled to mimic the fluid grace of the others, but each sharp Sanskrit command unlocked a new, bewildering shape in their bodies. *What kind of insane language was this?*

The students were the picture of tranquility and health, their sun-kissed skin glowing under the golden light. They moved in sync, muscles defined and lean, their bodies bending and stretching effortlessly, as if gravity were a suggestion they could politely ignore. Adorned in loose, natural fabrics, each one contributed to the serene aesthetic of the group. Eyes closed, faces calm, they seemed lost in their own meditative worlds.

But to Gemma, it felt as if each subtle glance and every rustle of movement was aimed directly at her—critiquing her every shaky pose and off-balance wobble. *They think I'm a mess. I look like an idiot. I should never have come.* Her mind spiraled as she awkwardly adjusted her foot placement for the third time. She could practically hear the whispers: *She doesn't belong here.* In truth, no one had paid any attention to her in the slightest. They were far too wrapped up in their own practice to notice her self-imposed turmoil.

The group moved as one for over an hour, breathing in whooshes of air. Gemma, a beat and a half behind, felt lost. The ordeal culminated in her lying flat on her back, as rigid as a sheet of plywood. She squeezed her eyes shut, holding back tears.

When Nihir approached, Gemma barely registered the soft padding of footsteps until his gentle hands rested on her shoulders. The touch was light but firm. He squatted down and placed a warm hand below each of her ears, delicately pulling to lengthen her neck and align her shoulders. Her breath slowed, and her muscles released with his touch. He lifted her legs, and in a pulling, rocking motion, shook the remaining tension from her body. She felt an immense release—stillness blooming within her.

A meditation gong sounded with a deep, resonant chime, a golden wave of sound expanding outward to fill the room with warmth. The initial strike was rich and full-bodied, vibrating through the air and settling into Gemma's bones. As it faded, the tone stretched thinner, unraveling in shimmering infinity that hovered at the edge of perception. She followed, her ears attuned to the vanishing frequency, chasing the retreating hum as it dissolved finally into silence. Her breath slowed, her body stilled—listening not just with her ears but with her entire being—until even the ghost of vibration was gone, leaving only her returning thoughts. Gemma lay like this for an unknown time before Nihir's kind voice reentered her consciousness.

"You are returning to your breath. To awaken your body, wiggle your toes and fingers. Rock your head from side to side, and when you are ready, roll over onto your right side."

Gemma complied. She curled into a tight fetal ball, her knees drawn to her chest, arms wrapped around herself as if she could make her body disappear into the earth. The coolness of the mat pressed against her skin. In that moment, the world felt too big, too open, and this compact position was her only way to feel safe, to contain herself.

"Push into the ground with your hand and return to your cross-legged seat."

Gemma sat up and found herself eye to eye with Nihir, seated in front of her.

"Namaste," Nihir said, bowing with his palms together over his heart.

The other students bowed and echoed a closing chant. With her eyes now open, she listened to the foreign words being sung and studied her teacher. His skin was a rich shade of copper, and his medium-length hair was glossy black. He seemed slightly older, not because his face had lines or he appeared aged, but because he exuded an ancient wisdom. Perhaps he was handsome, but he possessed a childlike quality that softened any overt sexiness.

"Thank you, Nihir," Gemma said.

"You are most welcome."

When the students finished rolling up their mats and left, Gemma lingered by the edge of the platform. The thought of returning to the chaotic churn of her own life made her stomach twist. She rallied her confidence and approached Nihir, who was tidying a pyramid of yoga blocks in the soft golden light of the afternoon.

"I need to talk to someone," Gemma blurted out, clutching the strap of her dry bag for reassurance. "I was hoping you might help."

Nihir paused, his hands resting at his sides. He gave her a calm, encouraging look. "Come," he said, gesturing toward the open-air kitchen.

Gemma followed him. The transition from the practice space to the shaded kitchen felt homey, the lush greenery of the garden framing the small space. She settled onto a low meditation cushion as Nihir retrieved a hand-hammered copper pot from a shelf and set it on a small gas burner on the floor.

"Where did you learn yoga?" she asked hesitantly, breaking the silence that only she felt was awkward.

Nihir glanced at her, his expression soft. "From my father. My parents were Jains. The core tenet of Jainism is *ahimsa*, or non-violence. They believe in existing without harm to any living being—not even the smallest insect."

Gemma raised an eyebrow. "That sounds intense. Is that what we were doing today?"

He chuckled, a quiet, melodic sound. "Not at all. Sorry to mislead you. Yoga isn't about religion. It's a method for awakening—an exploration of energy. It's about observing your body, your mind, and what is neither."

"That's—" Gemma started. "I'm not sure I'm cut out for yoga."

"You don't have to figure anything out or make a decision. Yoga isn't about having inherent talent, flexibility, or strength," Nihir said, pouring chai into two handmade earthenware cups as the spiced aroma filled the air. His voice carried the gentle authority of a teacher who had guided many before him. "Yoga meets you where you are. Consider it your refuge. Tell me, what brought you here today?"

"A free pass," Gemma hesitated, the weight of her embarrassment pressing down on her again. She sounded more flippant than she had meant to. She watched the steam curling from the brewing chai before finally blurting out a confession she had no intention of sharing.

"But it's not why I'm here. Someone offered me a job that pays a lot of money. The work isn't illegal, but it's not moral either, and the idea of it makes me feel awful. I can't stop thinking that it might be a mistake and a betrayal."

Nihir handed her the warm cup, his hands steady and calm. "A betrayal to who?" he asked.

"Myself. Other women. I don't know. I just want to be free. My own money. My own charter company."

"Unfasten your attachments to outcomes," he said. "Fear and desire cloud your perception. When you let go, you can see things as they truly are."

Gemma took a sip, the warmth spreading through her body. "I don't know if I can do that," she admitted. "I feel like I'm going nowhere, and I don't see a solution."

"With patience, the current will carry you where you need to go," Nihir said softly, his voice carrying the gentle authority of one who has navigated these waters before.

Her tears came suddenly, unbidden and unstoppable. She cried into her hands, her shoulders shaking with quiet sobs. Nihir didn't say anything more. He simply sat with her, his presence a steadying force as she let her emotions flow freely.

When the tears finally subsided, she wiped her face with the back of her hand. "Thank you," she whispered. Gemma looked around, her breath slowing as the surroundings seemed to absorb her anguish. The colors of the garden appeared brighter now; the air fresher.

"This place feels right," she whispered. "Being here, talking to you—it's the first time I've felt hope and peace in a long time."

"Hope is a powerful thing," Nihir finally said with a gentle smile. "Trust it, and trust yourself."

As Gemma rose to leave, Nihir stood as well, his movements fluid and unhurried. "Remember," he said, his voice following her as she stepped toward the path leading away from the studio, "you are already enough, Gemma. Everything you need is within you."

As she walked back down the hill, away from the yoga studio, the weight on her shoulders lifted. With some time off and her hangover subsiding, Gemma felt strong enough to visit her Yaya Mari. Her grandmother had asked her to come for a lesson. Despite feeling as bad as she did, Gemma knew her grandmother would be severely disappointed if she canceled. Nihir had cleared her mind; now she could keep her commitment and see her family.

6

MARIPOSA'S END

As the sun hung low over the western horizon, Gemma observed the routines from the walking path that led to her grandmother's house—women tending to gardens, children running along the shore, and a man stacking wood for a bonfire. This West Indian community had called The End home for hundreds of years, surviving by keeping to themselves.

This community owned nearly all of Sargasso Cove and a good stretch of St. Columba besides. Today, the beachfront alone was worth hundreds of millions. For as long as anyone could remember, developers had circled like sharks, turning cousins against cousins and fathers against sons. Now, a faction of the younger generation—louder, better organized—was pushing for a sprawling 150-slip marina.

Greed, like the tide, had always chipped away at the edges of things. To protect what remained, the elders' council, led by Mari August, placed the land in a trust. Still, rumors swirled. Many believed Cowboi Rivers was the real force behind the marina project, stoking the media-fueled ambitions of the island's young people. But Cowboi had his eyes on more than just the coastline—he had his sights set on Gemma, the future leader of Mariposa's End.

Gemma's roots in the village ran deep. The old women whispered her name and spoke of her bloodline, her ties to the old ways, and the stories that told of one who would return. Cowboi knew those stories too, and he had always had a knack for spotting valuable human assets long before anyone else recognized their worth. But Mari August understood this threat better than anyone. As leader of the council and priestess of Mariposa's End, she bore the weight of generations. Her only child, William August, had been killed by a drunk-driving tourist. Now his daughter Gemma was all that remained of the August lineage.

Here, the healer's mantle passed through the women. William, though cherished, had never been destined to inherit the spiritual crown, even if the land would have been his birthright. That gift now fell to Gemma.

But Gemma's mother raised her on the mainland, far from the rhythms of The End. And now Gemma worked for Taino Bay, a symbol of everything the elders feared: exploitation masked as progress, cultural erasure disguised as modernization, and the slow, insidious appropriation of local culture by tourist dollars. Her job selling timeshares represented the very forces threatening her ancestral home—commercial interests that viewed the island not as sacred ground but as real estate to be parceled and sold to the highest bidder. She hadn't fully grasped this painful irony yet.

If Gemma were to become trustee and spiritual steward, she had much to unlearn—and even more to remember. The Western mindset that valued individual success over community welfare would need to be shed like an outgrown skin, revealing the deeper connection to land and ancestry that had always flowed in her blood, dormant but never truly gone.

She had reached out to her grandmother upon her return to St. Columba. However, when she learned the extent of her duty as Yaya Mari's grandchild, she backed away and tried even harder to belong to town and Boon Dock Marine. The old ways seemed superstitious, and, with some guilt, Gemma even joked with her co-workers and Boon's Margaritaville crowd about being a Calypso Queen in waiting. Raised on Western values, Gemma measured success by status and material comfort. Everything Yaya Mari taught Gemma was counter to what she had learned growing up in Vermont.

For Mari, now in her 80s, the role had been a powerful legacy that demanded both reverence and resilience, but Mari couldn't force the practices of fasting and sacrifice on an unwilling granddaughter. Instead, Mari adjusted the training to match what Gemma was ready for, knowing that her granddaughter's journey would not follow the worn path from Africa. Rather than pushing her toward isolation and the grueling rites of initiation,

Mariposa's End | 57

Mari focused on cultivating Gemma's connection to the land and its spirits. She believed that Gemma's trial would come not through the traditional sacrifices but through the unique challenges her life would present.

The lessons began with bushcraft. Mari walked Gemma through the lush terrain, showing her the medicinal plants hidden in plain sight and the best times to harvest them. "See this vine?" Mari said one humid morning, holding up a tendril of soursop, her weathered fingers tracing the veined leaves with reverence. "Its leaves soothe fever and calm the body."

They continued along to where dappled sunlight broke through the canopy. Mari paused beside a slender tree with delicate, feathery leaves. "This is moringa," she explained, breaking off a small branch to show Gemma the intricate leaf pattern. "Our ancestors called it the miracle tree. The leaves strengthen the blood, clear the mind, and heal wounds that refuse to close." She crushed several leaves between her palms, releasing a peppery scent that hung in the humid air. "We dry this for tea when the dreams become too heavy."

As they ventured deeper into the green heart of The End, Mari pointed out plants for protection, for cleansing, for drawing boundaries between the living and the dead. Gemma tried to listen, though not always with the reverence her grandmother might have hoped for. How could weaving baskets or brewing herbal teas help Gemma navigate the trials facing her? But Mari's patience never wavered. "One day," she said cryptically, "this knowledge will save your life."

In place of fasting and isolation, Mari emphasized the importance of mindfulness and gratitude. She taught Gemma how to sit in stillness by the shore, to read the messages of the ripples on the sea's surface. One evening, as Gemma and her grandmother shared a breadfruit stew, Yaya said, "You only need to understand that everything you consume—food, water, even air—comes from the same force that sustains this island. Respect that force, and it will guide you." Gemma puzzled over the similarities between Nihir's and Yaya's teachings—meditation, sensations of the body, simple joys; even the ritual of tea was the same.

Despite Mari's approach, Gemma remained slow to accept her clairvoyance as more than a joke. She had grown up with her mother's fear of the spirits, but as the weeks passed, Gemma found herself drawn to the lessons of her lineage. On the deck of *Luna*, she had practiced tracking the stars and the moon's phases. Gemma looked out at the waves to read their signs. Without realizing it, she began to feel the weight of Mariposa's End shifting from burden to blessing. For the first time, she wondered if her grandmother might be right about her.

7
BOILER ROOM

But herbs and ghosts wouldn't pay the bills. Within a month, tourism would blow away with the coming storms. The Taino Bay Corporation had already pushed some of the fractional real estate sales team off the cruise ship mall and into the call center, and Gemma was among the reassigned.

The lead list Gemma dialed from was ice cold—colder, even, than the ironically named boiler room where she sat. Air conditioning units droned, and the overhead fluorescent lights buzzed, casting a sterile glow over rows of cubicles, while balmy breezes and warm white sands lay tantalizingly outside the windows and beyond the closed push-bar doors.

Gemma glanced around the room at the expressions of her fellow resort staff reassigned as telemarketers. Heads bowed, microphones jutted from tense jawlines. The air was thick with the monotony of forced enthusiasm, punctuated by the delivery of canned scripts repeated ad nauseam.

Gemma studied the goosebumps rising on her skin and suspected the room was chilled to the same temperature as the beer coolers in the lobby convenience store to keep the salespeople awake and selling. Some sat slumped in their chairs, their eyes glazed over, clicking the checkboxes for "no sale" again and again. Occasional bursts of laughter erupted, tinged with bitterness, as someone echoed a rude rejection from the other end of the line—the mirth, a small rebellion against the soul-sucking work.

No one wanted what Gemma was selling. The people on the receiving end of the calls had successfully dodged the in-person, high-pressure sales tactics while on the island, and they certainly didn't want to be sold a vacation condo now that they were safely at home. Their voices stiffened with annoyance; irritation became outright hostility as Gemma attempted to navigate her script. Some hung up immediately upon hearing "Taino Bay Resort" for the tenth time, while others let her get her pitch out before delivering a crushing "not interested" like a slap.

The Taino Bay sales managers seemed fine with a one-in-a-thousand success rate, but to the salespeople on the phones, it felt pointless—a Sisyphean ritual, pushing a boulder up a hill, only to have it bulldoze over them on the way down again and again. The whiteboard at the front of the room displaying the day's "winners" was nearly empty and only heightened the collective sense of futility.

This burden might have been tolerable if a living wage had been offered; however, it was a commission-only job. Gemma shifted in her chair, adjusting the headset digging into her temple, and glanced at the clock on the wall, its hands crawling with agonizing slowness.

In reality, it would not have made any difference if Gemma were pounding the pavement of Yacht Heaven Mall, working the phones, or taking the summer off. No tourists = no money. She wasn't sure what was worse—the monotony of the calls or the growing awareness that this drudgery was her life for the next few months—unless.

After an eight-hour shift, Gemma felt dirty and mean, but home was an hour bus ride away, and the cold-water showers at Boon Dock Marine wouldn't wash away her foul mood. The relief of Royal Asana floated briefly in her mind, a haven of peace where she could breathe, maybe even clear her head. The thought of the incense, the soft mats, and Nihir's oasis of calm was tempting. But as usual, the pull of Cruz and the familiarity of drinks at The Last Resort were stronger. It was easier to drown her cruel thoughts in rum than to face them head-on in meditation. Nihir's peace required effort, discipline—things she wasn't sure she had left in her after a day like this. Cruz would understand. The bar's dim lights would let her slip into a comfortable haze, if only for a little while.

"Meet me at the bar," she texted.

"Already here," came back.

Cruz's profile was a sharp outline illuminated by a

cone of overhead lighting. Gemma walked over, sat on her usual stool, and accepted her Dark and Stormy.

"Man, Cruz. This phone gig sucks. I don't know how much longer I can last."

"Cold shit on a paper plate in there. Beats me why you're dialing for pennies when Boon's offering you a thousand dollars a day to be his delivery girl. If we weren't friends, I'd call up Boon myself and ask for the job."

Cruz's description was spot on. The stench inside the boiler room was a nauseating blend of farts and the pungent odor of sweated-out alcohol. There was something almost cruel about how the air conditioning made the smell of bodies heating unwashed polyester fabric unbearable. Even thinking about it now made Gemma's stomach churn.

"Well, Nihir told me—"

Cruz interrupted by rolling his eyes outrageously. "Why are you listening to that dime-store holy man, anyway?"

Gemma had surprised herself by trudging up the hill to practice yoga at least twice a week since her first class. What had started as curiosity had transformed into something she now craved, a sanctuary where her perpetual internal chaos briefly subsided under Nihir's gentle guidance. These pilgrimages had started to supplant her long-established habit of drinking with Cruz after work, a change that visibly made him jealous.

"I don't know, Cruz. Nihir seems like a pretty happy guy. I think there might be some truth in what he says."

"Fine. Tell me, then. What does he say? Lay some divine truth on me."

Gemma continued, unperturbed.

"Basically, if I do something I'm ashamed of, especially for a living, it will haunt me. The money won't make a difference. It might cover up the shame for a while, but underneath, there will be internal conflict. According to him, my mind will always seek to stay occupied, so I should focus on something purposeful and beneficial."

"There you go. Problem solved. Just don't feel embarrassed by what you're doing. Take the job," Cruz said, gulping down the last of his drink.

He motioned for another by tapping the countertop with his index finger like a gambler. With Cruz's attention diverted, Gemma's mind drifted once again to Boon's proposition. With all that money, she could eventually start her own charter company, buy Yaya Mari a new house, and even invest in Nihir's yoga business. Why should her family and friends live and work in shacks when they could have villas or celebrity studios? And why was she a wage slave when she could have total freedom?

"You're making this harder than it needs to be," Cruz said, turning back to Gemma as the bartender slid a fresh drink across the counter. He lifted the glass and swirled the straw absentmindedly, eyes scanning the room like he was taking inventory. "Boon's offering you a golden ticket. People don't get those handed to them every day. Especially not people like us."

Gemma crossed her arms, leaning back in her chair. "People like us?"

"Locals. Nobodies. Wage slaves." Cruz said, taking a sip. "People who weren't born into wealth. Look around—half the people on this island would kill for a shot like the one that's been handed to you. And you're hesitating. Why?"

Gemma shook her head. "Why do you care so much?"

Cruz leaned back, exhaling through his nose in a huff. "I just don't want to see you waste your life. That's all. You've got potential, Gem. And if you don't take this chance, someone else will."

Gemma stared at him for a long moment. There was something about Cruz she couldn't shake—a nagging sense that he knew more about her than he let on. That his encouragement wasn't just about her future. He wanted her in the game, but why?

"That's not a real answer, is it?" she mumbled.

Cruz grinned. "It's the best one you're getting from me." He tipped his glass back, finishing the drink in one long gulp. "Take the job, Gemma. Trust me. It'll pay off."

"You know what? You've worn me down," she announced to Cruz. "I'm going to see Boon right now and accept his offer."

8
WATER TAXI

St. Lucy International looked more like an overgrown Pizza Hut than an airport, with its faded red roof and weathered stucco walls that had surrendered their original color to the relentless Caribbean sun long ago. Past the automatic sliding doors —which occasionally got stuck halfway—a red-roofed air traffic control tower gleamed in the sun, its windows reflecting blinding light as it stood perched on a cracked cement slab patched with tar and sprouting tall weeds between the cracks. Chickens and goats wandered the scrub bordering the runway with the casual confidence of longtime residents, occasionally causing ground crew to wave their arms and shout when the animals ventured too close to arriving or departing aircraft.

To combat the sweltering heat that pressed down like a weighted blanket, Gemma ordered a rum drink from a nearby bar cart with a hand-painted sign advertising island spirits. The bartender mixed her drink with practiced hands, adding an extra splash of rum with a conspiratorial wink.

Announcements crackled through aging speakers mounted in corners of the square building. The static sometimes overwhelmed the actual words, forcing travelers to strain their ears or check the apps on their phones for delays and announcements. Laughter-filled conversations swirled around her—a blend of local patois and tourist accents—suggesting delicious gossip being exchanged.

Half an hour later, the Boeing 737 touched down, rolling to a stop on the patched tarmac. A man in a sweat-soaked uniform pushed the mobile stairs into place, and the crew opened the door to receive the gangplank. Gemma tucked her Carl Hiaasen novel away into her bag and stood to greet Cowboi's human cargo. These girls came from all over, but they all had one thing in common: stars in their eyes and dreams of escaping lives that fell well below their expectations.

Cowboi had perfected his predatory harvests through movie casting calls and modeling agencies, dangling the glittering promise of fame before women whose desperation and naivete made them easy prey. He knew exactly which dreams to target and which vulnerabilities to exploit. The internet had made his work almost effortless—a few carefully crafted posts about "exclusive opportunities in paradise" and "life-changing photoshoots" were enough to fill his nets.

The girls dressed as if they were heading to an Instagram influencer party that existed only in their fantasies, their outfits a desperate patchwork of what they imagined glamour to look like. The aesthetic clashed in a way that felt both hyper-stylized and hastily thrown together, like a mood board assembled by someone who had never actually attended the parties they dreamed of.

Two girls in flouncy pink Lolita dresses with too-short hemlines clung together. Both wore hair extensions ratty from the journey and catching the light like spun sugar left in the rain. One leaned hard into goth vibes—wearing a pleated miniskirt, thigh-high boots, and a lace choker. Her fishnet stockings stretched over bruised and tattooed legs told stories she wasn't ready to share. Skyscraper heels threatened to send them all sprawling. Rhinestones peeled off their phone cases. They clutched their cheap handbags like lifelines, their expressions flickering between excitement and fear, their eyes widening with the uneasy realization that they had already stepped too far into something they couldn't control.

The alpha stepped forward, separating herself from the cluster of uncertainty behind her. She was tall, with striking, unnaturally red hair that hung straight and glossy down her back. She moved with what looked like confidence, shoulders back and chin raised, but Gemma had seen that particular brand of performance before. She knew the hubris was a mask, carefully constructed and desperately maintained.

This girl—she couldn't be more than eighteen—had appointed herself the protector of the group, the one who would negotiate their collective fate. But her hands shook slightly as she reclipped an oversized hoop earring that had come loose, and there was something brittle in the way she held her smile.

Behind her, the others waited in a loose semicircle, their body language a study in nervous energy. One wrapped her arms around herself despite the oppressive heat. This was a moment between the lives they'd left behind and what waited for them here in this sun-bleached prison.

"Are you our ride?" the redhead asked Gemma, her voice steady but her eyes darting around. "They told us to look for a pretty black girl with long dreadlocks."

"Yep. That's me," Gemma said, forcing a smile. "Welcome to the islands. Let's get you to the boat and then to Easter Cay. You're going to love your new home."

If the redhead was the alpha, then a tiny blonde girl, all in pink, who stood separately from the pack was the omega. She was nervous and fragile, dragging her scuffed Hello Kitty roller bag behind her like a dead body.

"Don't worry, it's a quick walk to the dock," Gemma reassured them. "And then a fun ride to the island."

"I don't want to go," the tiny blonde wailed, her voice cracking with desperation. She stopped abruptly in the middle of the baggage claim. Tears streaked down her flushed cheeks, cutting pale lines through her heavy foundation. "Please, I changed my mind."

Gemma's heart hammered against her ribs as she quickly moved to the girl's side, placing a gentle but firm hand on her shoulder. "Hey, hey, it's alright."

Two uniformed security guards by the exit had already turned their heads, their conversation halting mid-sentence as they assessed the commotion. One nudged the other, pointing in their direction. Gemma's mouth went dry. The last thing she needed was airport security asking questions. The other girls huddled closer, sensing the situation.

"What's your name, hon?" Gemma whispered, her voice low and soothing despite the panic fluttering in her chest. She needed to establish some connection, anything to get this situation under control before it spiraled.

"Lorna."

Lorna glanced at Gemma, her eyes red-rimmed and running with black mascara. Up close, her blonde extensions looked brittle and plastic—the hair tape grown out two months too long. "I want to go home."

"I don't know what to tell you, Lorna. This is your home now. Your flight was paid for. And not by me. Let's just get you to Easter Cay, and you can work out a deal there."

This was only Gemma's fourth delivery, but she already knew there was no negotiation waiting at the other end of this trip. Unless this feather-wisp of a thing acted like a total psycho when she got to Cowboi, she would be exploited until he grew tired of her, then she would be moved from location to location until she ceased to be a desirable commodity. When she had accepted her ticket, she accepted her fate. The illusion of choice would stretch just far enough to keep her pliant: the suggestion that she was there by her own design, that she could leave if she wanted, that the champagne and private jets to nowhere were part of some modern-day fairytale.

"I want my mom," Lorna wailed. Gemma glanced around nervously. Another guard directing the TSA line stiffened and started to move toward the group. Gemma put on her best salesperson smile, her face flushing. "Sorry about that," she called to him. "Custody issues. She doesn't want to stay with her father. I'm just the nanny."

The guard's posture relaxed despite the obvious lie. He didn't want to get involved, and his job was directing the customs line. They were almost out the door and, therefore, out of his jurisdiction. He gave a curt nod and returned his attention to his assigned task. Gemma smoothed her shirt and motioned for the girls to follow.

"Come on, let's get out of here before y'all cause an international incident."

Gemma's voice softened when they reached the sidewalk. "Listen, you're going to be okay. The job's not as bad as you think. You'll serve drinks, mingle with the guests, and look pretty. Nothing you can't handle."

Lorna looked at her, searching for reassurance. "And what about after?"

Gemma hesitated, the weight of her own complicity pressing down on her. "You'll figure it out. You're stronger than you think."

It was a lie, and Gemma hated herself for saying it. But she couldn't bear to see the fear in Lorna's eyes. This child should have been carrying a teddy bear, not a pink quilted Chanel knock-off.

"It's beautiful here," Lorna said softly as they walked across the parking lot toward the beach. Gemma nodded, not trusting herself to speak. She knew what Lorna was seeing—the crystal-clear water, the swaying palms, the promise of something better. But Gemma also knew what lay beneath that perfect-looking surface. This might look like paradise, but it was a cage, and the girls were walking into it willingly.

Lorna lingered at the edge of the dock, staring out at the ocean.

"Come on, Lorna. There's nowhere else to go," Gemma said, a little impatiently this time.

Once everyone was aboard, Gemma uncleated the lines and pushed off from the dock. The Sea Ray glided smoothly over the water, cutting through the gentle waves. The girls settled on the cushioned benches, chatting and laughing. Some took selfies, posing with the ocean behind them, trying to capture the start of their adventure. Lorna stared quietly at the horizon, hugging her knees to her chest. Gemma watched her for a moment before returning her attention to navigating through the harbor traffic.

She's gonna be okay, Gemma thought to herself. She swallowed the lump in her throat. The island of Easter Cay rose from the sea like Shangri-La for the rich and powerful. Gemma forced a new smile. "We're here."

The girls gathered their things, their excitement rekindled at the sight of the private island that was ten times as beautiful as St. Lucy's airport beach. Lorna hesitated, looking back at Gemma one last time. "Thank you," she whispered. Gemma nodded as the girls disembarked. She couldn't shake the feeling that she was sending them to their doom.

9
THE PARTY

Gemma sat in *Luna's* cockpit, watching the dazzling fireworks show unfurl above her head. Leading up to the 4th of July, Gemma had transported several boatloads of young women to Cowboi's island and was well paid for the task. Instead of the usual cheap rum that burned her throat and left her with splitting headaches, the glass she sipped was Barbancourt—fifty dollars a bottle with a taste like fine cognac over ice. She swirled the amber liquid, watching it catch the reflections of the fireworks overhead. The complex notes of vanilla and spice danced on her tongue.

Shells soared through the dark sky like the tails of comets, their faint whistles swallowed by silence, then suddenly—boom—an eruption into brilliant chrysanthemums of vibrant sparks. Dazzling golds and shimmering blues fountained down to dust the jungle-topped mountains. Each burst illuminated Gemma's face in the play of shadows and colorful glows.

Gemma heard the low roar of an engine cutting through the concert of color and sound in the night sky. She peered over *Luna's* port side to see Boon's dinghy materializing, its round, red shape bobbing like a port marker buoy. The Zodiac's inflated sides gleamed momentarily in the cascade of gold sparks as Boon throttled down the outboard, guiding the rubber craft until it bumped against Gemma's boat with a soft thud. Crab stretched a thin arm to grasp *Luna's* gunwale, his bony fingers holding the dinghy steady while Boon leaned forward to secure the painter to a nearby cleat with deft turns.

"Bad news. Flight's canceled. The new girls are arriving sometime tomorrow, or maybe the next day. But the good news is, you have the night off, and Cowboi is having a party! Jump in. We're going to Easter Cay," Boon said. "Cowboi wants to thank you personally for your good work so far."

"Personally?" she asked, raising an eyebrow. Her voice carried a mix of curiosity and wariness.

Boon leaned casually against the railing, a slight smirk playing on his lips. "Yeah, he's impressed. Says you're fitting in with the operation."

Gemma crossed her arms, the edge of skepticism sharpening her tone. "That's not exactly a compliment."

Boon chuckled, motioning for her to step down into his Zodiac. "Relax, Gem. It's a party, not a performance review. Cowboi throws these things all the time. You'll drink, eat, mingle—it's all good."

She tilted her head, eyeing him carefully. "And you think it's a good idea?"

Boon shrugged, restarting the outboard with a smooth pull. "Good idea or not, it's an invitation, and you don't ignore those from Cowboi. Besides, it's better to be on his good side, don't you think?"

"Okay, but I need to change into something presentable for a party," Gemma said.

"No time," Boon replied. "We're late—gotta leave right now."

Gemma glanced down at her faded batik sundress. This was hardly the attire for mingling with the elite at Cowboi's infamous gatherings. The thought of stepping onto Easter Cay looking like a dock rat made her stomach clench. But what choice did she have? Suppressing a sigh, she climbed down into Boon's boat for the trip around to the island's west side.

Phosphorescence washed over Boon's prop with such intense blue that it put the display in the sky to shame. Gemma scooped her hand through the water and held up a glistening glove that pulsed with azure light, the bioluminescent organisms dripping from her fingers like something magical and otherworldly. Whirlpools of illumination spiraled into the depths, coming to a point below the surface before disappearing back into black—tiny constellations born and dying in seconds.

As they approached Easter Cay, the channel markers

blinked their steady rhythm, casting emerald and ruby reflections across the water's surface. A gleaming metal dock reached toward them like a bony finger beckoning them closer. Along its length, uniformed attendants in crisp white shirts and khaki pants moved with choreographed precision, securing luxury tenders to steel cleats with practiced ease. Their movements betrayed years of training in the service of wealth. Each approaching craft was greeted with the same rehearsed smiles and subtle deference that marked the threshold between the merely rich and the truly powerful.

The gentle hum of Boon's Zodiac dropped to an idle, the craft bobbing in the swells. Gemma felt increasingly out of place in her faded sundress as they waited their turn, the water valet's white-gloved hand finally rising to wave them forward with a gesture that somehow conveyed both welcome and judgment.

Gemma scanned the crowd along the landing, recognizing celebrities mingling in tight groups, their conversations subdued yet full of intent as they waited for golf carts to whisk them up the winding incline beyond the trees. The air hung thick with unspoken hierarchy. Eyes flicked toward the rough-looking sailors and the island girl. When she made eye contact, the elite closed ranks like startled schools of fish, contracting inward, turning their backs to protect their numbers from the perceived threat.

A handsome teenage chauffeur arrived. The boy was polite, but hesitation flickered in his eyes as he ushered Boon, Crab, and Gemma aboard his cart. Gemma suspected he'd already pegged them as party crashers, their appearance poor enough to trigger quiet alarms in his well-trained instincts.

The wheels crunched softly against gravel on the ride up to the pool house. Uplighting revealed botanical treasures imported from Southeast Asia, Africa, and Central America—their forms like vivid brushstrokes against the darkness, as if an artist had painted this place from dreams. Night-blooming cereus unfurled waxy petals, wide and luminous and fleeting, destined to last only a single night. Their succulent vines cast snaking shadows while fragrant blossoms glowed like lanterns.

As they arrived under the rustic porte-cochère, gentle strains of Bossa Nova wafted through the air, the rhythm blending with laughter and the clinking of glasses. The rich, slightly briny aroma of grilling lobsters carried on the warm ocean breeze from an outdoor barbecue nearby.

A confetti of party girls frolicked along the multi-level infinity pool's edge, their laughter rising in bubbly bursts against the steady sway of the music. They posed and danced in their brightly colored bikinis or in the nude. Gemma recognized several girls from her pickups at the airport. She had tried to keep her distance from her charges, but she couldn't pretend to be ignorant of their names and fates—they recognized her and waved at her brightly. Behind them, the channel between the cay and the main island stretched out in a great barrier, a line where the black evening water met the starry sky.

From Gemma's office at Yacht Heaven, Cowboi's private island appeared idyllic with its sun-drenched beaches, lush greenery, and sprawling estate complete

The Party | 79

with pools and tennis courts. But beneath its picturesque facade lay the echoes of dark pursuits. The island's most infamous features were its enigmatic structures—high on a hill sat the temple, its strange blue and gold facade inspiring countless rumors. Some whispered about secret rituals and a satanic society.

Cowboi excused himself from his adoring flock, wove through the party in a bow-legged gait, and without speaking or even looking at Gemma, sat to admire the human display of his orchestration. He sprawled in the teakwood chair like a king, legs spread wide, arms draped over the armrests. His eyes gleamed with predatory satisfaction as he deliberately turned his gaze from the debauchery to Gemma, one corner of his mouth lifted in a knowing smirk. He tilted his head back, exposing his throat in false vulnerability while his fingers tapped a slow rhythm against his armrest, as if conducting the depravity before them.

Girls wearing only platform heels offered blow jobs to the line of men standing at the bar. The men—executives, politicians, and celebrities—accepted these offerings with an entitled casualness, some scrolling through their phones while manicured hands worked at their zippers. The scene unfolded with the precision of an assembly line wrapped in the veneer of hedonism.

Gemma fidgeted, feeling an intense imbalance of power. A handsome actor that Gemma couldn't quite name blew cigar smoke rings into the cowlicked blonde extensions of the petite beauty that bobbed on his cock. He sipped a daiquiri from a bright pink straw, barely interested in her ministrations. She couldn't remember the actor's name, but she couldn't forget the girl's name—Lorna.

"I'm glad you came," Cowboi finally said. "Thank you for your service. You are so much more reassuring to the girls when they arrive, you being closer to their age and female and all. You probably don't realize how hard it is to find good help."

"Oh, I know," Gemma said lightly, then realized she had spoken too casually. Cowboi exuded domination. Instinctually, Gemma knew that suggesting equality would put her at a disadvantage. She backpedaled to explain. "I mean, I know how hard it is to find help. I sell timeshares. The employee turnover in the Taino Bay sales office is astronomical. It seems like we're trying out new people every day," Gemma said.

"You sell real estate? And you're a boat captain? Interesting. Impressive, really. You're a very talented woman, Gemma. You know, I may have a bigger role for you soon. I have an idea. But for now, I insist you join in my little fun and games. I keep a few select studs in the stable for my lady guests. Please, help yourself to anything you like." Cowboi pointed out a stunning young man in swim trunks. "That one is five stars. Tried him myself. Highly recommend." He flashed his cold smile.

"Um. Thank you, but I'm fine just watching," said Gemma, although she would rather be anywhere else. Despite the luxurious surroundings and glitterati, even the boiler room at Taino Bay seemed better than this.

Deep conflict gnawed at her. She was involved in a prostitution ring and couldn't pretend otherwise.

Cowboi tapped an app on his smartwatch. A moment later, a slim, pale woman in kitchen whites appeared at his side.

"Sir?" she asked.

"Yes. Rebecca, Gemma is my special VIP guest for the evening. Get her whatever she wants. Table service. A private room. Whatever."

"Yes, sir."

"Thank you, Rebecca," Cowboi said as he gave his servant a parting slap on the ass.

"If America could see me now. Am I right?" Cowboi said. His grin was wide and a little crazy.

"I've wondered about that. You have such a squeaky-clean image back home. The all-American country boy. How do you keep the public in the dark about all this?"

"Ah—that. Well, it's expensive. But my guests are discreet. Perhaps out of self-protection. If they expose me, then they implicate themselves. That's not 100% watertight, though. My ex-wife, for example. But my lawyers took care of her. The bigger problem is the girls. Can't keep them here forever. They have a short shelf life, if you know what I mean? They're ancient by twenty-five. Week-old leftovers. But I have ways of keeping them in line."

Gemma didn't want to think too hard about what Cowboi meant by that.

He continued, "Gemma, listen. I have a more important job for you than the taxi runs. I've decided you're the right fit for my off-island operations. Boon agrees. My steward will pick you up at the main ferry dock tomorrow. We'll meet on my yacht and iron out the details. Be there at 9 a.m., sharp. But for now, I have a party to attend to."

She needed a stiff drink by the time Cowboi rejoined the orgy of his orchestration. She scanned the crowd for Boon and Crab, hoping they were ready to leave, but they were nowhere to be found. Trapped on Easter Cay, Gemma rang Rebecca for bottle service.

10

MEGAYACHT

Gemma wasn't sure what to wear for yachting with a superstar, but she knew from the party at Easter Cay that her Sargasso-sailor look wouldn't impress anyone in Cowboi's circle. Aboard *Luna*, turning this way and that, Gemma inspected herself in a hand mirror. The tight quarters made it difficult to get a full view, forcing her to contort awkwardly as the boat gently rocked with the morning tide. Her reflection revealed a woman struggling to belong in a world that wasn't naturally her own.

The belted, high-waisted shorts hugged her slim hips perfectly, complementing her long legs. The oversized white-collared blouse, crisp and pristine against her amber skin, was tucked in just so—not too casual, not too stuffy. Her tan espadrilles had tasteful heels, while the large-brimmed straw hat, banded with a blue ribbon embroidered with tiny anchors, completed the ensemble.

It was a close approximation of what the beautiful people wore on the covers of the leisure and sailing magazines that blanketed the Taino Bay timeshare office. Those glossy pages had been her guide, studied during slow afternoons between dream pitches to tourists.

She'd made a special trip to the club shop at the Taino Bay golf course, but Gemma could justify the splurge as an investment. This outing was a type of job interview. Besides the nautical-inspired outfit, she'd purchased an elegant bikini, a matching cover-up in sheer fabric, and— in a moment of daring—a little red evening dress that clung to her curves as if it were painted on. The saleswoman had assured her the dress wouldn't wrinkle in an overnight bag and was perfect for yacht cocktail parties. And Gemma pretended that jet-setting was a regular occurrence in her life.

Adjusting her freshly manicured dreadlocks so they cascaded perfectly from beneath the hat, Gemma sighed at her reflection. It would have to do. The women in Gemma's life were paragons of style, each expressing elegance in their own distinctive way. Yaya Mari always dressed impeccably for special occasions, wrapping herself in carefully arranged Caribbean fabrics that she wore with quiet dignity to church and on shopping excursions. Gemma's mother possessed an equally refined sense of style, though Gemma often dismissed her as "just a waitress." In reality, she was a skilled server at a Michelin-starred establishment who moved seamlessly between her crisp black-and-white work uniform and the flowing, elegant Bohemian pieces she favored for the countless music and art events that filled their community.

Feeling awkward, Gemma slouched in her bus seat. School kids in pale pink polo shirts and maroon slacks or pleated skirts jostled and laughed. The narrow aisle became an impromptu playground as two boys tossed a baseball cap back and forth, daring each other to keep it out of reach of a third child. Every so often, the bus jolted over a pothole, and the children squealed in delight. A cluster of girls sat in the back, their fingers busy braiding each other's hair while they whispered secrets between bursts of giggles. A small boy next to her tugged on his oversized collar, fidgeting with the nervous energy of a long ride still ahead, while another child leaned his head against the window, lulled by the bus's gentle rocking.

The morning commuters over Mt. Calabash scrutinized Gemma with undisguised interest. On the small island, where everyone knew everyone else, gossiping was a popular pastime, and today's topic was Gemma's attire. Instead of the polyester suit that was the uniform of the Yacht Heaven timeshare associates, she wore an outfit that cost more than most islanders made in a week. She felt judgment cling to her like the humid air.

On St. Columba, sudden leaps in status happened—a billionaire marriage or a real estate windfall that transformed fishermen's children into magnates overnight. Understandably, islanders had mixed feelings about these reversals of fortune—both jealousy and a secret desire to be next in line for such a transformation. The older women clicked their tongues, while the

Megayacht | 87

younger ones leaned closer, hoping to catch the scent of her perfume or a glimpse of whatever other expensive treasures might be hidden in that new handbag.

Gemma shook off the staring eyes, stepped down at her usual stop, but instead of heading toward Yacht Heaven, she turned and walked toward the almost deserted dock reserved for private luxury boats. Her footsteps echoed softly against the wood where Cowboi's man waited in a sleek yacht tender, its thrusters humming softly as it held position in the rolling tide.

"Welcome, I'm Aldo," Cowboi's steward said as he maneuvered alongside. He was a big, rough-looking man —not much of a steward in Gemma's humble opinion, more of a bodyguard. "Hand me your shoes and jump in. Cowboi is waiting for you on the *Freedom*."

She slipped off her espadrilles, took Aldo's hand, and accepted a flute of champagne while she took her seat. The transport skipped along the surface of the water, offering perfect views of the coral heads and rock formations that swirled with multicolored fish forty feet below.

As they drew closer to the enormous, gleaming white yacht anchored midway between St. Columba and Easter Cay, its sleek lines shone against the azure backdrop of the Caribbean. The *Freedom* was a floating palace, at least 300 feet of polished perfection with multiple decks rising like wedding cake tiers against the cloudless sky. The boat featured a drive-in bay for the tenders as big as a cathedral, its cavernous interior illuminated by recessed lighting that cast an ethereal glow across the gently lapping water. Aldo expertly maneuvered into the opening, the engine's purr echoing off the polished walls of the yacht's interior harbor.

"Watch your step," Aldo cautioned as he cut the engine and let momentum carry them the final few feet to the landing platform. He secured the tender with practiced efficiency, then took Gemma's hand to steady her as she stepped across the watery gap. Gemma's espadrilles dangled from her other hand as her bare feet touched the cool, glass-like surface. She could feel the subtle vibration of the yacht's idling engines humming beneath her, a reminder of the massive machinery keeping this floating luxury island operational.

"We'll get underway momentarily. Just follow the path of blue lights aft to the pool. Cowboi is expecting you," Aldo said as he stepped up behind her. Pinpoint LEDs inset like jewels ran in lines down the narrow gangway to the stern deck.

Gemma's heart sank a little when she saw that Boon and Crab had been included in what she thought would be a private meeting. Tables covered with the detritus of a catered feast overflowed with champagne bottles in melting ice and half-eaten platters of oysters. Shrimp tails littered the ground like the discarded fans of tiny geishas.

Crab noticed Gemma, waved, then cannonballed into the pool like a goofy redneck. The girls chosen for today's outing shrieked, throwing their hands up in a futile attempt to shield themselves from the shower of chlorinated water. Their expressions were a mix of laughter and irritation, eyes narrowing as droplets landed on their blingy cell phones and romance novels. Crab resurfaced, shaking his wet hair and grinning unabashedly.

Thankfully, only Gemma's sandals got sprinkled. She would have been furious if Crab had soaked her carefully selected outfit. Boon waved lazily from his chaise lounge, a half-empty champagne bottle dangling precariously from his thick fingers, while Cowboi blew an air kiss across the sun-warmed expanse of polished teak, his egg-sized diamond ring glinting in the Caribbean sunshine like warning signals she chose to ignore.

"Gemma!" He stood and met her with hands outstretched. "I'm so glad you made it. Come. Come. Follow me. Let's get you changed into your swimsuit." Cowboi wrapped her in a hug as if she were family.

"I have my bikini on under my shorts. I can just change here—" Gemma started. But Cowboi contradicted her by taking her hand and leading her away from the party deck, through a bulkhead, and down a ramp that narrowed into a corridor lit by recessed lamps. Every twenty feet, a small, round-edged door broke the smoothness of the hall's liminal yawn. Cowboi pulled the latch on cabin three, revealing a sleek room decorated in white acrylic, mirrors, and chrome.

"Get changed in here and stow your things. I need to talk to you in private before we rejoin the others," he said.

She closed the door between them, letting out a quick breath as she stripped down to her swimsuit. With a final glance in the mirror, she opened the door and stepped back into the hallway, where Cowboi waited, his eyes scanning her with a lazy, knowing smirk. It struck her that she was nearly naked for their so-called business meeting—the bikini's cut leaving little to the imagination. She straightened, lifting her chin to match his gaze, determined not to let the imbalance in their attire diminish her.

On the walk, the hall felt both expansive and confining; the silence between them was weighted with unspoken expectations as she reminded herself why she was there.

"Did you have this yacht built for you?" she asked.

"No, ma'am. Bought it used," Cowboi smiled boyishly. "The Sultan of Brunei wanted an upgrade. He thought this boat was embarrassingly small, but it suits me just fine."

She whistled through her teeth. "Too small, huh?"

"Yep. The sultan's new boat's 'bout 450 feet. Parked in Cannes right now," he chattered on in his affected country drawl, making the billionaire circuit sound like a monster truck pull.

Gemma followed Cowboi into a salon, past a bank of windows that wrapped them in a vista of blue. The mahogany glowed like liquid glass. Sofas snaked along the yacht's walls in an elegant and subtle cream and gold damask pattern. Built-in cabinets and silver monochrome stained glass windows curved gently back toward the guest cabins.

"Gemma, you're shaping up to be one of my most reliable captains," Cowboi said.

That Cowboi's redneck accent dissolved into bland,

efficient business-speak did not escape Gemma's notice. His country act came and went as frequently as the ocean breezes.

"I don't actually have a captain's license. I mean, I've been sailing since before I could walk, here and on Lake Champlain. But I never got certified."

"Well, you are an admiral in my book. Anyway, paper trails are not my style."

"Guess that makes sense," Gemma said. She crossed her arms over her chest and slumped forward slightly, an instinctive attempt to shield her exposed body. Her nervousness was so transparent it seemed to amuse Cowboi.

In resistance to his laughter, Gemma deliberately uncrossed her arms and straightened her posture. She squared her shoulders and lifted her chin, forcing herself to meet his gaze directly. The confidence felt entirely fabricated—her heart hammered against her ribs with each shallow breath—but she refused to let him see how deeply uncomfortable she felt.

"Listen. The whole reason I invited you here today is that I have a long-distance pickup in the Dominican Republic, and I need a crew and a captain I can trust. Boon's great, and so is Crab, but I've decided I'm going to put you in charge of this job. It's a test run, shall we say? If you do well, you'll get a promotion and more important work."

Gemma didn't know what disturbed her most—that she would be in charge of Boon and Crab as their captain, or the uncertainty of moving up the ladder in an organized crime ring.

"I don't have a boat that can make that trip. *Luna* is tiny—only twenty-eight feet and not open-water ready," Gemma said, hoping that Cowboi would lose interest in her for her lack of qualifications and allow her to continue to taxi the girls from the airport to Easter Cay in Boon's borrowed Sea Ray. That work was low risk and high enough pay to keep Gemma's anxiety in check.

"I talked to Boon already. He filled me in on your experience and your little boat problem. Tell you what, pick out a shiny new boat; whatever you want. Off the showroom floor, and I'll buy it for you as payment for the job, plus cash. It's got to be a sailing vessel, though. For this type of work, we want to limit your check-ins. And sometimes, you need to run silent."

"Any boat I want?" Gemma asked, astonished.

Her head was spinning. The trepidation of a moment before gave way to a rush of giddy excitement. A boat—not just any boat, but a proper yacht of her own—dangled before her like forbidden fruit, ripe for the taking. And not just the vessel itself, but also start-up cash—real money that could transform her half-formed plans into something tangible. This was Gemma's big break, the opportunity she'd been waiting for since she'd first returned to St. Columba with nothing but a suitcase and dreams.

It was everything she'd fantasized about during those long, grueling shifts at Yacht Heaven Mall, watching wealthy tourists casually discuss their maritime purchases while she struggled to make rent on her $500-a-month marina fees. Her charter business—no longer just wishful plans scribbled in notebooks—could actually materialize far sooner than she imagined. Turnkey. Her independence, her future, her chance to belong to the island on her own terms, all wrapped in pretty paper made of Cowboi's money.

"Any **suitable** boat," Cowboi amended. "Not too flashy. A production model. Something unremarkable. It needs to have a good-sized cargo area. We don't want to attract attention. A Beneteau would be my pick. They're a dime a dozen."

As Gemma absorbed the offer, her mind raced with the implications. She wanted to be her own boss, to quit Taino Bay once and for all, to own a decent boat and start her own charter company. Never mind that Cowboi's 'unremarkable' was her 'unobtainable.' A Beneteau was boat porn to her.

"Thank you for the opportunity, Cowboi. I won't let you down." She sat up even taller and accepted immediately.

Cowboi's grin widened, his approval clear. "I knew I could count on you, Gemma. Now that's settled, let's get back to the party."

Back at the pool, Cowboi flashed Crab and Boon a thumbs-up.

"Well, if it ain't our new captain," Boon teased. "Gemma's going to be the boss of us and work us to the bone."

Crab, who was lounging by the pool with a drink in

hand, laughed and raised his glass in salute. "To Captain Gemma!"

The sunbathing girls looked up with expressions that mixed respect with jealousy. Gemma's chest filled with confidence and pride. She realized she was ready to take on this new role, despite her initial apprehensions.

Cowboi drew his hand to his lips and released a piercing whistle between his forefinger and thumb, drawing everyone's attention.

"All right, everyone. We've got a beautiful day ahead of us. Let's enjoy it."

He picked up his acoustic guitar, mounted the diving board, and started strumming "Tennessee Waltz." Laughter filled the air as Crab grabbed one of the girls and dipped and twirled her around the pool. Gemma sat next to Boon, soaking up the sun's glow. She leaned back in her chair. The dream she had chased since arriving in St. Columba was now within reach, but the stakes were higher than ever. Cowboi's approval felt as intoxicating as the champagne fizzing in her flute. Yet, the shadow of what she was agreeing to lingered at the edges of her mind, a quiet warning she wasn't ready to heed.

The sounds of the party swelled around her, with Cowboi's guitar twanging as he transitioned into a raucous rendition of "Free Bird" and Crab hollering as he splashed into the pool yet again. Boon turned to her with a conspiratorial grin.

"You did good, kid," he said, his tone soft but carrying a weight of meaning that made her stomach twist.

Gemma raised her glass to her lips; the bubbles

Megayacht | 95

tickled her nose. She felt the eyes of the girls flitting toward her—maybe friendly, maybe curious, but all calculating. In that moment, she wasn't just Gemma August, the prodigal local girl; she was Gemma, Cowboi's chosen captain.

Cowboi tipped his hat back, laughing as he strummed an exaggerated outro to his song. The laughter and music faded into thoughts. For a moment, Gemma closed her eyes, imagining the life Cowboi had offered—a sleek boat and freedom from the grind. She turned back to the party, resolved for the moment. This was her chance, her turning point. She couldn't afford to falter now.

11

CONFESSION

Nihir sat cross-legged on the floor of the open-air kitchen, his spine perfectly straight yet relaxed. The gentle island breeze carried wisps of cardamom and clove-scented steam through the bamboo-screened space, mingling with the scent of tropical flowers from the garden. The creak of weathered wooden planks drew his attention, his serene expression brightening as he saw Gemma.

"Gemma! Join me for some chai," Nihir called out and waved her over.

Gemma's growing paranoia had pushed her here, seeking refuge in the one place where stillness seemed possible. The frantic thoughts that had been chasing her for days slowed in Nihir's tranquil presence; his measured breathing somehow calmed the storm inside her mind. The familiar tingle of peace that always seemed to emanate from him washed over her like a gentle wave, but it came coupled with an unwelcome realization that settled heavily in her chest: Cowboi's glittering world of wealth and exclusivity might not represent the freedom she had imagined. Instead, the golden cage she had willingly entered was beginning to reveal its bars, ornate but confining nonetheless. She was having second thoughts.

"You seem troubled," Nihir prompted.

"Can I trust you to keep a secret?" Gemma asked.

"Of course."

"Even if it's shady?" she inquired.

"Your secrets are perfectly safe with me," Nihir replied, his voice calm and grounded. "Please, take a seat."

Gemma sank onto a meditation cushion across from Nihir, adjusting herself awkwardly. The cushion's buckwheat seeds crunched beneath her weight as she tried to find a comfortable position.

He leaned over a small camp-style gas burner, its blue flame dancing beneath an intricately hand-hammered copper pot that gleamed with the patina of years of use, and poured their tea with quiet precision, his movements flowing with practiced grace. The aromatic chai arced smoothly into the cups placed between them. He whitened Gemma's with a small can of milk, tilting it just so, creating a perfect swirl of cream like a tiny maelstrom. The ritual seemed to slow time itself, offering a momentary respite from the chaos of Gemma's thoughts.

She picked up the cup and caressed the alternating rings of glaze and rough clay, its surface warm under her fingers. The tactile sensation grounded her, the cup's imperfect beauty somehow matching the conflicted feelings churning within her—both polished and raw, contained yet exposed.

Comfort spread through her body with the first sip. There was no urgency in Nihir's manner, just the quiet assurance that Gemma's words would come when she was ready.

"Nihir, I needed the money, so I took a job on this private island for wealthy people. At first, it was just running a water taxi—not the worst gig. I mentioned it to you briefly before. But now, they want me to do something illegal and dangerous."

"You are working for Cowboi Rivers?" Nihir asked.

"Yes."

"And this taxi you're running, it delivers sex workers?"

"How did you know?"

Nihir took a slow sip of his chai, his gaze drifting to the garden's edge where a hibiscus flower swayed gently in the breeze.

"You know, Gemma, this island isn't so different from where I grew up."

She tilted her head, curious. "Where's that?"

"Suriname. A small country in South America." He smiled faintly. "It's so small, you've probably never heard of it."

"I've heard of it," she said, her fingers tracing the rim of her clay cup. "But, honestly, I don't know much about it."

"It's a place with a complicated history," he said. "When I was growing up, it was poor. Dirt poor. There's

Confession | 99

oil money there, but that wealth has never trickled down to the people who need it most." He paused, the steam from his cup curling around his fingers.

"My parents were strict. Very religious. I ran away from home when I was sixteen."

Gemma's eyebrows lifted. "Sixteen? That's young."

He nodded, his expression thoughtful rather than regretful. "It was young, yes, but I believed I understood the world completely—as the young often do." He adjusted his position slightly on the cushion, his movements measured and deliberate. "After several weeks on my own, hunger became my constant companion, gnawing at both my body and my resolve. Still, I remained too proud, too certain of my path to return home."

Nihir's eyes met Gemma's with gentle intensity, his voice maintaining its warm, instructive cadence. "I encountered a businessman who offered a room in his beautiful home, provided elegant clothing, and delicious meals." He paused, allowing the weight of what would follow to settle between them. "But these comforts, as you might suspect, were not freely given. They came with expectations—a transaction I wasn't prepared to fully comprehend at that age."

Gemma set her cup down gently, sensing the weight of what Nihir was about to share.

"Sex work," Nihir said simply, not looking away. "For the political and investment elite who controlled all the wealth in my country. It seemed like the only way to escape my poverty."

Her expression didn't falter, though her grip tightened

slightly on the edge of the cushion. "I'm sorry," she said softly.

"I'm not," Nihir replied, his tone steady. "It shaped who I am. It could have been much worse. My clients treated me well—very well, in fact. Eventually, that same businessman brought me to Miami. There, I was marketed as a—well, a Kama Sutra fantasy, let's say." He smiled wryly. "It was a role I could lean into."

Gemma's gaze held his, her expression open but tinged with unease. "Did you meet Cowboi then?"

Nihir laughed. "I've more than met him. Yes, he booked me for his themed parties. Wild affairs, as you can imagine. During those trips, I discovered and fell in love with St. Columba." His voice grew warmer. "This place felt like a refuge. A chance to start over."

"How did you get out of that life?" she asked, her voice quiet.

"A benefactor. A client who saw more in me than what I was selling." He set his cup down and met her eyes. "He helped me buy my freedom. After that, I came back here and built this studio. I'm not ashamed of my experience, Gemma. It taught me resilience, empathy, and how to navigate a world that often feels impossible to live in."

She nodded, her cup cooling in her hands. "That's—a lot."

"We all carry something," Nihir said gently. "What matters is how and when we set it down." To illustrate, he set his cup on the floor.

It hit Gemma hard that someone like her had trafficked someone like Nihir, that he had worked on

Cowboi's island, that he had been with Cowboi. Tears streamed down her face as he scooted over to stroke her hair.

"Are you alright?" Nihir rested his hand on Gemma's back to steady her.

"I didn't expect you to have a past like that. I thought yogis were born in lotus pose."

Nihir laughed at her small joke but quickly composed himself in reaction to her dismay.

Gemma's voice hitched in her throat as she spoke. "Nihir, I'm so sorry. This world sucks. Now, Cowboi is offering me my big break. After what you told me, I don't know how to feel about it."

"My dear heart, you don't need to worry about me. I am free. Royal Asana is my perfect sanctuary. It may not seem like much, just some rough shacks in the jungle, but I'm truly content here. I want nothing bigger or fancier. What I know is that Cowboi isn't really offering you freedom. You already have that. You, too, must find satisfaction in what's real. The money isn't what you imagine. Do you understand me?"

Gemma gulped. "Shit. I don't know. What can I do? I'm stuck. Cowboi wants to promote me to captain. I've already said yes. This is a big job, and going back on my word might be risky, even dangerous. I don't think I can refuse it."

"It's your journey. It always has been. As I've told you all along, I'm here for you when you are ready to step outside of this reality you are creating. Your dilemma is an illusion. A narrative you've written. But I know that's hard to see. There is nothing to lose and nothing to gain. No matter what you choose, I am here for you."

Gemma sat quietly with Nihir. He had listened and demanded nothing in return. The students for the next class started to filter in, but Gemma didn't want to stay for practice. Her mind buzzed with conflict and embarrassment. Nihir had given her a brief respite from her thoughts, but she had known even before she sat down that he couldn't convince her to change her course.

"Gemma, listen to me," Nihir said, his voice carrying that familiar blend of warmth and quiet authority. "There's no immediate decision that must be made. Take a breath with that knowledge." He leaned forward slightly, his eyes meeting hers with compassion. "Please understand, I hold no judgment of you or your choices. I recognize actions as either skillful or unskillful—and even this distinction is merely our limited human discernment." He gestured with an open palm. "The path that seems most difficult may offer precisely the wisdom you need most. We can never truly know."

The sunlight filtering through the open-air studio caught the edges of his profile as he glanced toward the gathering students, golden rays illuminating the strong lines of his jaw and casting a warm glow across his serene features. "I'm here whenever you wish to continue this conversation, Gemma. My door remains open to you—day or night," he added, his voice dropping slightly lower on those last words. He paused, offering a gentle smile, lingering on her face with an attentiveness that hadn't been there before. The air between them seemed to shift, charged with a subtle new energy.

"The next class is about to begin—a gentle flow focused on finding stillness within uncertainty," he explained, his fingers lightly brushing her arm as he spoke. His touch was brief but deliberate, leaving warmth in its wake. "Would you care to stay and practice with us? Sometimes the body finds clarity when the mind cannot." He tilted his head slightly, his gaze holding hers with quiet intensity.

"I have the season wrap-up meeting at Taino Bay. I can't," Gemma replied.

"Okay. Well, how about you meet me tonight for dinner, then?" Nihir asked.

"Are you asking me on a date?" Gemma joked, secretly hoping it was true.

"Who knows which path opens before us?" Nihir smiled once more, this time with a twinkle of impish mischief.

Gemma had told a partial truth. She was indeed heading to Taino Bay, but the season wrap-up meeting was merely a convenient excuse. What truly pulled her there was far more pressing and complicated. She needed to expand her crew for Cowboi's job, and her list of potential candidates had narrowed to one name. Taino Bay was where she would find Cruz.

12

TAINO BAY

Under the sweeping shadows that crisscrossed the mosaic entrance of the Taino Bay business center, Gemma's co-workers gathered in small groups—servers with servers, maids with maids, managers with managers. Chatter filled the air, accompanied by the faint strains of steel drum music drifting from the live performer at the poolside bar. Every year, Taino executives dangled small perks—pool passes, discounted rooms, and vague promises of bonuses—hoping to entice current employees into signing contracts for another year of servitude.

The resort's slick veneer didn't fool anyone who worked there. Behind the charming cabanas lay a machine of ruthless efficiency. The annual ritual felt like watching people thrown into a shark tank, their desperation masked by forced smiles and pressed uniforms. Management circulated through the crowd, their practiced warmth as artificial as the coconut scent of the sunscreen they wore.

At last year's party, Gemma had been searching for a current that might carry her somewhere better than this purgatory—some invisible tide that would lift her above the cycle of tourist seasons and contract renewals. This year, her eyes swept the crowd not for salvation but for Cruz. On the private terrace of the conference room, she spotted him. He held the resort's signature cocktail, a Crystal Blue, in one hand. Employees jokingly referred to the drink as the Taino Drano—a mixed abomination of blue Curaçao and cheap rum.

Gemma walked over, brushing the ash from Cruz's lapel with a quick flick of her fingers. He flashed a sheepish grin, sweeping his hand over his hair as if to smooth away his embarrassment. Without a word, he stubbed out his cigarette in the glass ashtray balanced precariously on the railing. Below, the lazy river pool wound through plastic landscaping, its surface marred by an empty, deflated raft drifting listlessly on the water.

"When's the next party at Cowboi's?" Cruz asked suddenly, his eyes gleaming with anticipation for a night in the infamous world beyond the reef.

Gemma tilted her head and gave him a small smile. The opportunity to recruit Cruz might prove easier than she'd anticipated. "I don't know when the next party is," she replied casually, "but I can do one better. Cowboi wants me to do a job in the Dominican Republic, and I need more hands on the sail."

Cruz raised his brows. "Holy shit. Are you asking me to work for him?"

"Maybe," Gemma replied, keeping her tone even. "But listen—first, you don't even know what I need you to do. And second, are you really ready to jump into danger that easily?"

"Hell, yeah!" Cruz said with a shrug, grinning. "I don't care what the work is. If it's for Cowboi, I'm in."

Gemma held his gaze. She could see the flicker of excitement alive in his eyes.

"I'll be straight with you—Vaughn was the last guy to do this job, and he's missing. You remember Vaughn?" Gemma leaned in closer. "So, I want you to enter this with your eyes open. And that's not all. We'll be sailing. And not just sailing. Sailing in storm season. Hurricanes are no joke out there—they're killers. But the money is real. Five hundred grand in cash."

Cruz's grin faltered for just a second. "You're serious," he said, more a statement than a question.

"Dead serious. Cowboi trusts me to make this happen, but in turn, I need a crew I can trust. He's giving me the boat we're using for the delivery, and I'll be the captain. The trip will take a couple of weeks, maybe longer, depending on the conditions. My cut's higher because of my position, but a half-mill could be life-changing for you, or it could be a death sentence." She paused, letting the weight of the offer settle. "Don't answer right away. This is a big decision, and I don't want to drag you into something that might ruin your life."

He was silent. Deep calculation seemed to process

Taino Bay | 107

behind his eyes. Around them, the murmur of conversation grew louder. Gemma noticed a few glances in their direction; her conversation with Cruz had drawn unwanted attention. She leaned closer and lowered her voice. "Think about it. We can talk at The Last Resort if you're interested."

Cruz drummed his fingers against the table. "Forget that! Sign me up," he said, his grin returning twice as bright.

"When do we leave?"

"In two weeks, maybe sooner." Gemma smiled but continued with seriousness. "You can't breathe a word of this. No joke. Don't let those jerks over there know what's up." She nodded toward the Taino sales crowd, who were edging closer, their curiosity piqued by the overheard name of Cowboi Rivers.

"Welcome aboard," she said. "Listen, I have a date tonight. I'll text you tomorrow, and we'll firm up the details. I gotta run."

Cruz took a long sip of his drink. His eyes glinted with a calculated excitement that Gemma recognized. She held the key to the mysterious private island that everyone talked about.

"It's a deal, boss." Cruz winked.

Gemma rolled her eyes good-naturedly and left Cruz to his Taino Drano. As she walked away, she replayed in her mind the speech about life-changing money and death sentences and realized she had sounded like some side character on *Breaking Bad*. Heat crept up her neck at the memory of her own affected seriousness. Who did she think she was, speaking like that? It felt ridiculous, but the danger and money involved had forced her to frame the job in this type of tone. This wasn't a game of pretend. Perhaps sounding like a TV mobster wasn't so far off the mark after all.

13

BEFORE THE STORM

Waiting on the boardwalk, Gemma passed the time reading entrée specials and perusing the exotic cocktail list at the Neptune Bistro. The laminated menu boasted fresh-caught mahi-mahi with mango salsa for $52 and something called a "Castaway Cooler" that promised four types of rum. She traced her finger down the overpriced dishes, wondering if tourists actually paid these prices without flinching. She wasn't sure where Nihir would take her, but she assumed it would be one of these tourist spots on the beach.

"Gemma."

She turned at the sound of her name and found Nihir standing a few feet away, his silhouette softened by the tiki lights along the railing. He wore a simple white cotton button-down with the top few buttons undone and well-worn jeans. His leather sandals looked handcrafted, the kind sold by artisans at the island market rather than the mass-produced styles from Yacht Heaven.

His presence carried that unmistakable centeredness that made him seem like the only still point in a constantly shifting world, but tonight, there was tension in the air between them. His eyes held hers with an intensity different from their yoga sessions—more personal, more searching.

"Ready?" Nihir asked, his voice low.

"Sure," she replied. "Where do you want to eat?"

He nodded toward the beach. "There's a place around the point. We have to walk along the water's edge to get there. It's my favorite spot on the island."

Nihir took a seat on the wooden steps leading to the beach, slipped off his sandals, and rolled up his pants. Gemma followed suit, kicking off her flip-flops and clipping them to a carabiner on her dry bag. She felt a subtle shift in her energy, a loosening, as if Nihir's calm certainty had somehow spread to her.

They walked together, their footsteps pressing into the cool, damp sand while the tide lapped at their ankles. The shoreline curved gently ahead—a narrow strip of pale beach bordered by the shadowy silhouettes of night palms swaying in the breeze. The rhythmic sound of waves filled the space between them.

Nihir maintained an even pace, though every now and then, his shoulder brushed against Gemma's. As they approached the rocky point, the faint sound of music drifted on the wind. Nihir led her around the wave-kissed promontory and through a cluster of tide pools toward lantern-lit tables beneath trees at the base of a cliff.

"Here we are," Nihir said.

The rocky outcrop had concealed a small eatery—almost a shack. Fairy lights strung through a Cuban oak cast a gentle glow over sea grape hedges. The ambiance was intimate and quiet.

"I didn't know this place was here," Gemma said, genuinely surprised.

"Parking is above. You normally access it from that trail." Nihir pointed to a couple descending the rocky dirt path leading to the restaurant.

"Right! I've seen the sign on the road, but this is the first time I've actually come down here."

"As I said, it's my favorite, and I'm glad I get to share it with you," Nihir said. "It reminds me of home. My mother was a wonderful cook."

Nihir ordered samosas, curry vegetables, steamed fish with spicy herb chutney, and a bottle of dry white wine. They talked about the studio. Gemma's fingers traced the rim of her wineglass as her thoughts wandered—the drug run to the Dominican Republic would take her away from the island and pull her deeper into the dangerous orbit of Cowboi's operations.

"I have to say, you're really making progress with the intermediate poses," Nihir said, leaning back in his chair. "Solid. Strong stance, steady breath."

Gemma laughed softly. "Half the time, I'm just hoping I don't fall over."

"The balance comes naturally when you stop trying so

hard." Nihir smiled. "But enough about yoga. How are you enjoying the meal?"

"It's perfect," Gemma said, reaching for another samosa.

The weight of Nihir's easy presence made her feel both safe and exposed. The urge to fill the silence bubbled up inside her.

"My grandmother has something planned for me," she said suddenly. "At Mariposa's End—where my father's people live—my Yaya is insisting on this kind of ceremony. An initiation, she calls it." Her voice dropped as she leaned across the table. "It's happening right before I have to leave for—" She caught herself. "Before I leave on the trip."

Nihir's eyes softened with interest. "What kind of ceremony?"

"That's the thing," Gemma said, breaking the samosa apart with nervous fingers. "It's all very mysterious, very traditional. Something about connecting with spirits, talking to the dead." She shook her head with an uncomfortable laugh. "Mari says it's for protection, that I need a guardian to watch over me. She believes I have the gift—like she does."

"And do you believe that?" Nihir asked without judgment.

Gemma watched palm fronds sway in the evening breeze. "I don't know what I believe anymore. Sometimes I see things that..." She trailed off, then met his eyes again. "I'm both terrified and fascinated by it all. The End has this energy that's so different from anywhere else on the island. When I'm there, surrounded by all that history, all those expectations—it's like something ancient is pulling at me."

She took a sip of wine, trying to steady herself. "Mari keeps talking about a special tea. She says I'll be able to see my guardian spirits clearly afterward. That they'll be bound to me." Her fingers twisted her napkin beneath the table. "It sounds crazy when I say it out loud, doesn't it?"

Nihir's expression didn't waver. He nodded thoughtfully. "Not at all. I've always sensed there was something deeper to you."

Gemma shrugged, trying to brush it off. "Enough about this superstitious stuff. What about you? What are your plans for Royal Asana?" She tried to keep her tone light. "I've been thinking you could do so much more with it."

"Oh?" Nihir raised an eyebrow.

"I mean, the studio is gorgeous, and the classes are great, but you could expand. Partner with the resorts and offer private sessions to luxury tourists. Maybe even brand it with a line of yoga props. You could reach so many more people." Her words came out in a rushed stream. "Imagine hosting retreats for the wealthy elite. They'd pay premium prices."

Nihir took a sip of wine, studying her. "And what about the studio as it is now? The gardens, the community meals, the locals who find refuge there? Wouldn't expanding change all of that?"

Gemma opened her mouth to respond, then hesitated. Her fingers returned to the rim of her wine glass. "I guess—but maybe that's part of growth? Evolving into something bigger?"

"Bigger isn't always better," Nihir said. "Royal Asana isn't about fame or money for me. It's a place where people can come as they are and find peace. If it gets too big, too polished, it might lose what makes it special. Take this restaurant—it's hidden, family-run. Would it be better if it were exclusive and expensive?"

Gemma nodded, feeling the weight of his words. "That makes sense. I just thought—forget I said anything. I talk when I'm nervous."

Nihir leaned forward slightly. "Gemma, I think you're not really talking about the studio."

Her gaze shot up, meeting his. For a moment, she couldn't find the words.

He smiled knowingly. "You're carrying something—I can see that. A pressure to be impressive and successful. Maybe to prove something. It's okay to put that down for a little while."

Gemma looked out at the ocean, the horizon fading into the darkening sky. "You make it sound so easy."

"It's not, but it's worth trying."

They fell back into silence, the rhythm of the waves filling the space between them.

"I'm not sure how I feel about Cowboi," Gemma finally said, disrupting the comfort. She could no longer keep the imminent trip from entering the conversation.

Nihir nodded with understanding. "You don't have to

do it. You can stay here. Tell Cowboi you changed your mind. You have your family in Mariposa's End, your friends, me, and Royal Asana. Your life is a good one."

She sighed, leaning back in her chair. "If I don't play the game, I'll always wonder what could have been. It's not just about the money, though I won't pretend that it doesn't matter. I feel like this is my way out. You need a million to make a million."

Nihir reached across the table, his hand resting gently on hers. "I understand. But Cowboi isn't someone you can walk away from easily once you get in deep."

Gemma bit her lip, staring at their hands. "That's the thing, Nihir. I've spent my whole life scraping by, waiting for a break that never comes. People like me don't get ahead by working harder. We need luck—and luck isn't always legal."

Nihir's thumb gently stroked her palm as his eyes searched hers. "I get it, Gemma. Where one fits into society was everything in Suriname. But what you're talking about—it's risky. And I'm not just talking about money or the law. If you start down this path, how far are you willing to go? It's a road I have walked down, and one I chose to step off of. I may not have riches, but I have true wealth. I'm a person with purpose and satisfaction."

Gemma swallowed. She hadn't thought of it like that. Her mind was on elevation and freedom, not on the parts of herself she might have to sacrifice along the way.

"I won't pretend to have all the answers, Gemma. But you don't have to go through this alone. When you get back, I'll be here."

Her heart swelled with a mix of gratitude and guilt. She had been so focused on her needs that she hadn't fully considered the impact on those who cared about her. "I don't want to drag you into my mess," she said.

Nihir smiled. "Too late for that."

They both laughed, breaking the tension. The weight of her decision felt heavier than ever. As they continued to eat, their conversation flowed easily, the wine helping to loosen the knots. Yet the reality still hung in the air—she was sailing for two weeks, and the future felt uncertain, as though she were walking a tightrope with no safety net.

When the check came, Nihir insisted on paying, but Gemma waved him off. "No way. Let me handle this one."

He smiled without pushing the issue. Strolling back toward the boardwalk, the air had cooled, and the stars were whirls of milky galaxies against the clear sky. Gemma was approaching their goodbye. She wouldn't see him again before the trip.

"Gemma, whatever happens, be careful out there," Nihir said as they reached the bus stop.

Gemma looked into his eyes, feeling a pang of something she didn't want to name. "You know what? Why don't you come with me?"

Nihir blinked, surprised, his steady composure momentarily slipping. "What? Come with you? On the job for Cowboi?"

"Yeah," Gemma said, trying to keep her tone casual. "What do you say?"

Hesitation settled over him. He had just warned her to stay clear of this. She saw it in the slight shift of his posture, the way his gaze flickered to the horizon as if weighing something invisible and incredibly heavy between them. He'd been so certain a moment ago that she shouldn't get tangled up in Cowboi's world.

"I'm not a sailor," he said carefully.

She knew it was dangerous to ask, and judging by the way Nihir exhaled—a long, measured breath—he knew it too. But something in his hesitation wasn't just about the boat; it was about her.

"Well, the island practically rolls up its streets in August," Nihir said after a beat, his voice quieter now. "I'll be lucky to have a handful of students pass through the studio during the summer. Half the businesses are closed."

There it was—his excuse. The reason he could give himself, the thing that made saying yes seem reasonable. But Gemma could see through it. The way his fingers tapped his side, the way his jaw tightened before he spoke. He was choosing her, even if he wasn't ready to admit it.

She leaned in before she could second-guess herself. The kiss was brief but decisive—enough to taste the salt on his lips, to feel the way he stilled for a fraction of a second before responding. Enough to tell her that whatever this was between them, neither had control over it.

When she pulled away, his breath came a little uneven.

"Looks like you're coming with me, then," she murmured.

The bus arrived with a hiss of air brakes, its headlights

cutting through the glittering darkness. Gemma stepped back, the spell between them broken by the mechanical intrusion. Other passengers shuffled aboard—late-shift workers heading home, a couple of tourists clutching to-go bags from Neptune Bistro.

"I should go," she said, but neither of them moved toward the bus.

Nihir ran a hand through his hair. "Gemma, what we're talking about... if I come with you, there's no pretending this is just a sailing trip."

She nodded, understanding the weight of what she was asking. "I know."

"And your grandmother's ceremony—when is that happening?"

"Tomorrow night," she said.

The bus driver honked once, impatient.

"I have to think about this," Nihir said. "Give me until morning."

Gemma climbed the bus steps and turned. "Whatever you decide," she called through the open bus door, "I understand."

He stood in the circle of light from the streetlamp, hands in his pockets, watching her with an expression she couldn't read. The steady certainty she'd always associated with him had cracked, revealing something more complex underneath.

The doors closed with a pneumatic sigh, and the bus pulled away from the curb. Through the window, she watched Nihir grow smaller until the darkness swallowed him completely. Gemma closed her eyes and felt the weight of the choices she was forcing on others and the choices pressing down on her: Cowboi's job, Nihir's possible companionship, and whatever transformation awaited her in the ritual flames at Mariposa's End. By the time she reached the crossroads, one thing had become clear—there was no turning back.

14

YAYA MARI

Tonight was the ceremony, and Gemma didn't dare miss it. Expectation pressed down on her shoulders as she shifted on the unforgiving braided vine chair. She suspected her grandmother made her sit on the uncomfortable thing on purpose. Yaya's hand-knit blanket wrapped her thin frame in indigo, ochre, and crimson threads. Silver braids framed the old woman's weathered cheeks and penetrating black eyes.

The bitter herbal tea coated Gemma's tongue unpleasantly, but she continued to sip as Yaya Mari rocked in her ancient chair. The rhythmic creaking triggered something deep in Gemma's mind—the exact frequency that brought on her trances. Mari's expression shifted, a knowing smile playing on her lips as she acknowledged something unseen. After a moment of silent communion, she returned her gaze to her granddaughter.

Gemma fought the urge to look behind her. From

experience, she knew her grandmother's spiritual sight extended far beyond the physical world. Yaya's ghosts were something she had yet to grow used to. The evening breeze carried scents of bonfire and boiling whelks up from the beach.

"Your guardian has arrived! This spirit will be bound to you tonight. He is the key to your magic and protection. Your relationship with your guardian will grant you sight —near and far—into both the future and the past. The funny thing is, he's an old white drunk," Mari said conspiratorially, then released a squawk of mirth. "Not who I would have picked. The Fates have a wicked sense of humor," she said, her eyes twinkling.

"That's just creepy, Grandma. You're just trying to freak me out," Gemma retorted, grimacing as she took another drink from her handmade clay cup.

"Child, you and your modern sensibilities. Scared of the shadows." Gemma frowned but continued to listen. "You knew this spirit when he was alive. That's his boat right there, anchored just off the beach." Mari pointed to the abandoned boat named *Dream* floating on the horizon, a quarter mile from where she sat.

Gemma's eyes widened in recognition. "That's Vaughn's boat! I saw him by the dinghy shack on the other side of the island. Is he dead?"

Mari nodded, satisfied. "See! There's hope for you yet, girl. Yes, daughter, Vaughn is dead. And it appears he will be bound to you tonight."

Without a guiding spirit, Gemma's rites would have been nothing more than an empty performance and a hollow ritual that meant little in the grand scheme of things. Mari had confided in Gemma weeks before, "I'm worried, child. The spirits—they don't always come when called. It doesn't help that you are skeptical about the whole thing. And without a ghost to guide you, well—"

If Gemma couldn't join with her spirit guide, it would signify more than just personal failure—it could show a shift, a disconnection from the land and ancestors that bound her people together. It might even change how The End was governed. But Vaughn's arrival had shown that Gemma kept the gift of her family line.

The identity of the disheveled sailor whose ghost now lingered between worlds was a surprise. Of all the spirits that could have come to her aid, it was Vaughn—an outsider, a white man, a drunk. And yet, it was Vaughn who proved that Gemma truly had the gift. The moment his presence made itself known, something clicked inside Mari August. It didn't matter that Vaughn was flawed in life or unexpected in death. Perhaps this was cosmic irony designed to amuse mortals and gods alike.

The sun set behind the mountains, plunging the village into purple canyons. In the half-light, a young man ran up from the beach to tell them they were ready. Yaya Mari had orchestrated a coal-walking ceremony for the binding. Her dark eyes fixed on her granddaughter. Black tendrils from the tea of cohoba, marijuana, and jimson coursed through Gemma's blood—pulsing in her ears, building layer upon layer with the sounds of drums, laughter, wind, and crashing waves. Yaya Mari pointed down to a gathering of tall shadows shifting around a whirl of orange flames. When she reached out to Gemma, her fingers stretched like serpents.

Gemma followed Mari down the slope in her bare feet, but it felt as if she flew. The thunderheads of summer storms loomed and bristled overhead. Each flash of lightning cast her in webs of electric blue. When she reached the water's edge, everyone clapped. She stood, gathering power, her heart in rhythm with the beat of the drums. The weight of generations pressed down. The air was thick with the scent of sage and lignum vitae wood burning, glittering embers that rolled out like a red carpet across the sand. Heat shimmered, and the crazed surface of the coal pit became a glimpse of the earth's crust from billions of years ago.

Yaya Mari presented Gemma, her authority commanding silence among the crowd. "Gemma, tonight you stand at the crossroads of your destiny. You have chosen Vaughn, and he has chosen you, but it is the strength of our elders that is your birthright. Sankofa!"

Gemma felt a shiver run through her body. She glanced around, seeing the expectant faces of the living and something else—wavering, ghostly forms she couldn't quite make out. Yaya Mari raised her hands, and the flames roared higher.

"Tonight, you will undergo the rites of passage. You will face trials that will test your spirit, your strength, and your connection to this land."

Gemma stepped onto the fiery path. Heat singed her eyelashes, and the strange warmth from the tea climbed up her body. Voices and song wove a tapestry of sound that enveloped her. The pain seared through her feet, but she remained resolute as she walked. The tea's effects intensified. Ancestors stretched in an undulating chain to eternity—grandmothers, aunts, great writers, sailors, sacred artists—now dead but able to pierce the veil to welcome Gemma. The whispers of powerful words echoed in her ears, resonating with the weight of their experiences.

She embraced their presence and felt their strength. Some of their faces were etched with the deep lines of lives long lived, while others looked younger, their forms barely weathered by the early death that had claimed them. Among them was her father's face, his features both familiar and strange at once. His eyes held the same kindness she remembered from childhood, though his spectral form shimmered with an otherworldly light. He looked as if no time had passed since the accident, but vibrant, somehow. He nodded to her, a gesture so subtle yet so profoundly meaningful that Gemma felt her heart constrict with a bittersweet ache of recognition. Other whispers floated around the pit, soft as a breeze, yet filled with a mystical resonance. The sound wasn't frightening—it was gentle—but it carried an undeniable power. Some spoke in languages she didn't fully understand, words of the dead, words of other lands, yet she felt their meaning in her chest, each syllable a vibration in her soul.

Gemma's breath came quicker, shallow and uneven, as the burning heat under her bare feet enveloped her body and squeezed her lungs. Beneath the overwhelming sensation, there was a strange comfort, too—a sense of belonging, of being part of something much larger. She felt the weight of generations pressing down on her shoulders as her legs grew weak. The coals beneath her feet glowed red in the darkness, each step searing into her consciousness. Her vision blurred at the edges, the faces of the watching community members swimming before her. She lost track of who was dead and who was alive.

Halfway across the bed of fire, Gemma's knees buckled suddenly. She stumbled forward, her balance deserting her as the world tilted dangerously. A collective gasp rose from the crowd. Her body pitched, and for a terrifying moment, she hovered on the brink of collapse. The spirits around her seemed to hold their breath—her father's translucent form leaning forward with unmistakable concern etched across his features. Would she fall? Would the ceremony end in disgrace, confirming all her doubts about belonging here?

With a desperate surge of will, Gemma's hand shot out to steady herself against nothing but air. Vaughn rushed to her side, his form becoming momentarily solid. He righted her, then merged with her. Two now became one, and drawing deep from a well of strength she hadn't known she possessed, she straightened her spine and forced her trembling legs to continue. Each excruciating step was a testament to her determination, her heritage, her blood.

Finally, triumph. Gemma reached the end of the fire walk and emerged from her trance. Yaya Mari smiled and took her granddaughter's hand, her weathered palm cool against Gemma's overheated skin. The old woman's eyes shone with fierce pride and something deeper—recognition of the power that now flowed through her lineage. Fingers intertwined, she raised their joined fists into the air, the silver of her braids catching the firelight as she proclaimed Gemma's victory without words. The people of The End cheered with passionate abandon and so did the spirits that only Gemma and Mari could see, their ethereal forms dancing in jubilation around the sacred space, welcoming her into their eternal communion.

"You have shown great courage, Gemma," Mari said.

Mari knew her granddaughter would face trials far more challenging than the one she had passed tonight. She could take the path of ease and embrace her role as the protector of this land, or Gemma could walk through the fire of modern life and lead her people to the knowledge of what capitalism really meant for Sargasso Cove.

15

DEPARTURE

Gemma's new boat changed hands at Boon Dock Marine with little fanfare. The yacht dealer, in his Sperry topsiders and Maui Jims, cast a disdainful glance over the scruffy boatyard and its keeper. Rusted boat stands held aging hulls, their bottom paint flaking into the dust. Drunks sprawled in the shade, their wet snores emitting loudly over the buzz of mosquitoes. Seagulls swooped to pick at bait tied to fish pots in the shallows.

"Congratulations, Boon," the salesman said, his smile as polished as the gleaming chrome fittings of the Beneteau Oceanis 46 he had delivered, which was now bobbing at the end of the dock. "I mean, look at her."

Boon sat in his downcycled office chair, his hands resting on his oil-smeared overalls. His eyes flicked toward the boat, her hull pristine white, reflecting diamonds of sunlight. She looked too clean for Boon Dock Marine, too out of place among the disintegrating hulls. And that suited Boon just fine.

"She'll do," Boon said, his voice tinged with a drawl.

"She'll do? I mean, Boon—she's brand new, straight from France. In-mast furling, retractable swim platform. Hell, she's got enough automation to practically sail herself."

"Fancy," Boon said, giving the dealer the barest smirk. "A boat that sails itself... I reckon that takes the fun out of it?"

The dealer's laugh was chummy with a hint of something more judgmental. "Depends on your definition of fun. Most people buying boats like this are looking for comfort. Sunset cruises, a bottle of Dom, and maybe some Sinatra." He gestured at the Beneteau's silhouette, his gaze lingering on her lines. "Just smooth sailing." He looked out over the water like his luxurious retirement lay just past the horizon.

Boon shrugged, his posture loose. He didn't feel the need to impress. Boon Dock Marine wasn't the kind of place that saw half-million-dollar boats pulling into its slips. Sun-bleached fishing boats, a center console Whaler, a hurricane haul—sure. A few new inflatables here and there. But a brand new Beneteau? Not a chance.

The dealer lingered, keys jangling nervously in his hand as he glanced back at the sleek yacht. It gleamed like a pearl in a mud puddle.

"You, uh..." The dealer turned, flashing a smile. "You lined up a buyer for her already?"

Boon let the question hang in the air. He said, "Yep. She's spoken for."

"Spoken for?" The dealer echoed again. His smile didn't fade. "Anyone I know?"

Boon didn't flinch. His eyes stayed fixed, and his lips still. The dealer tried again.

The broker slipped back into his pitch, his words scripted. "You've got something special here. A boat like this doesn't just look good; she's reliable and capable. Open ocean, island hops—wherever you want to go. I mean, a Beneteau? Not exactly the usual stock for Boon Dock, right?"

Boon had reached his limit with the line of inquiry. He gave the dealer a look that was equal parts annoyance and amusement.

"You done talking up the boat?" Boon said, his voice flat. "Or do you want to stay for a beer?"

The dealer laughed—quick, a little too loud—but a faint blush crept over his cheeks. His gaze flicked to the cracked vinyl chairs and overturned 5-gallon buckets Boon had gestured to and the grease-streaked cooler lurking in the shadows of the tarp-covered shack. Diesel and drying seaweed scented the air. He pinched his cufflink, straightened his crisp sports coat, and jingled the car keys in his hand, as if the idea of setting foot inside the grimy clubhouse might soil more than his slacks.

The dealer paused, weighing his next words. "Just seems... unexpected, is all. You sure the buyer's not someone I know? These big-ticket sales usually stay in the same circles, you know what I mean?"

Boon's jaw tightened. His tone stayed easy, but the edge underneath was hard to miss.

"You asking *me* for my customer list?"

The dealer raised his hands, grinning again. "No, no. Just curious."

"As I said, she's spoken for." Boon's voice had gone flat. Any remnants of country charm turned off like a switch.

The dealer held his grin a moment longer. "Right. Well, you're good to go, then. If you need more of these, just let me know. I'll give you a bulk deal." His sarcasm was a play for the final word.

"Appreciate it," Boon replied simply, winning the game.

Boon watched the dealer retreat across the potholed parking lot toward his shiny black sedan. Once he was out of sight, Boon pulled out his phone.

"Gemma," he said when she picked up. "She's here. Get your tail to shore, pronto."

Minutes later, a wash of spray announced Gemma's arrival at the dock, her dreadlocks misted and wind-tossed. When she walked up to the clubhouse and her eyes landed on the *Beneteau*, her jaw dropped.

"No way," she whispered.

Boon gave her a rare smile.

"Way," he said. "She's all yours."

"She's a beaut."

Boon tossed her the keys. Whatever the dealer thought—about Boon, about the boat, about the kind of people who came and went from places like this—he didn't know the half of it.

"You know," Boon said, glancing up at her, "there's a tradition with boats—you name them after women. Brings good luck and fair winds."

Gemma smirked, leaning against the weathered post. "Mari. My grandmother," Gemma said, her voice softening. "You know her full name is Mariposa."

Would Yaya be pleased to have this boat named after her? Gemma wasn't so sure, but there was something about the name—*Mariposa*—that felt right. A butterfly, delicate yet capable of traveling vast distances. It wasn't lost on her that butterflies could also be fragile, crushed if they flew too close to the wrong things.

"*Mariposa* it is," Boon declared. "Let's make it official."

"We can't do this without our crew. I'll call Cruz and Nihir," Gemma said suddenly. "And we might even sail tomorrow. No reason to delay the trip. The longer we wait, the deeper into storm season we'll be, and I want to get this over with."

Crab joined them in the blue shade of the shack. He rummaged in the cooler and extracted a fresh Heineken, grunting as he twisted the bottle cap off with his teeth.

"I'm lucky I still got any molars," Crab said by way of greeting.

"Stop gnawing on that thing, ya heathen," Boon muttered back, shaking his head.

Gemma could hear the noise of The Last Resort in the background as her call to Cruz went through. "What's up?" Cruz's voice was full of cheer. "Don't tell me. We're shipping out."

Departure | 135

"Tomorrow," Gemma said. "But tonight, we're christening the boat. Stay put. I'll have Nihir pick you up."

There was a pause. "Sure thing, Captain. I'll grab another round while I wait."

Gemma ended the call with Cruz and dialed Nihir next. He picked up on the second ring.

"Nihir! The dealership delivered the boat, and she's beautiful. We're having a party tonight, and we're sailing tomorrow," she said. "Cruz is at The Last Resort. Can you pick him up and swing by his condo to grab his bags on your way to Boon Dock? Make sure you both pack warm clothes and a waterproof jacket. Whatever you don't have, we can outfit you from the Boon Dock store."

"I'll be there in two hours," Nihir replied without hesitation.

By the time Cruz and Nihir arrived, the Boon Dock crowd had taken on a festive, ramshackle energy. The radio crackled with Cowboi Rivers tunes, as usual. Gemma saw Nihir's Jeep pull up, and she crossed the dirt lot to welcome her crew members.

Nihir closed the distance and swept Gemma off her feet in an exuberant hug. He held up a humble canvas knapsack.

"Is that all you brought?" Gemma said, smiling sweetly. She raised an eyebrow. Nihir's minimalist approach was both elegant and enviable. She took his hand, leading him toward the party, while Cruz trailed two steps behind. Nihir's confident stride and easy smile turned heads as he approached, his presence commanding attention without effort, and no one at Boon Dock had met Gemma's crush yet.

"About time you got here," Boon called out, raising a Solo cup as Cruz and Nihir joined the gathering of folding chairs by the water's edge.

"Wouldn't miss it," Cruz replied, admiring the sleek Beneteau tied off to the dock. "Damn. Look at her. I mean, look at her." He shook his head in disbelief, a grin stretching across his face.

Gemma caught Nihir's eye. "Everything okay?"

Nihir nodded slowly, but his expression was thoughtful. "Cruz was talkative on the ride over. I mean, he could be a superfan of Cowboi, but fans rarely know about what really happens on Easter Cay."

"I told him all about the parties," Gemma concluded, but she turned over the possibilities in her mind that there was something between Cruz and Cowboi that he wasn't telling her.

Before Gemma could ask more, Boon shouted for everyone to gather around. "Christening time!"

The ceremony began in true Boon Dock Marine fashion—no speeches, no fancy champagne, just a Heineken bottle.

"To *Mariposa*. May she get us where we need to go!" Gemma called to the small crowd.

"And back again," Cruz added.

"You're supposed to say something fancy," Crab added.

Boon waved a dismissive hand. "Just smash the damn bottle."

With a flick of her wrist, Gemma brought the bottle

Departure | 137

down against the Beneteau's cranse iron. The green glass shattered with a sharp pop, foam spraying onto the dock and into the water.

Crab let out a cheer, raising his drink.

Someone changed the station on the radio, and Bob Marley belted out "Redemption Song" as the little party took hold. Laughter bubbled, the sound easy and unguarded. It felt good—too good, Gemma thought as she looked out at the horizon, where the sun had melted into the line between land and sea. *Mariposa* looked like a mirage in the fading light.

Nihir stood apart for a moment, gazing at the boat as if lost in similar thoughts. Gemma approached him, a beer in hand, and led him back to the gathering. They settled into the circle of folding chairs.

"She's somethin' else," Boon said, tipping his beer toward *Mariposa*.

The party lingered as twilight set in. Gemma watched her crew with a beer clutched loosely in her hands. She knew this was a moment they'd remember. Beneath the camaraderie and the rough jokes, the reality of what they were about to do loomed like an undertow.

Cruz tilted his beer toward her, snapping her out of her thoughts. "To Captain Gemma and the *Mariposa*."

"To Captain Gemma," Crab echoed, raising his bottle high.

Nihir clinked his bottle against hers without a word, his gaze steady on hers. The quiet acknowledgment felt more meaningful than any toast.

THE FOLLOWING MORNING, Gemma awoke in her new cabin. For the past three years, she had slept in *Luna*'s single bunk on a stiff foam rubber pad no wider than a military cot. Now, her queen-sized mattress was as soft as the goose down bedding in the cottages at the five-star inn where she grew up. In a stolen moment of rare comfort, she sank into the duvet. Morning sun filled the master cabin, which offered warmth and elegance.

Turning her head, she saw Nihir, one arm draped over his eyes to block out the sunlight peeping through the port lights. His shirt was rumpled, and a faint scent of salt and rum lingered between them. The sight of him there, so at ease, startled her. Now she remembered. Everyone had gotten so drunk last night; she had invited the crew to sleep aboard. Gemma's heart gave a small, nervous flutter before she settled back into the pillows, letting herself enjoy the moment.

Nihir stirred, lowering his arm to glance at her. "Morning." His voice was low, gravelly with sleep.

"Morning," she replied softly. "You don't have to get up yet. It's still early. Today's the big day."

"Aye, aye, captain," Nihir said, and he slipped back into slumber.

For a fleeting moment, the weight of their mission lifted, replaced by the promise of a new adventure—and maybe, just maybe, something more.

Gemma had never been on such a luxurious boat, except for Cowboi's yacht. Now, *Mariposa* was hers—or

Departure | 139

nearly hers. The amenities were more than she could hope for—on-demand hot water, a bidet, a vanity, and even a heated toilet seat. In the main cabin, Boon's orange Crocs swished back and forth, sticking out of the bilge as he waterproofed a compartment to conceal their valuable cargo. When Boon heard Gemma's steps, he scooted across the floorboards like he was floating across a still pond.

"Nearly done," he said. "Cruz and Crab went to grab coffee at Paradise Burger," he said, wiping his hands with a rag that looked suspiciously like an old pair of boxer shorts.

Gemma had expected to hear complaints about Boon's subordinate duties. Cowboi was giving her a chance in a leadership role, but the upside-down pecking order made her uncomfortable. She had worked with enough older men to know that apologizing for her assignment would only diminish her authority. Not that she needed to say she was sorry; she would prove herself as captain through her actions. The weight of responsibility sat heavily, but there was a thrill to it, too—finally being trusted with something significant.

They motored *Mariposa* from the seclusion of Boon Dock's slips to the bustling fuel dock around the point, the sleek vessel cutting smoothly through the morning-still water, drawing admiring gazes from the pump personnel.

Gulls circled overhead as Cruz and Crab met a panel van filled with provisions from town. The creaks and thuds of the fenders against the weathered pilings soothed Gemma's frayed nerves like a sailor's lullaby, while Crab filled the water and diesel tanks with practiced efficiency. Cruz loaded packages of vacuum-sealed meat into the freezer, methodically stacked cans of beans, vegetables, and fruits in the hold, and hung fresh produce—mangoes, papayas, and tomatoes—in canvas sacks and baskets that swayed gently with the boat's movement. To everyone's surprise, Cruz turned out to be a more than competent galley manager, as though he'd spent years at sea rather than behind a timeshare sales desk.

Gemma studied her charts at the nav station, tracing her finger along her course marked in pencil to the only section of water she was concerned about—the Mona Passage. This notorious eater of boats distinguished itself with shifting shoals and roaring currents. The twin islands of St. Columba and St. Lucy lie just north of Grenada, near the southern end of the Lesser Antilles. *Mariposa's* northwest course would take them in a diagonal of five hundred miles to the Dominican Republic. The first few days of their Caribbean Sea crossing would be a nice beam reach across open water. But the Mona Passage, their final eighty miles, would not be easy. Gemma had crossed this stretch before, and the trauma and nausea of it resurfaced in her memory.

When Gemma finished her sailing plan, she climbed to the helm to check on the wind. The boys were ready and waiting, so she gave the all-clear, and Boon pushed off with a boot kick against a steel piling. Once *Mariposa* cleared the harbor markers, Gemma raised the main with the power winch. It inched up the mast like a creeping spider. She eased off slightly, unfurled the headsail, and adjusted the heading to catch the wind. The automation of the Beneteau was a new game compared to the boats she had sailed before. The jib ballooned with a whomp, and she trimmed the sails into an uneasy peace. Lines, canvas, and steel vibrated in perfect balance with the wheel. The rhythmic creaking of the rigging and the gentle sway of the boat beneath kindled the sense of adventure and freedom she always felt when sailing. All the worries of the past weeks melted away. That was the beauty of this all-in endeavor.

Mariposa began to stretch into her sea legs while the crew tidied up the deck. Once the boat settled onto her course, the men retired below for a nap.

A few hours later, Cruz popped his head up into the cockpit.

"It's chilly up here," he said.

"It's nice once you get used to it. Grab a sweatshirt and mix up some cocktails."

Cruz rummaged below and reappeared with two rum and pineapples topped with maraschino cherry garnishes. The breeze snatched the smell of nutmeg from the plastic cups.

"Are you ready for your first watch?"

"I'm a little nervous, to be honest," Cruz said.

"You'll be a seasoned hand in no time," Gemma said, giving Cruz a reassuring pat on the back. "Okay, here's the deal. *Mariposa* has a fancy autopilot—you just press this button to hold our course. But don't think that means you can zone out. Stuff happens out here: other boats, debris floating around, and squalls can come out of nowhere."

She leaned against the helm, her tone easy but firm. "And things *will* break. They always do. If you hear anything weird, see anything off, or even feel like something's not right, call me. No heroics. We're a team out here, so don't try to handle it solo."

Cruz nodded, taking it all in, but his brow furrowed slightly. "Okay. Anything else I should know?"

Gemma smirked. "If you fall asleep, you might wake up with a shaving cream mustache or worse."

Gemma observed Cruz sip his drink. There was nothing uncomfortable about the quiet. On the contrary, it was intimate. Assured that Cruz would be all right, Gemma climbed down below. It was still daylight, but she needed some sleep. The party last night and the trip preparations had been exhausting.

"Okay, Cruz, you got this. I'm beat. I'm gonna get some shut-eye," Gemma said as she excused herself from the cockpit. On her way through the galley, she gulped water from a gallon jug left in the sink, the cool liquid soothing her dry throat before she retired to her cabin. The gentle tilt of the *Mariposa* wedged her snugly into her berth, the familiar motion of the boat cradling her as she settled in. Above her, a gear hammock swayed with the rhythm of the crossing, lulling her into slumber.

Vaughn felt the shift in Gemma's consciousness like a door creaking open—her brainwaves slowing, defenses weakening as sleep pulled her under. This was his chance. He had to make her understand the danger she was walking into. He had to plant the seed of suspicion that might save her life.

Drawing upon every fragment of energy he could muster from the ethereal plane, Vaughn pressed against the barriers of her sleeping mind. The connection was fragile, tenuous, but it held. He would show her what they had done to him—what they were capable of doing to her.

Let me in, he willed. *Let me show you.*

The memory unfolded like a film reel clicking into place. Gemma became Vaughn in the dream plane.

Hippie girls spun in lazy circles, their bare feet kicking up clouds of dust in the courtyard of Paradise Burger. The air was thick with wood smoke and burger grease, while conversations and laughter wove like invisible threads.

I needed to piss. The line for the toilet stretched halfway across the yard—one pathetic water closet serving the whole crowd. So I did what any sensible guy would do and walked out to the beach.

The relief was immediate and satisfying, my stream carving a shallow trench in the soft sand. I was still mid-flow when the world exploded.

Rough canvas slammed over my head from a sail bag, heavy with mildew and salt. Before I could react, something hard and heavy cracked against my temple. White-hot pain bloomed across my skull as I crumpled to the ground.

Inside the suffocating darkness, spots danced like fireflies gone mad. Something wet and warm trickled down my cheek—blood, pooling at the bottom of the canvas. My wrists were yanked behind me and bound tight. Then came the dragging—my heels digging into the sand, then scraping across wood as I was hauled down the dock.

The familiar clang of steel beneath me told me where I was:

my own skiff. Cold water soaked my knees as I knelt helplessly. The engine roared to life—my engine, my boat, turned against me.

We were flying across Sargasso Bay, the hull slapping against the waves in a beat I knew by heart. Then, abruptly, the engine died. In the sudden silence, I heard the gentle lap of water against the hull, the distant cry of night birds.

The second blow came without warning—

Gemma wrenched herself from the dream. She had died in first person, and the psychic backlash severed the link between her and Vaughn. She reeled, disoriented, grasping at fragments of a bond that had snapped.

No—

Gemma's mind recoiled, her subconscious rewriting the nightmare into something safer, something her psyche could handle. She was rejecting the dark truth Vaughn had tried to show her. Her emotions churned like a storm—fear, anger, confusion—but their very volatility made what happened impossible to grasp. She wasn't ready. Not yet.

The door to her slammed shut left Vaughn alone in the darkness, his warning unfinished, his murder unrevealed. Gemma was still blind to the danger closing in around her. And without Gemma, Vaughn was nothing more than a drifting shadow, unable to influence or protect her or anyone, unresolved and unable to move on.

PART II

16

THE WATCH

Cruz

Cruz stood his first solo watch at the helm as the sailboat pitched beneath him. The vessel responded to his slightest adjustment, a living creature beneath his hands. One sharp turn—just one—and they'd flip, the mast slapping the water's surface like a felled tree. The idea sent electricity down his spine. Not that he would do such a thing, but knowing he could... that sweet, dangerous knowledge hummed in his blood.

He adjusted the starboard wheel and smiled as the port wheel followed suit. The double-wheel setup gave the impression that a ghost was his copilot. Crab's and Boon's muffled voices carried from below deck to Cruz's finely tuned ears. Minutes slid into hours, and Cruz allowed himself to ease into the routine. When Boon climbed into the cockpit to take over, Cruz looked up and flashed a proud grin.

"I think I'm getting the hang of it," Cruz said.

"You're a natural," Boon said, his tone insincere.

Cruz shrugged. "I've never felt so free."

"Ironic, isn't it?" Boon said, leaning on the rail, his eyes scanning the horizon. "You're trapped on a thousand square feet of wood and fiberglass floating in an unforgiving environment that will kill you in a minute if you're not careful, and the inescapable prison feels freeing." He chuckled softly. "Pretty soon, sailing will be in your blood. It's why I've been doing this for decades. It's like nothing else."

Cruz nodded, letting his gaze drift back to the water, satisfied.

"You think Gemma's a good captain? She seems solid, but..." Cruz trailed off, glancing at Boon for a clue about how loyal he was to Gemma.

Boon chuckled, shaking his head. "Gemma's got grit, I'll give her that. She's determined. But sailing isn't just about guts. It's instinct. You can't learn instinct. You either have it or you don't."

Cruz frowned, letting the pause stretch. "I mean, she's been doing all right so far, hasn't she?"

"Sure," Boon said with a nonchalant shrug. "She's good with a chart. I'll give her that. But let me tell you something, kid." He leaned in slightly, his voice dropping. "The sea doesn't care about your plans. It doesn't care about your confidence. Out here, when things go south, it's muscle memory and guts that save your ass. And between you and me, I don't think Gemma's been out here long enough to develop the feel. She sailed Sunfish and Lasers as a kid and has done a couple of crossings, but that's not enough."

Cruz shifted uncomfortably, gripping the wheel a little tighter. "I don't know, Boon. She seems pretty capable to me."

Boon laughed, low and conspiratorial. "Sure, she's capable, but that's not why she's the captain. Cowboi has other plans for her. That's why you've got me and Crab on board—to make sure things stay on course."

Cruz nodded slowly. "What plans?"

"Never mind that," Boon said, straightening. "And don't get me wrong. She's done a fine job so far. I just think we should keep an eye on things, you know? Be ready to step in if we need to. A captain's only as good as her crew and her vessel, after all."

Cruz shrugged, letting the tension from Boon's overshare ease slightly as the conversation shifted. "Fair enough. By the way, thanks for saying I'm doing okay out here. I was pretty nervous at first."

Boon's tone warmed, the grin on his face almost genuine. "You did fine. And I gotta say, you seem to know your way around a galley."

Cruz brightened, allowing the praise to land. "Yeah?"

Boon said, clapping him on the back again. "Good food is just as important as knowing how to handle the wheel."

"Well, I guess I'll take that as a win," Cruz said,

genuinely pleased. Cooking was Cruz's hobby, a pastime he used to unwind from the pressures of his job.

"Take it as more than that," Boon said, his tone turning serious for a moment. "Out here, morale's everything. A good cook can keep a crew together when nothing else will. Don't let anyone tell you different."

"Now, get some rest, Cruz," Boon said, stepping up to the helm. "I'm up. If you're really wound up, there are some sleeping pills in the medicine cabinet."

Cruz hesitated, then nodded. "Thanks, Boon."

Boon

Boon took over the wheel, his eyes scanning the horizon for any signs of trouble. The sea stretched endlessly, frosted with whitecaps and clear of any ships or land. A steady breeze hummed through the rigging as he zipped up his windbreaker and crossed his arms over his chest to keep warm. The familiar rhythm of the sea usually cleared his head, but not today. His thoughts circled back to Cowboi Rivers, the man pulling the strings.

This assignment wasn't just another run—it was a demotion. His drunken slip-ups and bad decisions had made Cowboi very angry. Boon knew the man well enough to understand that second chances came with strings. But recruiting Gemma? That had probably saved his hide.

He adjusted his grip on the wheel. Gemma August— young, stubborn, and oblivious to just how valuable she was. Cowboi had made it clear that *she* was the one he wanted at the helm of *Mariposa*. Not for her sailing skills, but for what she controlled.

Cowboi would let Gemma believe the boat and cash were payment—her reward for a risky job. But that was the trap—there was no turning back. The *Mariposa* wasn't just a half-million-dollar yacht; it was a spotlight, a marker tying her to Cowboi's empire. He would have dirt on Gemma, enough to puppet her every move, and this was a highly visible and highly illegal job.

The *Mariposa* glided forward, smooth and fast, as if the boat knew where she was heading.

"Cards?" Crab called up.

Crab climbed into the cockpit, settling in the other pilot's chair, and dealt out a hand without another word. The men had been sailing together so long that their routines were as predictable as sunrise. Crab tucked the deck away from the wind, and they fell into their normal exchange of half-finished thoughts and insider jokes, like twin-speak. Each understood the other's meaning without full sentences.

The bond ran deeper than their work for Cowboi, forged in rougher days when they'd worked sailing jobs for next to nothing—deliveries, charters. Crab, in particular, couldn't help wishing they could go back to that simpler time.

Boon furrowed his brow as he stared into the distance.

"You remember that time we hauled those big-screen TVs from Mexico to Grenada?" Crab said, breaking the silence.

Boon snorted, shaking his head. "How could I forget?

Half of them didn't fit in the hold. The deck looked like a solar array."

Crab chuckled, dealing out the cards. "And that customs guy? What was his name? Lewis, Louis, or something?"

"Louis," Boon said with a grin. "Slipped him a couple of bottles of rum and one of those TVs. The man acted like we'd handed him the keys to a palace."

Crab laughed. "You think he ever got that thing to work? We gave him one that got water-damaged."

"Not our problem," Boon replied, smirking as he picked up his hand. "Besides, it wasn't half as ridiculous as those counterfeit Levi's. Remember that?"

Crab groaned, rubbing his face. "How could I forget? And the labels—'Levi's' with a Y."

"Hey, they sold, didn't they?" Boon shot back. "Haitians loved them. Practically hacked each other to pieces at the market for a pair."

Crab leaned forward, shaking his head with a grin. "Yeah, but you remember what you said when we finally unloaded them all?"

"What?"

"'Next time, let's stick to rum and TVs.'"

Boon chuckled, leaning back in his chair. "Simpler times, Crab. Simpler times."

Crab's smile faded slightly, and he looked out at the horizon. "Felt like we were just two guys against the world, doing what we wanted, following the wind. No Cowboi. No strings."

Boon's expression turned somber, and he nodded.

"Yeah. But the world's a different place now. We can't go back, no matter how much you want to. And I like the money."

The silence settled between them again, comfortable but weighted with their shared history. Crab dealt another hand, the worn cards guarded in each man's weathered hands.

"Got any sevens?" Crab asked, his leathery features betraying nothing as he arranged his cards.

"Go fish," Boon replied, stifling a grin.

Two hardened men who'd spent their lives smuggling across international waters now played a children's game with the intensity of high-stakes poker. The juxtaposition was almost comical—these grizzled sailors with their weathered faces and checkered pasts, utterly absorbed in Go Fish.

Crab leaned back against the cockpit cushion, studying his cards. "Remember that beat-up Catalina? Loved that boat."

Boon didn't respond right away. He shuffled the cards in his hand, then glanced up, his expression tightening. His tone stayed level, but his fingers tapped against the wheel. "Ya know, nobody's forcing you to be a part of this, Crab."

Crab shot back, his frustration bubbling over. "Cowboi doesn't let people walk away, and you know it."

Boon's smirk returned, colder this time. "Then stop pining and play your damn cards. Got any threes?"

Crab sighed, sliding a card across the bench.

They played in silence for a while, the only sounds the

slap of cards and the faint hum of the boat slicing through the water. Finally, Crab broke the silence with a sigh. "You ever think about Gemma?"

Boon raised an eyebrow. "What about her?"

"What will happen to her? She is a beautiful girl with talent and smarts, and she doesn't know what she's gotten herself into. Good kid. Got deep ties back home, too. You shouldn't have brought her into this."

"She's tougher than she looks," Boon replied, his tone dismissive. "And besides, she's not the one calling the shots. This is an opportunity for everyone. Not just us and her, but the entire island of St. Columba."

Crab shook his head, his lips pressed into a thin line. "You keep telling yourself that."

Crab dealt another hand, but his heart wasn't in it anymore. The weight of what they were sailing toward loomed heavy over both men, a silent specter that neither the cards nor their easy banter could chase away.

Gemma

On their fourth day, Gemma woke to relieve Boon from his watch. She glanced at Nihir's sleeping form in her bed, uncertainty gnawing at her as she considered everything that had led to this moment. Her grandmother had never tried to dissuade her from taking this job. Considering that the ownership of their land hung in the balance, her grandmother's faith was remarkably brave. Silence on the matter wasn't approval but a quiet acknowledgment that Mari trusted the spirits' plans.

The first hours alone on Gemma's watch proved ideal to practice the meditation techniques Nihir had taught her at Royal Asana and the trance work Yaya Mari favored. She focused on a single point of concentration—the space between her in-breath and out-breath—and in that fleeting, delicate moment, she dropped into a profound emptiness. This didn't separate her from her surroundings; instead, it deepened her awareness of the present moment, anchoring her to the vastness of the ocean and her own small place within the universe.

By her calculations, land should be visible by morning. Her eyes scanned the horizon, alert for the lights of freighters that might drift across their path. In the distance, waves rose and fell in gentle crests, glistening under the moonlight. The iridescent light cast slicks of silver over the empty seascape, transforming the night into something luminous and otherworldly.

Vaughn's presence slipped into her awareness like a shadow hovering at her side.

"Vaughn? I know you're there," Gemma said to the wind.

So far, she had channeled only fleeting, disconnected messages from Vaughn in dreams but learned nothing of real consequence, other than he was murdered. By whom or why remained hidden. To harness the spirit's full energy was a loud affair—at least with her imperfect technique—and the boat was relatively small. In a full possession, her voice would deepen, words tumbling out in a fevered torrent as her body jerked and swayed like a marionette. If she tried, there was a real danger that she would lose control and pitch into the dark water.

Gemma hadn't told Boon and Crab anything about the ritual at Mariposa's End or the spectral castaway that sailed with them, especially since they had all known Vaughn in life. Nihir knew more, but she hadn't shared her whole experience with him either. She feared the men on the boat would think she was crazy or, worse, be terrified or saddened by the presence of their departed friend.

She could feel Vaughn's essence blending with her own, his voice threading through her in a way that felt alien. The boundary between herself and Vaughn dissolved into a flow of power.

"Vaughn," she murmured again, barely above the sound of the wind and waves. "I know you're there."

The surrounding air seemed to shift, growing heavier. She closed her eyes and focused, drawing the power up her spine but keeping it throttled. Then she heard his voice—a whisper so soft it could have been mistaken for the rustling of the sails.

"I'm here," Vaughn said, the words emerging through Gemma's mouth. She curled forward to muffle the sound. After a pause, Vaughn continued, "Cowboi's got plans for you. For Mariposa's End. This job is not what you think it is."

Gemma swallowed hard. "What plans?"

Her pulse raced. She tried to hold on to her guide, but her effort to keep their communication at a whisper weakened the connection.

"Vaughn, wait—what plans?"

Then he was gone, leaving Gemma alone on the deck with the weight of his vague warning pressing down on her. She drew her knees to her chest and stared out at the dark expanse.

The faint creak of footsteps on the ladder startled her, breaking the stillness of the ghost's departure. Gemma quickly straightened, brushing a hand over her face to compose herself just as Nihir climbed into the cockpit, balancing a steaming mug of tea in one hand. Ah, now she understood why Vaughn had fled.

Since the night of Mariposa's christening, she and Nihir had shared the captain's cabin aboard the *Mariposa* —a practical choice at first, born of limited space and mutual trust, but one that had gradually grown into something unspoken, something closer. His company felt natural, as if the boundaries between them had shifted without either acknowledging it. He offered her a small, knowing smile, his eyes glinting as they caught the light of the LED nav screen, and she felt a warmth rise in her chest that had nothing to do with the teacup he handed her.

"You've been up here a while," he said softly, handing her the mug. "Figured you could use some tea and company."

Gemma accepted the cup with a nod, her heart still racing. "Thanks."

Nihir settled into the seat next to her, his gaze sweeping over the horizon before landing back on her. "I

The Watch | 159

heard an unfamiliar voice. Sounded like a man. Must have been the wind."

Gemma blew gently on the tea, keeping her hands steady. "Must have."

Nihir studied her for a long moment, his expression unreadable. "You seemed deep in thought when I came up. Everything okay?"

Gemma forced a smile. "Just thinking about landfall."

She sipped again in silence, Vaughn's warning still weighing heavily on her mind. She kept her secrets close, knowing that the truth could change everything—for better or for worse.

17

HISPANIOLA

It had been a near-perfect sail, but the mood of the water changed as they approached Puerto Rico. Gemma prepared for the sea change as she read the vibrations of the boat. The morning's gentle waves became powerful swells. Clouds formed out of nothingness, towering hundreds of feet high, the fists of gods raised skyward.

"How's she handling?" Boon shouted over the building wind.

"She's holding," Gemma replied, her voice steady. "But we need to stay sharp."

Crab and Boon, both seasoned sailors, exchanged smiles through the spray from the waves breaking over the bow. Sharing a grip on the inner forestay, they barely flinched, accustomed to witnessing nature's fury. Cruz and Nihir, however, looked about to hurl their breakfasts over the lifelines at any second. Gemma tightened her grip on the wheel, feeling her heart race as the pressure shifted.

The first raindrops hit like needles, and within seconds, a torrent poured from the sky, pounding against the deck with a force that sounded like thunderous applause. The waves swelled, growing monstrous, lifting the boat until it seemed to ride the crests of towering, liquid mountains. Each gust tore fiercely at the sails, straining the rigging and threatening to unbalance the *Mariposa* with every surge.

"Okay, guys, let's get these sails reefed!" Gemma shouted.

Boon and Crab rushed to drop the sheets while Cruz closed the hatches, and Nihir stood by, too sick to be much help. A wrenching creak sounded like squealing brakes. A halyard had jammed the main, and the *Mariposa* leaned at an alarming angle. There was no alternative; someone had to climb the mast and shake the line free.

Gemma's eyes locked with Boon's, a silent command passing between them. Without hesitation, he sprang into action, leaping to the center of the boat and climbing the spar steps with practiced ease. There was no time to grab a harness. The line had jammed higher than the steps reached, forcing him to scale the last few feet by sheer strength, gripping with his thighs and arms as he pulled himself up. His hands moved swiftly, shaking the halyard free.

Water streamed from Gemma's dreadlocks and into her eyes. Soaked to the bone, she fought to keep the *Mariposa* on course. The boat groaned and shuddered with each powerful impact as the waves battered its hull, but she held fast as she steered into the raging wind. Time dissolved into a relentless blur of rain, wind, and crashing waves, each gust and swell seeming to blur the edges of reality. The storm showed no mercy, its force undiminished as hours dragged on.

At last, the winds began to ease. The waves calmed as their ferocity waned. The rain tapered off to a light drizzle, and the sky brightened. Gemma finally exhaled in a long, trembling sigh, the tension draining from her body as relief and exhaustion washed over her. But this was just the beginning. The Mona Passage stretched before them, a restless expanse of blue-gray water heaving beneath their hull.

Worse than the storm, the slow, grinding pitch and roll gnawed at their nerves. The monotonous rhythm wore them down hour by hour. Conversation dwindled to sparse essentials, then to nothing at all as each person retreated into their own private misery. The crew moved in silence, their faces drawn and eyes glazed.

By dusk, the sky turned featureless with low, gray cloud cover that hung oppressively close, blocking out stars and moon alike. It created an enclosing limbo of slow progress, a purgatory where time seemed suspended, leaving them adrift in a dimensionless void where sea and sky merged into continuous gloom. The only sound punctuating their isolation was the persistent creak of rigging swaying with each roll, a haunting melody that followed them like a ghost's whisper through the darkness, marking a passage that felt like

Hispaniola | 163

days. As dawn unraveled, even the sky seemed bored, with only the occasional ghostly shadow of a frigate bird sleeping on the wind before vanishing into the mist again.

Crab stirred, dragging himself upright from his cat-like slumber on a cockpit bench. "Christ, this stretch is always a washing machine," he muttered, sprawling back with his arms crossed behind his head.

Gemma smirked from the helm, adjusting their course slightly. "A couple more hours and we'll be through it," she called, secretly pleased that she had a strong stomach.

Nihir's face was pale and drawn. His usual composed demeanor was nowhere to be found. The rise and fall of the waves had turned him into a hollow-eyed shadow of himself.

Boon ambled over, a mischievous grin spreading across his face. "You alright there, Nihir ol' buddy? You're lookin' a bit green, mate." Boon, too, seemed to be immune to seasickness. Nihir answered by spitting into the ocean.

Boon chuckled. He couldn't resist ribbing a man when he was down. "Didn't think a man of your skills would be knocked flat by a little roll."

"Inner peace," Nihir muttered, his voice hoarse, "is riding it out. I feel it. I accept it. It'll pass, one way or another."

Boon slapped his knee, laughing. "Guess that makes you human after all! For a while, I thought you were some kind of Zen robot."

"I'm no robot. And right now, I feel like I'm dying,"

Nihir replied, managing a weak grin despite his misery. He wiped a hand across his sweat-slicked forehead.

"Oi, Boon," Crab said, joining Boon in the fun-making. "Think we should get him a bucket?"

"Too late for that. He's already chummed the side more than once."

Gemma rolled her eyes. "Alright, boys, that's enough. Nihir's handling this crossing better than most first-timers." She glanced over at Nihir, her expression softening. "You're doing fine. It's rough, but we're almost there."

Nihir nodded, grateful for Gemma's steady voice cutting through the relentless teasing.

THE INLET of Luperón's harbor, hidden behind rugged headlands, opened into a wide, shallow basin wreathed in bougainvillea. Boats anchored precariously close to one another swung in synchronized arcs on the tide, leaving only a breath's width between them. Along the shoreline, the remains of beached boats lay half-buried in the sand, reminders of Luperón's long history as a haven for smugglers of all types. It was a place where time moved slowly and where cruisers lingered, lulled by the community's embrace of outlaws.

Following Cowboi's instructions, Gemma navigated *Mariposa* to a predesignated mooring, keeping her movements swift and purposeful. She bypassed the customs dock entirely, slipping into position through morning traffic, her eyes scanning the harbor for any sign of unwanted attention. The risk of evading customs and immigration loomed, but she blended seamlessly into the busy routines of the maritime morning.

Boon scooped up the floating lead with the boathook, threaded the chock, and cleated the line, then repeated the procedure on the other side. The boat drifted back with a tug, relaxing into a comfortable roll. Small shacks painted in faded pastels clung to the hillsides. The air was thick with the scent of overripe mangoes. A handful of ramshackle bars and eateries, adorned with hand-painted signs, offered cold beers and fresh-caught fish. Gemma took a deep breath and picked up the VHF handset.

"Casablanca, Casablanca, Casablanca, this is Mariposa. Come in, Casablanca."

Silence. She tried again. "Casablanca, Casablanca, Mariposa."

"Mariposa, this is Casablanca. Go to channel 71."

"Going to 71." Gemma dialed in the new frequency. "Casablanca, this is Mariposa. Are you there?"

"Yes, go ahead," said a staticky voice.

"We have a reservation for Captain Blaine. What time do you open? Over." Gemma recited the code Cowboi had given her. The radio waves crackled for a long moment, then the voice returned.

"I'm sorry, but check-in isn't until ten," said the voice.

"Ten o'clock is fine. We're on our mooring. Will you come pick us up? Over."

"Roger that. Ten o'clock pickup. Over and out."

A little over an hour later, Gemma heard the low growl

of the sleek go-fast before it came into view. It sliced through the water like a black shark, cutting effortlessly through the calm surface. The pilot, neatly dressed in a polo shirt and crisp cargo shorts, expertly guided his Pantera alongside *Mariposa* with precision. A remora, startled by the prop wash, darted out from under *Mariposa's* hull, seeking refuge in the deeper waters. Gemma steadied herself, taking a gulp of the coffee that Cruz had thankfully spiked with whiskey, now grown cold.

"¿Estás en Mariposa?" said the man at the wheel.

"Do you speak English?" Gemma asked.

"Sí. I mean, yes, I speak English. My name is Carlos."

"Tie up and come aboard, Carlos." Gemma gestured to a cleat, maintaining the etiquette she had been taught, which demanded an invitation and perhaps a cup of coffee.

"No need. I'll take you to see Domingo now," he said. "He's waiting for you at the resort. Bring a swimsuit."

Gemma whispered to Boon, "Will you come with me? I don't want to go alone."

"Of course," Boon said.

Gemma ducked below and grabbed a few things for her day bag. She spoke to Cruz, Nihir, and Crab. "We'll be back as soon as possible. Gotta take care of business. Hold down the fort."

Onshore, black mud and decomposing debris at the waterline appeared and disappeared from view as Carlos expertly maneuvered alongside the battered courtesy dock. The craft bumped gently against the worn rubber

Hispaniola | 167

bumpers, the sound rolling across the quiet beach. Gemma stepped onto the sand, her legs adjusting to the unfamiliar stillness after many days at sea. Immediately, a powerful stench of rotting fish and brackish water erupted from the muck, assaulting her senses with unexpected ferocity. The odor hung heavy in the humid air, almost visible in its intensity.

Flies buzzed in thick, undulating clouds above piles of seaweed and unidentifiable organic matter that formed dark mounds along the tideline. The insects created a constant, irritating drone that seemed to intensify the oppressive heat. Her stomach lurched violently, a wave of nausea washing over her as her body struggled with the abrupt transition between sea and land. Boon steadied her with a firm grip on her elbow, his fingers digging in as he prevented her from stumbling into the fetid muck.

"Are you okay?" Boon asked.

"Everything is moving. I feel sick."

"Ha! You're land sick! Freakin' hilarious. Folks who don't puke their guts out at sea usually get hit way worse on dry land. Just somethin' I've noticed over the years." Boon smacked her back with a good-natured thump.

"Don't tease me. I feel awful." Gemma wobbled like a newborn colt.

"Come on, you'll be fine," Boon said.

He helped her straighten and pointed to where Carlos was waiting a few yards away next to a wall of branches that separated the beach from a gentle slope of vegetation. As they caught up, a break in the dense, tangled underbrush narrowed into a winding path that meandered like a stream.

On the walk, the trees canopied them in a cathedral. Humidity rose from the damp, spongy ground, along with clouds of gnats and sandflies that buzzed around their ankles and faces. The rich, earthy scent of decomposing leaves mingled with the salt air. Towering palms and ancient mahogany trees rustled overhead, their leaves whispering secrets while the raucous caws of palm crows and the melodic twitters of Caribbean tanagers scored the air with music. Occasionally, a flash of brilliant red or yellow would dart between branches as birds went about their morning rituals.

The dirt trail gradually gave way to a cement pathway curbed with low walls artfully embedded with shells and polished stones in shades of white, gray, and brown. Through the jungle canopy, indistinct conversation and high-spirited laughter floated toward Gemma, growing louder with each step they took toward the unseen resort.

They rounded a bend, and a swimming pool appeared like a mirage—a turquoise oasis framed by lush greenery. Girls in bikinis clustered around a waterfall fountain that adorned the pool, perched on underwater stools as they ordered colorful, fruit-topped drinks from a submerged bar, their voices mingling with the soft splash.

Even from a distance, Gemma could tell these weren't first-class travelers. The laid-back crowd had the telltale look of hostel-hoppers and liveaboard sailors savoring a brief escape from cramped bunks or long passages. Some lounged in plastic deck chairs, others swapped tales of hidden beaches in animated voices, and a few wore the far-off, thousand-yard stare of those who had been at sea too long.

The resort was a dream in poured concrete, with courtyards, cabanas, and snack bars nestled in undulating lines, each structure seamlessly connected to the next. Whitewashed walls curved organically around stands of native trees, preserving the landscape while creating intimate spaces. Flowering vines cascaded down trellises, their vibrant purples and reds stark against the pale buildings. The entire complex seemed to have grown from the hillside.

Carlos broke the spell. "Domingo is this way. Come," he said, leading them along a winding path of inlaid stones past the pool area to a latticed atrium displaying overpriced pepper sauces, rum cakes, and knock-off sunglasses. A ceiling fan spun lazily overhead, barely making a dent in the hot air. Past the unmanned reception desk with its polished mahogany counter and abandoned guest book, Carlos guided them into a private courtyard where light filtered through flowering vines.

"Sit. Domingo will be with you soon," Carlos said and left to return to his duties elsewhere.

The décor was inexpensive but festive—sea fans woven into hanging nets over a red-tiled floor. Gemma settled into a rattan chair painted white with a high, round back while her fingers drummed an anxious rhythm against the matching side table.

A woman in a bold floral caftan drifted into the garden. Her extraordinarily long hair, the color of hot cocoa, brushed the backs of her knees as she moved with liquid grace. She carried a tray that clinked softly with glasses and a pitcher of herbs and fruits suspended in honey-colored liquid.

"Mamajuana," she said, her voice surprisingly high and childlike despite the silver threading her temples and the age spots mapping her hands. "Our family recipe and the national drink of the Dominican Republic." After filling cordial glasses with the amber liquid, she said, "Enjoy," and vanished just like Carlos had.

Gemma took a cautious sip. The herb liqueur bloomed across her tongue—sweet, spicy, with an underlying medicinal bite that somehow settled her churning stomach.

"They have no reason to poison us, right?" she asked Boon.

Boon answered by downing his shot with a theatrical hoot and immediately pouring another. Gemma had tipped back her glass, following Boon's lead, when footsteps echoed on the paving stones behind her.

The man came into view and looked like he'd been forged in a jeweler's crucible of gold. His blue summer suit—impeccably tailored to his slight frame—shimmered like Caribbean waters, and his hair, slicked back to the color of varnished teak, caught the dappled sunlight filtering through the overhead canopy. Rings adorned every finger, and a thick chain of interlocking gold links rested against his chest. The diamond-encrusted watch on his slim wrist caught fire with every gesture, sending prisms of light dancing across the garden walls whenever he moved his hand. He trailed a sharp, green cologne that reminded Gemma of money.

"Bienvenido. I'm Domingo," he said with genuine warmth as he took Boon's hand in his, then turned to Gemma. She bowed almost imperceptibly. "I'm Gemma, and this is my colleague, Boon Sanderson."

A light kiss on each cheek was her reward—his cologne now overwhelming and his lips cool against her skin.

"Sit, sit, please," Domingo said, his cheer carefully measured. "You're here. And punctual—I appreciate that. Cowboi told me you were efficient and trustworthy."

Gemma savored the way he drew out the vowels of Cowboi's name, making it sound both exotic and musical.

"Since we can't load your boat with our cargo until nightfall, please be my honored guests for the day. Luperón Bay crawls with spies, so we must be cautious." His eyes narrowed theatrically, hands moving with dancer-like fluidity, a puppet show of creeping villains. "For now, you'll join me at my private pool! You met my older sister, Carmilla—she's a remarkable cook. I'm told you have three more crew members still aboard. I've sent Carlos to radio your boat and collect them. Meanwhile, please excuse me. I must coordinate with Carmilla for our little celebration." He spread his arms wide. "Mi casa es su casa."

Another sweeping gesture directed them toward an opening in the landscape before he disappeared in the opposite direction, calling over his shoulder, "Please, make yourselves comfortable."

The path, bordered by vibrant hibiscus, opened into a private sanctuary at the center of the compound. In the clearing, a gem-like pool reflected dappled sunlight filtering through swaying palms. Cream-colored lounge chairs invited relaxation around the perimeter, while potted orchids and bird-of-paradise burst with tropical color. Luxurious white towels were rolled and stacked on a marble-topped table for guests.

"I'll go back and grab that mamajuana," Boon announced with obvious enthusiasm, clearly relishing the prospect of a day spent drinking and relaxing. "Back in two shakes." He vanished before Gemma could respond—not that she objected to more of the spiced rum drink.

Left alone with the steady thrum of cicadas, she explored the pool's perimeter. On the far side, she discovered a vintage bamboo bar beside a cabana. The drawers and cabinets yielded a treasure trove of pool party essentials: premium liquor, mixers, sunscreen, insect repellent, and a collection of dog-eared paperbacks and glossy travel magazines.

All set, she thought, though unease still intruded upon her thoughts.

Selecting a sunny lounger, she opened the umbrella over the poolside table, arranged two towels into a comfortable nest, and sorted through Spanish fashion magazines from the bar. She'd just settled in with a three-year-old Condé Nast Traveler when Boon returned, taking the chaise lounge beside her, but his restless energy soon shattered the postcard-perfect peace.

"I don't trust that bastard," Boon muttered as he

Hispaniola | 173

returned with his bottle, casting wary glances back toward the path.

She patted the lounger next to her, indicating that Boon should sit. "Domingo? Come on, Boon—he's a drug lord. We're not supposed to trust him. Just chill. We'll be in and out before you know it." Gemma kept her voice deliberately light to mask her own discomfort. Something nagged at her—a sense that the rules could shift without warning, that hidden agendas lurked just beyond her sight.

Boon caught the flicker of doubt crossing her face, his mouth setting into a grim line. "You feel it too. There's something about him. My gut's usually pretty damn solid." He raked his salty blond hair back from his forehead.

Gemma tried to ease his mind. "Relax. Have another drink, Boon. It'd be rude to turn down Carmilla's cooking. Besides, aren't you starving? A salad or some fruit would hit the spot right now."

Boon snorted. "Can't argue with that. Fresh food wouldn't hurt, and I guess there's jack shit we can do to speed things up anyway." Another shot of mamajuana disappeared in one swallow.

Nearly an hour passed before Domingo returned, leading Crab, Cruz, Nihir, and a parade of local women toward the pool. Crab swaggered forward like a conquering hero, brandishing a fifth of tequila and whooping with delight. His goofy exuberance was amplified by mint-green shorts dotted with pink flamingos, a bright pink Izod polo, and his ever-present Greek fisherman cap.

The women efficiently transformed the space, setting up a buffet that made Gemma's mouth water: platters of arroz con pollo, fresh ceviche, crispy tostones, creamy avocado salad, and pyramids of tropical fruit that gleamed like jewels. Carmilla placed a fresh pitcher of mamajuana beside Gemma and Boon with a knowing smile.

Crab couldn't contain himself—like a caged animal suddenly freed, he bounced between the pool's edge, buffet, and bar. He splashed his feet in the water, knocked back tequila shots, and bellowed off-key renditions of "Pink Pony Club."

Gemma watched with mounting exasperation. She understood his restlessness after five days confined to the *Mariposa*, but his manic energy was wearing thin, especially when she needed to focus on business. This wasn't the place to cut loose.

"Hey, Crab," she called, fighting to keep irritation from her voice. "Why don't you make some of your famous margaritas? I'm sure Carmilla can find ice, limes, whatever you need. I saw a blender at the bar." Gemma gestured toward the bamboo setup, hoping a task might occupy him long enough for her to conclude the exchange with Domingo and get her crew safely back on the water. The unexpected party was pleasant but dangerous—especially with her crew growing drunker by the minute.

"You got it, Cap! Coming right up!" Crab bounded toward the bar with renewed purpose.

Domingo claimed the lounger on the other side of Gemma, saying nothing at first, letting the atmosphere of leisure wash over them. When Nihir approached with ice water, Gemma sent him away with a barely perceptible head shake.

"You know," Domingo said, eyes fixed on the pool's surface, "this resort is merely the beginning. I have much grander plans. This place was in ruins when I inherited it. Cowboi has been... generous in that regard. New cabanas, the swim-up bar at the main pool, upgraded kitchen facilities. But it still doesn't attract the glitterati, the real money. Cowboi promised this would become another Easter Cay. Currently, it serves sailors, backpackers, and the occasional cartel boss passing through. I need to elevate my brand, and I've waited long enough." His gaze shifted to her. "Do you understand what I'm saying?"

Gemma shifted uncomfortably.

"Sounds like you have significant investment at stake," she said carefully, avoiding any impression of interest in his hospitality ventures.

The crash of breaking glass and Crab's explosive "Aw, shit!" made Carmilla shriek. Gemma started to rise, muttering, "Dammit," but Domingo's hand on her shoulder stopped her cold.

"Sit, Gemma. I have a proposition requiring privacy. Boon, would you be so kind as to give your friend a hand over there?"

Boon's questioning glance met Gemma's quick nod. "Yeah, alright," he said reluctantly, retreating to join cleanup efforts at the bar, while Nihir cast worried looks between Gemma and Domingo before following.

Once they were alone, Domingo's mask slipped—easy

charm dissolving to reveal something colder, more calculating.

"Gemma, surely you realize Cowboi has more money than he could spend in ten lifetimes," Domingo began, his voice dropping to conspiracy levels.

"I suppose," Gemma replied. She wrapped her arms around herself, the tropical sun suddenly feeling cold. From her peripheral vision, she noticed Cruz hovering near the pool's edge, his casual posture failing to hide the tilt of someone absorbing every word. Her eyes met his briefly before he looked away.

"Cowboi bankrolls these transport runs and warehouses drugs here to fuel his endless parties. That's what I've become: a warehouse."

Gemma studied his face, searching for subtext. "It sounds like you disapprove."

"Not disapprove," Domingo said, swirling amber liquid in his glass. "But Cowboi doesn't treat me as an equal. This is my home, yet it never becomes the luxury destination he promised. He invests but delivers only so much." He leaned forward, his voice dropping further. "Always dangling carrots I'm tired of chasing."

Gemma crossed her arms defensively. "So you're done playing along?"

Domingo's smile crept up his cheeks. "The world still sees us as a cheap tropical escape. The Dominican Republic's image improves, but news about Haitian gangs drags us down, negatively affecting the work I do to elevate the resort."

"A public relations problem," Gemma said flatly. She

wanted nothing so much as to leave this conversation and get back to the *Mariposa*.

"Exactly." He pointed at her like she'd solved a puzzle. "When I met you, I thought, 'Domingo, this woman sees things differently.'"

"And what makes you so certain?"

"Cowboi usually sends me loud, unpleasant white men. The last one? A complete drunk." His dismissive wave carried contempt. "But you? You're independent-minded. Most importantly, you're smart enough to cut out the middleman."

Gemma's blood chilled. "Cut out the middleman?"

Domingo leaned back, watching her like a cat studying prey. "You're supposed to deliver this shipment to St. Columba, correct? Instead, we tell Cowboi that you were hijacked. You remain here, and we distribute the goods through my networks. Buy more. And repeat."

He paused, letting the words sink in. "I'll triple what Cowboi pays you."

Gemma's fingers drummed against her thigh, her mind racing.

"Think about it," Domingo continued, his voice softening like silk hiding steel. "No more scraping by. You'd work for me exclusively. I have vision, and I see you here with me."

The offer hit like a physical blow, stealing Gemma's breath. For a moment, words failed her completely. "Domingo! Don't ask me to do that!" she finally managed. "You've just met me! The boat I arrived in, the charter company I plan to start—that's my payment. How could

178 | DAY DRINKERS

you possibly triple that? What you're proposing is impossibly complicated, and I don't have the stomach for this kind of work. I have family in St. Columba. I can't abandon everything and relocate here." She steadied herself, desperation creeping in. "I just want my boat—to start a legitimate business, a fresh start. This was supposed to be one job, nothing more."

Her gaze held his, defiance and desperation flickering in her eyes like competing flames, as if hoping he'd reconsider and release her from this path that twisted far beyond her original plans.

Domingo's smile died, replaced by thinly veiled disappointment—and something colder. Mistrust crystallized in his expression.

"That's unfortunate," he said. The words flowed smoothly, but a razor's edge crept into his tone. His gaze hardened. He'd revealed his hand, and now Gemma wasn't just a missed opportunity—she was a liability who knew too much.

Cruz had drifted closer, pretending to thumb through a weathered magazine Gemma had discarded.

Domingo's jaw tightened. His glance at Cruz was brief but loaded—a silent calculation passing behind his eyes. His discomfort manifested in the rhythmic tap of his ring against his cocktail glass.

When his attention returned to Gemma, the warm charm had returned—but it was thinner now, stretched over something much darker. "No problem. These things have a way of resolving themselves," Domingo said.

But his menacing look at Cruz communicated something entirely different.

The atmosphere sent ice through her veins. *Why can't this go according to plan*, she thought, the mamajuana rising in her throat.

"I've misjudged the situation," Domingo continued with false lightness. "Carlos will return you to your boat after you eat. We'll load the cargo after sunset as originally planned. Think no more of my offer. Please, enjoy yourselves. But remember, Gemma—opportunities like this appear once in a lifetime. Buenos días."

With that, he shot a deadly look at Cruz and disappeared down the lush path toward his office, leaving the rest of the party by the pool. Gemma understood that her arrangement with Domingo had fundamentally shifted, though she couldn't yet fathom how. Her hands trembled as she reached for her glass. Nearby, Boon, Crab, and Nihir continued their jovial conversation by the bar, oblivious to the danger that had just brushed past them like a shark in the deep.

18

BAIT AND SWITCH

The radio had been nothing but static since they'd left the meeting with Domingo, its low hiss gnawing at Gemma's nerves through the long crawl to evening. She watched the jagged green silhouette of Luperón's hills catch fire in the dying light. As night settled over the harbor, cabin lights began flickering to life across the anchorage like emerging stars.

Unheralded, Carlos's Pantera materialized, its sleek black hull cutting through the water like a blade.

Crab and Cruz moved efficiently to load the cargo, their earlier pleasure of being on dry land replaced by a need to leave the Dominican Republic as soon as possible. Gemma hadn't told them the whole of the conversation with Domingo, but she filled them in on what they needed to know about the danger. They worked in grim synchronization as Carlos hoisted duffel bags up onto the *Mariposa's* deck with a solid thud. The chemical and earthy smell of the concealed cocaine left no doubt about what they were handling.

Carlos stepped aboard once the last bag was on the *Mariposa's* deck, his movements crisp and deliberate. He helped the crew pass the bales concealed in black nylon down the hatch.

Carlos nodded approvingly at the hidden compartments, already open. "You did this carpentry? Good work."

"I'm experienced at moving goods," Boon muttered. He avoided Carlos's eyes, his focus locked on sealing the contraband away from inquiry. As the last panel clicked into place, it betrayed nothing of the fortune within.

The crew gathered topside to finish the deal.

"Until the handoff is made to Cowboi, you are the responsible party," Carlos concluded, his tone clearly relaying Domingo's terms—and disapproval. Gemma gave a curt nod that felt like a signature. Carlos climbed down to his Pantera and peeled away, engines purring as he vanished into the night.

Crab exhaled deeply, his shoulders relaxing as he turned to Nihir. "That's it. No drama. Let's hope it stays that way."

Cruz stood nearby, observing the process in silence.

"Well, let's get out of here," Gemma said. "This place gives me the creeps."

After casting off the mooring line, Crab, Boon, and Cruz moved in the red and green gloom of the running lights, stowing sail bags and lines, while Gemma motored the *Mariposa* through the tightly packed boats and cleared the channel as chop threw spray over the deck and misted her hair and windbreaker. The engine undulated between a purr and a roar as the hull rose in and out of the waves. She waited to turn into the wind and raise sail when they were well out of visual range of Domingo's surveillance. She didn't want anyone guessing at their exact course.

Nihir approached her at the helm, leaning against the second wheel. "One and done, right?" he said quietly.

Gemma gave a nod of understanding. Nihir was reminding her of her vow to give up this criminal path as soon as they returned. "Let's hope so. You get some sleep. I'll take this watch."

Twelve knots on the quarter beam swept the boat back into the Mona Passage. Gemma had been preparing herself for this, but now the reality sank in—this wasn't some story from an airport crime novel. This was real. She was trafficking 100 kilos of cocaine.

As the divided island of Hispaniola receded into the distance, Gemma gazed at the twinkling lights of the Dominican Republic, a bright web of electricity stretching along the coast. In stark contrast, Haiti's dark border lay behind them, broken only by the sporadic flicker of charcoal fires in the black hills. The difference between the two nations was striking. Haiti, with no petroleum resources and dwindling supplies of wood fuels, seemed to cling to survival while the Dominican Republic flourished, growing more prosperous as its neighbor sank deeper and deeper into the grips of failed statehood.

Gemma's thoughts drifted to world politics, the sharp reality of suffering, and the unrelenting grip of poverty that so many faced. She thought of the intricate systems that allowed inequality to persist—the hidden deals, the power plays, and the compromises made by those who justified their actions as necessary. It was the same logic that had ensnared her: one job, all for the sake of her better future.

Cocooned in the solitude of her watch, Gemma unraveled her own choices. *Maybe I'm no different, an oppressor,* she thought, the weight of her decisions pressing down on her. The promise of returning home lingered at the edge of her mind, an anchor in the haze of moral ambiguity.

When this job is done, I'm going to give Cowboi my resignation. I'm a free agent, and the Mariposa will be mine. She repeated in her mind, letting its clarity solidify, and realized there were two Mariposas—the one under her feet and her family land. Her original thought was of the boat, but Mariposa's End perhaps meant more to her now.

Vaughn's presence beside her became tangible, a quiet specter keeping watch at her side. She didn't need to hear him to feel his approval of her decision; the ghost's silent companionship was enough. Gemma tightened her grip on the wheel, her resolve strengthening. The stars above seemed brighter, as if they, too, recognized the shift within her.

It was time to wake Crab for his shift. With a long exhale, Gemma stood, the chilly night air clinging to her skin. *Get through this first,* she reminded herself, her thoughts drifting toward the long sail ahead. She checked the heading, scanned for traffic, and engaged the autopilot before heading below. The adrenaline from yesterday's events had faded, leaving Gemma bone-weary after her night watch.

Gently shaking Crab's shoulder, she said jokingly, "Good morning, sunshine."

"Five more minutes, Mom," Crab replied with a sleepy smile. He smelled faintly of cornflakes.

Once Crab got settled in the cockpit, she retreated to her cabin. A faint snore from Nihir marked his position on the darkened bunk, his face partially buried in their pile of pillows. In the pale moonlight seeping through the hatch, his dark lashes looked impossibly long against his cheekbones, and his features softened into peace.

She was careful not to disturb him, but her eyes lingered longer than she intended. A tender ache stirred in her chest, unexpected and undeniable, as she realized how much she had grown to care for him.

She sat on the bench and stripped off her clothes. Nihir shifted in his sleep as she lifted the covers and slipped into the warm bunk, pulling the comforter snug around her. She lay back, staring at the ceiling as the ship swayed, lulled by the rock of the waves. The cushions cradled her as she surrendered to heavy, dreamless sleep.

When she woke to check on the helm, Crab gripped the wheel like a vise, his knuckles bone-white. Morning light washed over his face, accentuating the creased, leathery skin and wide, alert eyes.

"You seem spooked," Gemma said, her voice low. "What's up?"

Crab shifted his weight, jaw tight. "I think we're being followed, and I have a bad feeling about who it might be."

The words hung in the air like frost. Gemma's heart kicked against her ribs. "Really? What did you see?"

Crab nodded toward the expanse of water behind them. "I noticed it a few hours ago—a light, just barely visible on the horizon. No AIS number. When I scanned for a visual, I couldn't see anything. But every so often, I'd catch these flashes in my peripheral vision." He paused. "At first, I thought it was a passing yacht or freighter. But it hasn't changed course. It's been keeping pace with us ever since."

Gemma squinted into the distance, seeing only endless water shimmering under the morning sky.

"Shit. You should've woken me," she said, her voice sharper than intended. She softened her tone. "If anyone's really out there, they're probably staying out of range and running dark. The light you saw could've been the moon's reflection, phosphorescence, anything. But if you're right..."

She pushed down rising panic, her mind racing. Better to discuss this with the entire crew. "Go below and wake everyone. Have Cruz start breakfast, and then we'll meet," she told Crab, taking over the wheel. Grabbing binoculars from the console, she scanned the horizon.

Despite the pressing matter, she knew the crew would need fuel for whatever lay ahead. There was an unspoken understanding aboard her vessel—crisis or not, routines were important.

Soon, the aromas of buttery eggs and coffee wafted up

from the galley. Cruz emerged groggily, unfolded the topside table while squinting against the harsh morning light, then retreated back to the galley like a badger withdrawing into its burrow.

Gemma rested a hand on her queasy stomach. The vessel's rhythmic swaying seemed to intensify with her growing anxiety. The possibility of being followed had transformed the boat's motion from friend to enemy.

Nihir emerged from below to set napkins and forks on the table. His dark eyes narrowed as he scanned behind them for trouble.

"Crab told me what's up. What's the plan if we are being followed?" he asked quietly, his voice pitched low enough that only Gemma could hear. "Do we change course? Try to outrun them? Or continue as if nothing's wrong?"

"Come and get it," Cruz called to both above and below deck. "Nihir, take these cups." He handed coffee mugs up one at a time. The entire crew soon filled the cockpit and settled around the table.

"Fuck me. I hate to say it, but I think you were right, Crab. We're being followed," Gemma said. "It's a powerboat. Only a dot right now, but I'm guessing it's Customs or Coast Guard. Listen up—if those guys are officials of some sort, they'll look for erratic behavior. I don't know if the rules for probable cause are the same at sea, but let's assume they are. This could be nothing, just traffic going the same way, but we need to stay sharp."

"We're unmarked and unregistered. Doesn't matter, though. Maritime law is not the same as on land. The

Coast Guard has a pretty broad authority to stop, search, and board any vessel without cause," Boon added.

"That's bad. But let's stick to our schedule. Take watches as usual. If we panic, that'll really catch their eye," Gemma said.

Five untouched breakfasts sat cold and forgotten until Cruz tipped them overboard and cleared away the dishes.

19

PIRATES!

Their pursuers played cat-and-mouse with the *Mariposa*. Now, with the open expanse of the Caribbean Sea stretching ahead, Gemma hoped the ominous steel vessel would veer off toward Puerto Rico. Instead, it surged forward, shifting into top speed and slicing through the churning water with predatory intent. The distance between them shrank. The hum of engines deepened, reverberating through their hull.

Then came the voice—booming through a public address system, cold and commanding.

"Unidentified vessel, heave to and prepare to be boarded."

Gemma yelled back against the wind, "Who are you? Identify yourself!"

"Narcotics," they broadcast back.

Panic shot through Gemma's body, her heart

hammering against her ribs. She exchanged a glance with Nihir, who sat beside her on the cockpit bench. His usual serene demeanor held steady, but she caught the subtle shift—shoulders tensing beneath his linen shirt, gaze sharpening as it swept the approaching vessel. For a moment, genuine fear flickered across his features before vanishing behind a mask of resolve.

He leaned toward her. "Look at their boat. No flag, no numbers. This isn't an official operation."

The words grounded Gemma amid her spiraling thoughts. He was right. The boat bore no markings, and the crew appeared to be civilians—filthy ones at that. As she scanned their rough faces, dread settled in her stomach.

"Narcotics with who? What agency? What country?" she shouted, her voice strained over the distance.

The Interceptor's captain didn't respond directly. Instead, he issued another command.

"Drop your sails and prepare for boarding, or we'll fire on your vessel."

The pretense vanished. They weren't DEA or Coasties. The pirate crew moved swiftly, lashing the vessels together with boarding lines, their motions fluid and synchronized. Crab and Boon scrambled across the deck, snatching up boat hooks and winch handles—anything that might drive the intruders back.

Nihir dashed below to help Cruz retrieve the boat's guns. Gemma heard muffled thuds and the gun locker being thrown open. She caught Nihir's eye as he emerged briefly at the companionway, his placid expression replaced by focused resolve.

The pirates moved in a terrifying dance of efficiency. Their grimy faces remained emotionless, communicating through hand gestures. One muscular man with a jagged scar bisecting his left eyebrow leaped across the narrowing gap, his movements quick and deliberate as he tied the two vessels together with expert precision.

Others tossed thick rubber fenders into the shrinking space between boats. With the collision of hulls, the pirate leader leaped across, an automatic rifle slung across his back. His imposing figure radiated menace, his breath foul with the stench of decay.

"Do as you're told, and we might let you live."

Gemma met his eyes, refusing to show her terror even as her palms grew slick with sweat. The leader's lips curled into a cruel smile as he pressed the cold barrel of his gun against her temple.

"Everyone below deck!" he bellowed. "Come up with your hands up, or I'll put a bullet through this one's pretty little head!" His finger twitched against the trigger for emphasis, making Gemma's breath catch.

Tense seconds passed before shuffling sounds emerged from below. Cruz appeared first, a .38 strapped at his side. Behind him came Nihir, clutching a weathered Beretta over his head.

"Throw your guns on the deck," the leader commanded, pressing the gun harder against Gemma's temple. "Now!"

Nihir's and Cruz's firearms clattered on the teak. Two pirates surged forward, kicking the discarded weapons out of reach. With rough hands, they patted down the men, shoving Cruz against the cabin wall while yanking Boon's arms upward. Crab winced as thick fingers dug into his shoulders.

"Mira esto," one called out triumphantly, displaying a .22 he'd retrieved from Boon's ankle holster. Cruz's jaw tightened as this last weapon was confiscated.

"Tie them up and get the drugs from the compartments in the galley. There are false fronts behind the cabinets," the leader ordered.

They knew! Someone had tipped them off.

A tattooed pirate marched them midship, his blackened fingers working the ropes with efficiency. He leaned close to Gemma, his eyes revealing cruel satisfaction.

"Amarrados bien." He breathed out rummy fumes and nodded in approval.

Gemma's stomach churned, but she refused to look away. The man smirked at her defiance before turning to Boon, tugging unnecessarily hard on the older sailor's bindings.

"Cocaine aquí!" The shout rose from below deck. Cheers erupted from the pirates as the few that remained up top descended to haul up the loot. Heavy duffels were heaved and dragged through the companionway.

Gemma strained against her bonds, the rough rope burning her wrists. Every movement sent sharp pains through her arms, but she welcomed the sensation—it meant she was alive and fighting. She twisted her hands, testing for slack, her breath hitching as she felt the faintest give in the knots.

The tattooed subordinate who had left to help transfer cargo had abandoned his AK against the cabin top.

"What do we do?" Crab whispered from behind the mast, panic lacing his voice.

The pirate leader reappeared, machete drawn, its edge gleaming.

"Stay calm and keep quiet," Gemma called back softly. She had to act before the inevitable kill order came. The pirates were completing their mission, and she was fairly sure no quarter was their endgame. However, why they hadn't gunned down Gemma and her crew on the spot remained a mystery.

She whispered to Boon, "I think I can get free. I'm going to pull hard. Don't make a sound when I do. And be ready to grab that gun." She turned to Cruz. "No matter what happens, do nothing until I give the word."

Pain shot up Gemma's arm, and she bit back a cry as she freed one hand.

"I've got it. Don't move."

Waves crashed against the gunwales. Fenders squealed between the boats like trapped pigs. A line snapped free, and the bows pulled away from each other. As the pirates moved to re-secure the separating boats, the *Mariposa* rolled hard. Her mast slapped the raised pilothouse of the Interceptor, sending debris from a plastic radar dome flying. With the sudden lurch, Gemma's second hand pulled free.

Victory surged through her.

"Run! Arm yourselves!"

Boon and Cruz hauled Nihir and Crab forward, bound in a twisted human chain. Crab stumbled, nearly taking them all down, but Boon planted his feet and steadied them. The pirate leader noticed his quarry was free and lunged with his machete. Boon snarled, bending low to sweep up the abandoned AK-47. His fingers wrapped around the stock just as the pirate reached him. Without hesitation, Boon squeezed the trigger.

The leader crumpled, his machete clattering across the deck. Gemma seized the blade amid the chaos.

"Hold still!" she shouted.

Boon yanked at the rope around Crab's wrist while Gemma raised the machete, slicing through bonds one by one. Nihir staggered back, shaking his bleeding wrists.

"Cover us! Get the guns!" Armed with another fallen weapon, Nihir positioned himself.

"Now!" Boon barked.

They burst into action, embodying fierce determination to reclaim their freedom. Crab scurried to retrieve the confiscated guns kicked against the gunwale. Cruz fired, the crack echoing across the churning sea. Boon followed, spraying bullets into the fray. A sickening crunch erupted as the hulls crushed a pirate who'd fallen between the boats.

Movement on the pirate boat caught Gemma's eye.

"Get down!"

The navigator in the pilothouse fired across the decks, bullets whipping through the air like angry hornets. Boon retaliated with automatic fire, mowing down the remaining intruders aboard the *Mariposa*—except for their leader, who leaped across the gap despite his wounds. Blood trailed from the shots Boon had inflicted, the man's face twisted in fury.

Adrenaline surged through Gemma's veins as she scrambled toward the helm, fingers trembling as she started the engine. By her count, only two or three pirates remained alive.

"Boon! Shoot out their engines! Crab, cut the boarding lines!"

Crab grabbed a knife and ran along the gunwale with surprising agility. As the ships separated, Gemma felt a surge of triumph. She engaged the engine and pulled away at full throttle.

They had escaped—for now. But she knew the pursuit was far from over. The pirates still had their radio, and backup would come.

20

WHERE TO RUN?

Gemma's arms throbbed from neck to fingertips. The ropes had cut into her skin, leaving welts that oozed tiny drops of blood, but there was no time to rest. She handed the helm to Boon with orders to put as much distance as possible between the *Mariposa* and the disabled pirates. However, they were still in a shipping lane. The cocaine needed to be restowed and the ship repaired as soon as possible.

Crouching in the dim cabin lights, Gemma shoved duffels back into their compartments, wincing as her shoulder flared with pain. She gritted her teeth and reached for another bag.

Pressing her forehead against the edge of the floorboard, she considered dipping into the cargo to dull her pain and wipe away her exhaustion, but the thought made her stomach turn. She hated how cocaine made her feel—sharp, restless, brittle from the inside out. She needed to heal, not artificial energy, and her hatred for these drugs grew with each passing day. Instead, she unfastened the first-aid kit clipped to the wall and dry swallowed three Tylenol.

"Every splinter, all the evidence—throw it all overboard," she ordered, passing up an orange plastic pail to Cruz. "Nothing stays that could raise questions."

The crew moved like the walking dead through the wreckage. Nihir swept jagged fragments of teak and fiberglass into a large dustpan and dumped the evidence overboard. Crab tackled the worst of the damage, laying patches over the scarred hull and deck. The bullet holes were clean and round, but the machete gashes were something else entirely—ragged, splintered tears from which glass needles protruded. He worked methodically, sealing and disguising each one. Boon examined the spot where the *Mariposa's* mast had slammed into the pilothouse of the pirate boat. The dent was substantial—a crater the size of his fist—but the damage appeared superficial. He pressed his ear to the cool surface, listening for the grinding or knocking that might betray a failure, and heard none.

Despite the crew being battered black and blue, nerves stretched to breaking point, and eyes hollow from exhaustion, the *Mariposa* needed to be made respectable again, not just for their own psychological benefit but as a practical necessity. If they were stopped and boarded, a normal-looking boat might be their only salvation.

Gemma sat at her charts while the others did repairs. They had cleared the Mona Passage and now lay south of the Dominican Republic. She was fairly sure Domingo would send another boat—maybe several. If he did, his men would guess the *Mariposa* was on its original route back to St. Columba or taking refuge in either Puerto Rico or the Virgin Islands. They would sweep those areas, while the *Mariposa's* evasive maneuvers would be limited. The engine, designed only to supplement the sails, wouldn't be enough to outrun the pursuit of a powerboat.

Her finger traced an eastern route to St. Martin, but her gaze snapped west, to Cuba on the map. Could they backtrack, cut up the Jamaica Channel, and hide until she devised a better plan? Running west would be unexpected. With luck, they'd become invisible.

"Boon," she called up to the wheel. "Get down here for a sec. I need your opinion."

Boon climbed down and stood over the nav table. "I don't know, Gemma. Those waters are dangerous. There are shoals and brutal currents around the Tiburon Peninsula. The sea gangs there are low-tech but vicious," Boon cautioned.

Gemma frowned, crossing her arms. "I'm not saying it's perfect, but it's an evasive route they won't expect. This gives us a shot at backtracking unnoticed."

Boon tilted his head, considering. "I mean, you're right; no one will look for us in the Windward Passage. But clearing customs and immigration in Cuba will be tough, if not impossible, and I certainly don't recommend making landfall on the south coast of Haiti. We need fuel, food, and water, though. We have to stop somewhere."

Gemma let out a slow breath, her fingers drumming against the table. "We just need a good cover story."

"Well, if you're set on this idea, Crab was born in Grenada, so he doesn't need a visa to enter Cuba," Boon said, his voice picking up as an idea took shape. "I can forge paperwork to make it look like Crab is soloing the *Mariposa* on a delivery to Miami."

Gemma raised an eyebrow. "And you think they'll buy that? This boat's pretty big for one sailor."

"The agents will probably come aboard to confirm," Boon admitted, shrugging, "but as long as Crab keeps his cool, it's plausible. He could sail this boat alone, especially with all the automation; he's been sailing all his life."

Gemma rested her hand on Boon's shoulder. "I'm going to make the call." She gave Boon a squeeze, though she wasn't entirely sure who she was trying to reassure— him or herself.

She called up to the deck. "Hey, boys! We're going to Cuba," hoping for an enthusiastic cheer or at least some sign of relief, but heavy silence was the only response. After a moment, the murmur of discussion filtered below.

Cruz climbed down the steps, followed by Crab and Nihir. "That's not the best move," he protested.

Gemma turned. "We don't have a lot of options."

Cruz folded his arms like he was ready to argue. "Puerto Rico. It's U.S. territory, and it's only hours away." He let the words settle, then added, "We'll be safe there."

Gemma frowned. "Safe? I don't think so."

Crab let out a sharp laugh. "That's exactly where

Domingo's guys will look for us—Puerto Rico or the USVI."

Cruz shook his head. "They won't be looking for us in U.S. waters. They'll assume we won't head straight for the one place with the highest law enforcement presence."

"Well, that's another problem," Nihir said from behind Crab. "Customs and the Coast Guard will be crawling all over us."

Cruz's jaw tightened, but he didn't back down. "It's still the best shot at protection. If we hole up in Cuba, we're on our own. No U.S. protection, no backup."

"Who said we need legal protection? We're drug runners, for Christ's sake," Gemma countered, eyeing Cruz. "We need to disappear. And that means avoiding any place that flies a U.S. flag."

Silence stretched between them, tension spanning the space.

Cruz shifted his weight. He was outvoted, and he knew it. "Fine," he said, his voice carefully measured. "Cuba it is."

THE HAITIAN PENINSULA welcomed *Mariposa* with fair afternoon winds. So far, Boon had been wrong about the poor sailing conditions, but the relief didn't last. As they skimmed the rugged coastline, a chaotic minefield of floating debris came into view. At first glance, the brightly colored detergent bottles, battered water jugs, and faded plastic soda containers seemed like innocent flotsam. But Gemma knew better. Each one marked the location of a

Where to Run? | 201

fish pot below, tethered with invisible nylon filaments that snaked through the water like ghostly fingers waiting to ensnare unsuspecting vessels.

"Watch the lines!" Gemma called from the helm, her voice carrying a sharp edge of urgency. She adjusted the wheel with precision as she wove through the maze of makeshift markers.

Tension on deck grew palpable as the crew took up positions along the rails, their bodies leaning over the sides. Their eyes scanned the water ahead, searching for the shimmer of nylon beneath the surface or the bob of yet another plastic bottle. Boon stood with legs braced wide apart, his substantial frame tense as he pointed out potential hazards with quick, jabbing motions.

"Port side! A huge bunch coming up!" he barked.

The fish pots grew as thick as weeds in every direction, a seemingly random pattern that Gemma was forced to solve in real-time.

"These guys don't give a damn about anyone else," Cruz muttered, leaning over the bow to spot the barely visible lines. "It's like they're trying to foul every boat that passes through here."

"They're just trying to feed their kids," Nihir responded.

Gemma's gaze flicked between the shore and the floating minefield. She nodded, her focus unwavering. *Mariposa* pushed forward with just enough speed to maintain control. Finally, after what felt like hours, they emerged from the maze. The open water ahead was a welcome sight. Gemma exhaled deeply, her shoulders relaxing as she eased the wheel into a steady course. She was sure the prop had caught some of the lines, but they had evaded the majority, or so she hoped.

"That was fun," Cruz said sarcastically, flopping onto the bench.

The *Mariposa* glided into open water, leaving Haiti's treacherous coastline in its wake.

As evening shadows began to stretch across the water, Gemma announced, "We need to set a rotation: two men for two hours. We're clear of the peninsula, and we need rest, so we'll double up and take short shifts."

"I'll take first watch," Crab volunteered.

"I'll double up with Crab," Boon followed.

"Nihir, will you take second watch with me?" Cruz asked. "You look half-dead, Gemma," he said. "You need to get some rest. Four hours, at least."

Gemma hesitated, responsibility weighing heavily. "Okay. You're right. Wake me in four. No heroics, no extended shifts."

After reviewing their heading, Gemma finally descended into the cabin. The gentle rocking of the boat felt like being cradled. She collapsed onto her bunk, sleep claiming her before she could even pull up the blanket.

The vision came like a wave washing over her dreams.

Wind whipped through a patch of turpentine trees where I lay tangled, but I felt nothing. One remaining flip-flop cut into the top of my ballooning foot. Tiny crabs in translucent shells, no bigger than the knuckles of my dead fingers, nipped at my bloated body. Ghost crabs, they were called. I used to watch them scurry along the edge of the tide from the deck of my beloved sailboat. Now, they were eating me away slowly but surely.

My eyes had gone milky and blind, yet somehow I could see everything. Not the narrow, focused sight of the living, trapped behind the prison of pupils and lenses. This was something else entirely—vision unmoored from flesh, stretching in all directions like ripples on still water. I saw in fragments and echoes, in threads that wove backward through memory and forward into possibility. Time folded like paper, each crease revealing another moment, another truth.

Above, a helicopter hovered over the crest of the encircling mountains. I tried to shout at the search-and-rescue spotter hanging out of the sliding door, but I could not yell, and my arms could not wave. In frustration, I strained, forcing myself out of my motionless husk. I took flight and soared over the bay, leaving the dead meat that had been my body behind on the sand. Free from rot, the chopper forgotten, I spiraled through the sky to my boat, bobbing at anchor, dismasted and desperately in need of a paint job. Once the winner of many regattas, Dream had been a beauty in her day.

She floated at her mooring like a broken promise. Once the pride of every regatta, her hull gleaming white above the waterline and royal blue below, Dream had been transformed into something pitiful. Seaweed hung from her neglected bottom like funeral shrouds. Her topside paint had faded to the color of old bones, her decks cracked and peeling under an uncaring sun. Even her sails were gone—sold at the sailor's swap meet for beer money, traded away like pieces of my soul.

A ghost ship for a ghost captain. Whoever killed me had only finished what neglect had started.

I drifted down into her cabin, and shame hit me harder than any physical blow ever could. Cockroaches scattered across the sole, weaving between towers of moldy takeout containers and empty bottles. The air reeked of decay and abandonment. This had been my sanctuary once, my floating home. Now it was a monument to how far I'd fallen.

Yet death had brought unexpected clarity. The fog of self-pity and alcohol that had clouded my final years was gone, burned away like morning mist. I could see the bigger picture now, understand the connections I'd missed while stumbling through my last days alive.

The motive lay scattered across my navigation desk: pages of notes—my exposé of Cowboi's empire.

The damning evidence I'd uncovered about his operations, his trafficking routes, the people who'd simply vanished after crossing him, was hidden on encrypted drives in a lockbox behind the water tank. And most damaging of all was safe in cloud storage, but here were the breadcrumbs, the pages that led to the truth.

Yet the papers lay exactly where I'd left them, gathering dust and black mildew. Would anyone even bother to salvage Dream? Probably not. Sargasso Cove was already a graveyard of abandoned boats, hulks that floated until their bilge pumps failed and the sea finally claimed them. Another ghost vessel in a bay full of ghosts.

I rose through the cabin top, drifting over the helm I'd never steer again, gazing toward shore where Mariposa's End sprawled like a painting. The settlement's buildings scattered themselves across the hillside in no particular order. I knew that place—knew its reputation, its *unspoken rules. You didn't visit Mariposa's End without an invitation.*

But today, for the first time since my death, I felt something calling me there. A presence, ancient and patient, that had been waiting for this moment. The swirling indigo that marked the spiritual heart of the community pulsed like a beacon, drawing me toward answers I'd never found in life. The summons had come.

A shout from topside jolted Gemma awake, the vision of Vaughn's body and spirit dissolving. But the image lingered—the derelict sailboat, those scattered papers. And somewhere in the back of her mind, a whisper of danger, but Vaughn's vision was from the past, not now, and she had more pressing matters, like being pursued by pirates.

"Shit, what is it?" Gemma asked, checking her watch. She'd been asleep for nearly four hours—it was well past midnight now.

"A boat! I don't know how they found us, but it could be Domingo's men. Just like before, there's nothing on the radar. But I definitely saw a light right in front of us," Boon said, his tone frantic and edged with paranoia.

Gemma joined Boon and Crab at the wheel, forcing herself to stay calm. Cruz and Nihir should have been on watch by now, but somehow Boon and Crab were still up here. "Why would they be in front of us? It's probably just a commercial ship," she replied, but even as she said it, her gut twisted. PTSD was already setting in from the gunfight and the intense stress from everything that had happened since joining Cowboi's organization.

"But it could be Domingo," Boon pressed, his eyes wide. "They could have come around the West Point."

Crab stood near Boon, gripping the ship's binoculars tightly. His hands trembled as he adjusted the focus.

"Directly ahead. See, there?" Crab pointed and handed Gemma the binoculars.

She raised the glasses, peering into the dark expanse. A point of light danced on the horizon. Crab's nervous energy felt contagious, and she couldn't shake the feeling that something was off.

"It might be one of the Haitian gangs that control this point. But the gangs have small boats at best. Whatever that is, it seems big," Crab muttered, his voice shaky.

Gemma lowered the binoculars and studied his face. His pupils were dilated, and there was a jittery quality to his movements that made her stomach sink. She glanced toward Boon, who stood near the chart plotter, his eyes darting between the screen and the sea. His demeanor was no better—restless, his jaw grinding.

It hit her—the cockpit was a mess. The ashtray overflowed, and Heineken bottles and rum glasses filled every cup holder. That wasn't unusual. However, a razor blade flashing in the console and a set of faint, parallel cuts in the smooth plastic face of the plotter were new.

While she, Nihir, and Cruz had been catching some much-needed sleep, Boon and Crab must have dipped into the cargo, and it was enough to fray their nerves and warp their judgment.

"Did you check the vessel ID?" Gemma asked, keeping her voice steady as her eyes flicked again to the blade glinting under the dim light. A confrontation about what they'd clearly been snorting wasn't worth the aggravation at the moment—not with the way Crab's eyes darted wildly across the water.

"Of course I checked!" Boon snapped. "The AIS didn't show anything, but I saw the light."

Gemma sighed and stepped over to the plotter. Pinching her fingers and spreading them across the scratched screen, she zoomed out until the shallow depth markers and a small landmass came into view.

"There it is," she said, pointing to the screen. "The abandoned lighthouse on Navassa Island. The glare off the lens must have caught your eye. It's a trick of the light that made it seem much closer, guys. Nothing to worry about."

Crab looked down, his shoulders slumping with embarrassment. Boon bristled, muttering something under his breath about how it could've been anything. But the tension in their faces didn't ease, and Gemma knew it wasn't just exhaustion fueling their paranoia.

"Anything I should know about?" Nihir poked his head up, stifling a yawn, roused by the commotion. Cruz appeared behind him, both men clearly having been woken from deep sleep.

"No worries," she said, her voice intentionally light. "Crab. Boon. Get some rest. It's another eight hours until we near Cuba, and it'll be late morning before we can anchor. Since we're all awake now, Nihir and I will take the next watch. Cruz, you can spell us at dawn."

Boon hesitated, his jaw loosening a little. He nodded

and disappeared down the ladder. Crab followed, mumbling something about a glass of water. Gemma took a steadying breath and turned to Nihir and Cruz.

"Just a phantom lighthouse and two jittery crewmen who need to sleep it off," Gemma explained quietly. She handed Nihir the binoculars. "Let's keep an eye out."

As Gemma settled at the helm with Nihir as her co-pilot and Cruz preparing to go back below, the faint glow of Navassa's lighthouse shimmered in the distance, a reminder of how easily the mind could play tricks when the stakes were high and her crew was on edge.

An hour later, *Mariposa* sailed eerily close to the cylindrical tower of decaying masonry. The once-pristine whitewashed façade had crumbled away, revealing the rough, weathered stone beneath. Waves pounded relentlessly against the jagged rocks, casting shining slivers of silver. Ghostly and forgotten, the place stood in ruins—its windows shattered, roofs collapsed, and vines, like greedy fingers, dragged the structure down, piece by piece. Mysterious moans and rhythmic creaking floated on the wind. The lighthouse, once a beacon of safety, now stood as a decaying monument to time's relentless march.

Gemma gripped the wheel, her body heavy. An infinity of stars winked above, so clear and dense that she could see spirals and whorls of the galaxy's geometry light-years away. Nihir slouched beside her, dropping in and out of sleep. Gemma's eyes burned from exhaustion, despite her brief rest. The weight of responsibility pressed on her shoulders as she scanned the water, her mind fighting to stay alert. Gemma forgave Crab and Boon for their little theft. If she were partial to cocaine, she might have done the same.

∽

CRUZ CALLED everyone up on deck as the first hints of dawn touched the eastern horizon. As the sun rose, so did the mountainous coast of eastern Cuba, emerging like a dark silhouette from the cobalt waters of the Caribbean. The craggy peaks of the Sierra Maestra loomed in the distance, their rugged outlines sharp against the deepening hues of dawn, bathed in shades of violet and gold.

Gemma stood in quiet awe as the landscape unfolded. Patches of dense, emerald-green jungle clung to the steep slopes, while scattered palms swayed in the earth-scented breeze. Below, the coastline jutted out into rocky headlands and hidden coves, where the waves crashed against the shore, sending sprays of white foam into the air. Ahead, the entrance to the bay came into view. Beyond a narrow passage, the harbor opened.

Without thinking, Gemma took over the wheel and turned the ignition, and the engine gave a wheezing roar before sputtering to a stop with a gut-wrenching squeal and a metallic clunk. The sound echoed across the water, loud and final.

"Damn it!" she hissed, slamming her hand against the wheel.

"What was that?" Nihir asked.

Gemma's stomach sank as the realization hit her like a

punch. The fish traps. She had been so focused on the excitement of nearing their destination that she had forgotten about the tangle of nylon lines from the Haitian fish pots they had passed through yesterday.

"We've got a problem," Gemma said, her voice tight with frustration. "The lines are tangled in the prop."

Gemma didn't mince words when Boon and Crab appeared, both looking worse for wear after their drug-fueled night watch. "The prop's fouled. Fish trap lines. We're dead in the water until it's clear. Boon, take the wheel."

"All right," Boon muttered, holding up his hands.

Cruz groaned. "Can't we just sail the rest of the way in?"

Gemma shook her head. "No way. Santiago Bay's entrance is a maze of shallow channels, and I mean a maze. I've never seen a more complicated approach. Even if we somehow managed to make it through the entrance under sail, the harbor itself is enormous, and we can't be seen on deck. Even Crab can't single-handedly sail into that marina."

"There's no way around it. We need the engine." Leaving the crew up top, Gemma dashed to the gear locker to retrieve her wetsuit. Her movements were swift, her frustration channeling into action. She knew she was the best diver aboard, and if this was going to get fixed, it would have to be her.

She stripped down to her underwear, pulled on the neoprene suit, threaded her dreadlocks through the top of her diving mask, and twisted them into a messy bun,

Where to Run? | 211

securing them out of the way. Her mind raced as she considered her options. She might be able to free dive this, but she knew using the scuba gear would make the job quicker and safer, especially if the lines were as tightly wrapped as she feared.

"I'm going in," Gemma said simply, pulling a tank from the gear locker. She slipped the straps of her BC over her shoulders. "We don't have time to waste. I'll cut the lines and get us moving again."

Boon's brow furrowed, but he didn't argue. The sails flapped like the wings of a bird trapped in a net as Boon turned the wheel hard over, set it, and adjusted the trim. He backed the jib and eased off the mainsheet slightly, stopping the forward progress of *Mariposa* to a near standstill. With the rudder hard over, the equivalent of an emergency brake at sea, *Mariposa* was hove to.

Gemma trailed a length of rope in the water and tied it around her waist as a safety line. With a nod, she pulled her mask down over her eyes and slipped the mouthpiece of the regulator between her teeth. With practiced motion, she plunged in. As she sank into the blue expanse, she equalized, adjusted her buoyancy control, and came to rest on the surface. Kicking with bare feet, she cleared water from her mask. Crab threw in her fins, and she pulled them on her feet. Patterns of darkness moved in the layers of shifting depth, just below the penetration of the morning sun.

Gemma unsheathed her knife as the *Mariposa* drifted sideways on the current, her heart pounding in her ears. Adjusting her buoyancy, she hovered underwater at eye level with the propeller, now enmeshed in a mess of tangled fishing lines. The tangle was far worse than she had expected—a tight, impenetrable knot of nylon threads and plastic filaments as large as a grapefruit.

The water pressed against her, murky in the early light. Gemma threaded the knife's edge through the Gordian knot, sawing steadily, her strokes quick but controlled. The lines resisted, their monofilament threads biting into her fingers with every movement. Threads of blood twisted like ribbons, dispersing in the current. She glanced upward; the surface shimmered above her, but there was no time to waste. Her crew was counting on her.

The mass loosened with each deliberate slice, the propeller gradually revealing itself from its plastic prison. Finally, with a decisive yank, she freed the last stubborn chunk. The tangle floated away like a defeated adversary, drifting off in the current.

Gemma felt the rush of relief for only a moment before an icy jolt of dread replaced it. Her instincts screamed as she turned her head against the water's resistance, feeling the oppressive presence of something behind her. The space around her had grown noticeably darker, as if a cloud had passed over the sun, but she knew better. Something large was blocking the light.

Her eyes widened in horror as a sleek, shadowy form glided into view, its movements languid but purposeful. The scent of blood from her cut hands had drawn a deadly visitor. The shark was massive—easily twelve feet long—its gray bulk moving with predatory grace. Dark, lifeless eyes fixed on her as its massive head swayed slowly from side to side, testing the water for more blood.

Gemma's training kicked in even as terror flooded her system. Don't panic. Don't splash. Don't run. The shark circled her in a wide arc, its dorsal fin cutting through the water like a sail. She could see the pale undersides of its pectoral fins as it banked, the rows of serrated teeth barely visible in its slightly open mouth.

Her heart hammered so loudly she was certain the predator could hear it. The safety line around her waist suddenly felt like a trap. But the boat was her only refuge.

The shark completed its circle and began to tighten the radius, moving closer with each pass. Gemma forced herself to remain still, her breathing controlled through the regulator, even as every instinct screamed at her to flee. She needed to get to the surface, but sudden movement could trigger an attack.

The massive creature made another pass, this time close enough that she could see the individual scars along its flank and the rough texture of its skin. It was a bull shark—aggressive, unpredictable, and perfectly comfortable in these warm coastal waters.

On its next pass, the shark bumped against her leg— not a bite, but a test. The contact sent a surge of terror through her body, but she forced herself to remain motionless. The bump was almost gentle, but she could feel the incredible power behind it, the muscle and sinew capable of tearing her apart in seconds.

That's when she realized the shark wasn't just investigating—it was positioning itself.

Filling her BC, Gemma surfaced as slowly as she dared, fighting every instinct to rocket upward. When she finally breached, she spat out her regulator mouthpiece and shouted, "Shark! Bull shark! Grab the spearguns!"

Panic clawed at her chest as she swam toward the stern with measured strokes, fighting the urge to thrash. The sleek form moved beneath her. The swim ladder seemed impossibly far away. Behind her, the creature's massive head broke the surface before sliding back down. It was getting bolder.

Her hand finally found the swim ladder, and she sacrificed her fins, kicking them away like an offering to the sea gods as she scrambled onto the swim deck. Her breath came in ragged gasps, and her hands trembled. She looked back as a dorsal fin sliced through the surface like a knife.

The shark had followed her right to the boat, its massive bulk visible just beneath the surface. As Gemma watched in horror, it rolled on its side, one black eye fixed on her as if calculating whether she was still within reach.

"Hold on!" Boon's voice rang out, commanding authority. She heard a sharp whistle as the spear discharged with a metallic twang, followed by the unmistakable splash and solid thud of the barbed spear finding its mark deep in the predator's thick hide, just behind the dorsal fin.

"Got the bastard!" he shouted.

The shark's reaction was immediate and violent. A slick of crimson bloomed in the sea as the massive shark thrashed wildly, its tail whipping the surface into foam.

The spear shaft protruded from its flank like a flag, and the wounded predator rolled and twisted, trying to dislodge the foreign object. For a moment, it seemed it might turn its fury on the boat itself.

Then, as if making a calculated decision, the beast went rigid. Its black eye fixed on them one final time before it suddenly darted away into the deep, trailing a ribbon of blood that dispersed in swirling tendrils behind it. The massive tail disappeared into the depths, leaving only disturbed water and the metallic tang of blood in the air.

Crab pulled Gemma onto the cockpit bench, his expression grim but focused. She tried to stand on shaky legs, then collapsed back down. Her hands stung from the cuts, and her chest heaved with exertion, but she was alive. The crew cheered, the tension giving way to relief as they prepared to head for the harbor at Santiago de Cuba.

21

THE DEAL

Gemma's muscles ached as she peeled off her wetsuit, the neoprene clinging stubbornly to her wet body. She toweled off quickly and changed into a faded hoodie and a pair of khaki shorts. Her hands were still damp as she gathered the customs and immigration paperwork from the nav station.

"Here," she said, handing the stack of forms over to Boon and Crab to complete. Everyone aboard had been through hell in the last twenty-four hours, but survival now depended on making everyone disappear on paper—everyone except for Crab, who would still have to face the authorities.

The two graying men argued in hushed tones over passports and fabricated itineraries, their voices low and conspiratorial. Crab squinted at the small print, the creases around his eyes deepening with concentration. The men's bickering had the practiced rhythm of old friends who knew exactly how to get under each other's skin, especially in a crisis.

"You're writing like a damn kindergartner," Boon muttered, snatching a form from Crab's hands. "That scrawl will have them scratching their heads for hours."

"At least I can spell 'declare' correctly," Crab retorted, pointing at Boon's paperwork with a nicotine-stained finger.

"Why are you changing our departure to Tortola when I'm Grenadian?" Crab argued.

"Because it's the least suspicious route, Einstein," Boon snapped back.

Scraps of pink and yellow paper from aborted forms littered the sole of the main cabin, but the actual issue wasn't logistics. It was stress. Everyone aboard had been through the wringer. Gemma ran a hand over her face and exhaled. There was no room for error. One inconsistency, and Customs would search them from top to bottom. If that happened, it was all over. She reached for a pen. "Let's get this perfect," she said.

On the approach, Gemma twisted her dreadlocks tightly under the hood of her sweatshirt and slid her wrap-around sunglasses onto her face. The boat hummed beneath her as she expertly motored past the weathered concrete sentry house standing sentinel at the mouth of the channel, its peeling paint and watchful windows making her skin crawl with apprehension.

Santiago de Cuba's strict maritime protocol required all incoming vessels to call in before entering the harbor proper—a formality they couldn't bypass without raising immediate red flags. Gemma's stomach knotted as she watched Crab fidget with the radio. She desperately hoped his natural charm and sailor's gift of gab could somehow convince the harbor officials to waive the standard inspection, but she knew the chances of that were slim. A bead of sweat trickled down her temple.

A single man arriving alone in a restricted country aboard a 46-foot sailboat practically screamed irregularity. No matter how confident Crab sounded on the radio, the harbor officials would almost certainly insist on coming aboard. Gemma's fingers tightened around the wheel as she contemplated the consequences. If they were boarded —when they were boarded—it was absolutely critical that the inspectors remain on deck and out of *Mariposa's* cabin. The evidence below would destroy them if discovered.

"Okay, ready," Gemma announced to the crew. "Crab, tell them you don't need a pilot and that you'll check in at Marlin Marina."

A woman's voice responded to Crab's hail. The operator acknowledged Crab's message but then fell silent for a beat too long.

A man's gruff voice came back. "Prepare for boarding."

Fuck.

Defeated, they anchored off, and Gemma, Nihir, Boon, and Cruz gallows-walked to the hidden door behind the bed in the V-berth. A low-ceilinged corridor through the chain locker led to a compartment that was five feet wide at the opening and narrowed to a point at the other end. The claustrophobic panic room was terrifying. Lights would turn off after five minutes, so they scrambled to get

The Deal | 219

comfortable as the timer counted down with a tick, tick, tick. They squeezed in and squatted like toads in the dark.

The silence was oppressive, broken only by shallow breaths and the faint creak of the hull as the boat shifted with the waves. Gemma's chest tightened, her pulse racing in the suffocating blackness. Boon let out a nervous chuckle, quickly stifled by a sharp hiss from Cruz.

"Alright," Nihir's voice cut through the tension, so quiet it was almost imperceptible. "Everyone, close your eyes. Focus on my voice." His calm was a tether in the overwhelming darkness. "We're going to breathe together. In for four counts, hold for four, out for four."

At first, their breaths were uneven and shaky, but as Nihir continued to guide them, the rhythm took hold: inhale, hold, exhale. Slowly, the tightness in Gemma's chest began to ease, and the pounding of her heart dulled to a manageable thrum.

"The walls don't matter. Just picture an open sky, endless and calm," Nihir said.

Gemma clung to the image, letting the imagined expanse replace the suffocating reality of their cramped hideaway. Cruz and Boon, who rarely indulged in anything remotely spiritual, followed Nihir out of pure necessity. For a moment, the fear of discovery, the press of the walls, and the weight of their situation faded, replaced by the simple act of breathing in unison. It was a fragile peace, but it was enough to get them through the next stretch of waiting in what felt like coffin.

Thirty minutes later, the rumble of an outboard approached. Soon after, heavy boot steps echoed above them through the chamber. A strange man's voice mixed with Crab's, but Gemma couldn't make out the words.

What if they go through the drawers in the captain's cabin? How would Crab explain women's clothes? Gemma's mind raced. *Fuck. Who cares about clothes? What if they find ten million dollars' worth of cocaine?*

She and the crew had done everything they could to make the story of Crab's solo crossing plausible, but it wouldn't stand up if the inspectors were very nosy. So far, the officials hadn't ventured further than the cockpit. More indistinct voices, closer to the fore this time. Gemma's heart pounded so loudly she was sure the officials could hear it thumping through the deck. Up top, the voices stopped, and the footsteps retreated. The outboard started again, then was gone. Gemma let out a long breath of relief. They waited for Crab's signal.

"All clear," he called through the tunnel.

Gemma found the latch, and four bodies tumbled out. Cruz and Boon desperately pushed from behind. No time to waste. They needed to get *Mariposa* out of sight. She ordered Crab to motor into a finger bay that ran deep inland, far away from the customs and immigration office.

From Gemma's low vantage at the bottom of the companionway, she could see San Pedro de la Roca towering above, a stone fortress built into a rocky promontory. Ancient stairs connected the terraces, one above another. Three hundred years of guano whitewashed the crenellated walls and turrets. Glimpses of cannons peeked through the scrubby brown overgrowth.

The Deal | 221

As the inlet faded to murky brown, they gained confidence that no one had followed them into this secluded backwater. The depth finder showed increasingly shallow readings, mud clouds billowing in their wake as *Mariposa's* keel occasionally kissed the soft mud bottom. Mangrove roots reached like gnarled fingers into the water on either side, creating a natural privacy screen.

Crab finally gave the definitive "all clear" with a satisfied nod.

"Over there," Gemma pointed toward a particularly dense cluster of trees. "That spot should keep us hidden."

Crab maneuvered the boat with practiced ease. Once satisfied that their location was out of sight of any officials, he dropped anchor with a reassuring clank of chain. The boat settled on the still water as he moved to the stern and began lowering the dinghy from the davits. The craft hit the water with a splash that echoed across the quiet inlet.

With surprising agility for his age, Crab clambered down into the bobbing dinghy, his Greek fisherman's cap firmly in place. He fired up the outboard motor with one efficient pull.

"They want me to check in right away. Back before you know it," he called up, then disappeared around the mangrove-covered point, heading toward the marina office to finish the paperwork that would make their precarious situation nominally safer.

Gemma's stomach jumped when she saw a returning boat far too soon. *Did he forget something?* But no. It wasn't

Crab. A local skiff, loaded with fruit, came racing toward them from around the point.

Apparently, someone had seen their approach and watched them anchor. A weathered man stood among the piles of produce, operating the long-tillered outboard motor from a standing position.

"Buenos días. ¿Habla español?" he hailed Gemma and grabbed hold of *Mariposa's* gunwale.

"No hablo español," Gemma said, hoping he'd go away, but he switched to English easily.

The skiff was so overloaded that its rail was nearly level with the waterline.

"Whatever you need, I'm your man. Fresh fruit? I have the best fruit in Cuba. Look!" He gestured to heaps of bananas, pineapples, oranges, and other fruits and vegetables of all shapes and sizes. Without allowing for a negative reply, he chattered on. "You need water, fuel, laundry service. I can do it all for you!"

The fruit looked delicious, but Gemma didn't want this man's eyes on them when Crab returned. He would inevitably use any information he gathered to his advantage. And even if he didn't, Gemma knew the ways of the tropics. Rumors spread like viruses. Gossip on the trade winds was faster than light. She had to think.

"What's your name?" she asked.

"Alberto," he replied.

"Tell you what, Alberto, I'll take three pineapples, a hand of bananas, and I'll gather up the crew's laundry. You have it washed and bring it back tomorrow, and we'll have more work for you then. Lots of business—but I want something special in return. What I want more than anything is privacy. Do you understand? You tell the others we're your customers and that they need to stay far away from us. On shore, if anyone talks, tell them we are scouting properties for a real estate development. Can you do this?"

"Bueno, bueno! Sure, I can! I'm your protection. My specialty. No problem! What kind of money do you have?"

"Only ECs," Gemma replied. A dark cloud of disappointment crossed Alberto's eyes.

"Okay, ma'am. Sure. No problem," Alberto said. "I can exchange EC in town."

She had plenty of US currency on board, but she didn't want it to be known that they were worth robbing. Eastern Caribbean dollars were never popular because they were hard to spend directly, and although they were pegged to the US dollar, in reality, their value fluctuated wildly. Gemma had judged it right. She knew the drill—hire the right man, and you bought security, at least until your money ran out.

Gemma told Boon to load up the boat's canvas ditty bags with dirty clothes. The equivalent of ten US dollars bought them privacy until morning. Hopefully, they wouldn't be in prison by then.

"We're checked in," Crab said upon his return. "It was sketchy as all fuck, but I explained I was a boat brat—born and raised on the sea. Did my overly friendly and stupid routine. A little too much bottom paint in my veins, if you know what I mean. It helps that Cuban technology is from the 1950s. They had no way to check my background or our registration, so we're good for now."

Relieved, Gemma sliced up the pineapple she'd bought, poured warm glasses of rum, and gathered the crew at the cockpit table. She made a mental note to ask Alberto for ice when he returned with the laundry tomorrow.

"First, here's to Crab. You saved the day!" Gemma toasted.

The crew joined in the toast, their glasses clinking together.

"Now, we need to figure out what to do. How do we get home? Let's go round-robin and throw out some ideas. Rules of the game: good ideas are great, and bad ideas are even better. Don't be shy."

She used a brainstorming technique her mom had taught her—rewarding silly ideas often sparked creative solutions.

"I'll go first," Gemma said. "Should we call Cowboi?"

Nihir shook his head. "Cowboi's just gonna tell us to turn around and deliver the drugs as planned. That's risky. Domingo's got people looking for us."

"All right," Crab said, hesitating. "If we're throwing out bad ideas... we could call Domingo and try to renegotiate. No details on where we are. Maybe we set up a neutral drop point. He wants the cargo; let's give it to him."

Cruz scoffed. "Right, because *that's* gonna end well. His men tried to kill us."

Gemma sipped her rum, letting the tension dissolve

momentarily as she collected her thoughts. "All right, Cruz, your turn. Hit us with your best bad idea."

Cruz leaned back in his chair, his gaze sweeping over the group. "Let's cut the bullshit. There's no easy way out of this. Here's the truth: I'm not who you think I am."

The crew froze. Gemma sat up bolt straight and raised an eyebrow. Suspicion ran rampant across her face. "What do you mean?" she asked.

Cruz reached into his pocket and pulled out a leather billfold. With a flick of his wrist, he tossed it onto the table. It slid to a stop in front of Gemma, who hesitated before picking it up. Her breath caught at the sight of a gold badge topped with an embossed eagle. Opposite it, a laminated credential card bore **CENTRAL INTELLIGENCE AGENCY,** Cruz's photo, and a classification code.

"You're CIA?" she said, her voice tight.

"Undercover," Cruz confirmed, his voice taking on a sharper, more professional edge that Gemma had never heard before. "For over two years, I've been embedded here, gathering intelligence on Cowboi's entire operation. That cocaine you're all worried about? It's not just contraband—it's critical evidence in an international investigation that spans three federal agencies and two governments."

He exhaled sharply before shaking his head. The practiced casualness he'd maintained seemed to fall away with each word. "I wasn't working alone on this. Vaughn was digging for me too, though he didn't fully comprehend the scope or the danger. He didn't know he was essentially functioning as an asset." Cruz's eyes changed from wide and friendly to shrewd and calculating. "Vaughn had natural access, local connections, and a disarming way of asking questions that didn't trigger Cowboi's defenses. He could float through spaces where someone like me would raise red flags."

Cruz leaned forward, elbows on his knees, his expression haunted. "Cowboi treated Vaughn like the court jester—harmless entertainment, too drunk to be a threat." He hesitated, his jaw tightening as muscles worked beneath his skin. "But when Vaughn disappeared..."

He turned to Gemma, meeting her eyes directly. "You became my contingency plan, Gemma. I systematically positioned you, cultivated your trust, and groomed you to be an informant. I engineered circumstances to place you in Cowboi's orbit." The hard edge in his voice softened slightly. "And I'm genuinely sorry for that manipulation. You deserved better than being pulled into this without your knowledge or consent."

The crew fell silent, save for the gentle lapping of waves against the hull. Then Crab laughed. "You're telling me you've been playing us this whole time?"

"All that time drinking in the bar? That was a frame-up?" Gemma added.

"Undercover intelligence comes from being where the targets are. Bars are perfect. Everyone trusted me because I played the role. I trained for months to make it believable and spent years cultivating relationships connected to Cowboi."

The Deal | 227

He glanced at Gemma, his eyes reflecting a weight beyond their current predicament. "Look, I get that this sounds insane, but Cowboi's network goes deeper than you can imagine. We're talking systematic drug and human trafficking operations, offshore money laundering schemes that hide billions from taxation and scrutiny. Easter Cay isn't just a playground; it's the epicenter of an exploitation empire."

"The FBI has had surveillance on Easter Cay for nearly a decade, documenting everything from suspicious flight manifests to the parade of underage victims. We've compiled reports on dozens of confirmed minors who've been flown in from South America, Eastern Europe, the U.S., of course, and even France. Some as young as fourteen." His voice dropped lower. "But the St. Columba government protects him. They've blocked every attempt at international cooperation."

Cruz leaned closer, his intensity palpable in the confined space. "We needed a way to draw him to U.S. soil where we could actually touch him. His network of lawyers and fixers has constructed an impenetrable shield offshore—they've negotiated immunity agreements, buried evidence, and intimidated witnesses. But on American soil, with the right documentation and testimony?" He fixed Gemma with an unwavering stare. "You cooperate with us now, help bring him into our jurisdiction, and I guarantee you walk away clean. No charges, no record of involvement. A complete separation from all of this. It's your way out."

Nihir shifted in his seat. "How?"

"Gemma will call Cowboi," Cruz said. "Tell him about Domingo's double-cross. He'll want the details, but just say we've got the shipment secured and we have a buyer." Cruz glanced at Nihir. "That's where you come in."

Nihir stiffened. "Me?"

"Yeah. Cowboi knows you. Knows you had connections in Miami." Cruz leaned in.

"We'll tell him you lined up a buyer through your old manager."

Nihir's jaw tightened. "You mean my pimp? You think he'll buy that?"

"He'll have to," Cruz shrugged. "If Cowboi thinks there's a way to make this mess disappear and he doesn't lose money, he'll make a deal. Especially now. Word's already spreading that he's losing control. Domingo's stunt didn't just put the shipment at risk—it made Cowboi look weak. We'll use that vulnerability."

Cruz leaned back, his eyes darkening as he continued. "For years, Cowboi has operated with impunity on his private island, protected by powerful friends and a network of enablers."

He turned to Gemma, his voice dropping. "You'll contact Cowboi directly. Make it clear this is a crisis that threatens his entire operation—something that requires his personal touch to resolve. We'll lure him to Florida with the promise of both profit and discretion. When he steps off that plane in Miami thinking he's about to handle some routine damage control, he'll walk straight into a federal trap."

Cruz's fingers drummed against the table. "We've been

The Deal | 229

building a case for years—witness statements, financial records, everything. Vaughn was instrumental. The moment he sets foot stateside, he's done."

"Cowboi's not stupid. He'll just send his errand boys," Gemma said.

Cruz shook his head. "Cowboi's hold is slipping. People in his network—Domingo included—are circling like sharks. He can't afford to send his thugs this time. If something goes wrong again, it's over. He needs the respect of his partners." Cruz leaned in, lowering his voice. "Look, in every major crisis, he handled things personally. He can't afford to send someone else."

Gemma noticed Boon's fingers twitching against his glass. His small tell, one she had learned from their many games of cards, made her stomach churn. He wasn't just upset—he was angry. Too angry. But now wasn't the time to address it.

"And if this goes sideways?" she pressed.

"It won't." Cruz's confidence was cold, absolute.

Boon stared at him. "You expect us to just trust you?"

"I don't expect anything. But here's the deal: you've painted yourselves into a corner. You follow my plan and walk away free."

The group fell silent again.

Cruz stood, his tone shifting to operational. "Gemma, keep the story simple: Domingo's double-cross failed. The shipment is intact. We have a buyer in Miami through Nihir's connections. Cowboi needs to be there in person to make it happen."

As the crew dispersed, Gemma lingered at the table.

The stakes had risen higher than she'd ever imagined—they weren't just running cargo anymore; they were setting a trap for one of the most powerful men in the Caribbean, maybe in the world. A man with connections that reached from island governments to mainland billionaires, from entertainment moguls to political leaders. The kind of man who could make people disappear without a trace, just as Vaughn had vanished.

More secrets were hiding beneath the surface of Cruz's plan—layers of deception and danger she couldn't fully comprehend. The whispers about Easter Cay had always been there, floating through the harbor like Sahara dust. Gemma had transported women, telling herself she was just a taxi. But deep down, she'd known how very wrong it was.

Boon's reaction troubled her most. The secrets would have to come to light soon. If Cruz's intelligence was accurate, federal investigators had already been building a case against Cowboi for years—trafficking minors, facilitating abuse, blackmailing the powerful and not-so-powerful. The private island paradise was just the visible tip of an operation that extended across continents—an iceberg of corruption.

The others sought solitude to reflect on their situation. Gemma sat alone in the cockpit, watching life teeming in the roots of the mangroves. The revelation about Cruz had shattered everything she thought she knew. For two years, he'd been playing a role— their friendship, the routine of comparing sales at The Last Resort, even his encouragement to take Boon's job—all calculated moves in an intelligence operation.

She traced her finger along a machete gash in the teak table, wondering how many other "friends" in her life might be something else entirely. The thought made her chest tighten. Tomorrow, she would have to look Cruz in the eye and pretend nothing had changed. Smile at his jokes. Trust his guidance. Act like he hadn't just revealed their entire relationship was built on lies.

What choice did she have? They were stranded in Cuba with millions in cocaine hidden below decks. Her dreams of running her own charter business had twisted into this nightmare of federal agents and international drug lords.

Gemma took the last sip of her rum, letting the burn slide down her throat. The irony wasn't lost on her—she'd returned to St. Columba seeking a connection to her roots, only to discover she had never truly belonged anywhere. Now, she was trapped in a web of deception with no way out except through it.

Tomorrow, she would call Cowboi. Like it or not, the were stuck with Cruz and his plan.

22

SANTIAGO DE CUBA

Alberto's approach woke Gemma. She popped her head outside to see who was motoring up. Large, paper-wrapped parcels and the inventory of a small grocery store weighed down the little boat. She smiled at the handsome man in his frayed cargo shorts, a white T-shirt, and a Mount Gay ball cap, so sun-faded that the red had turned to pale pink. Clearly, these clothes were cast-offs from the pleasure cruisers who passed through these bays. Gemma guessed Alberto's age to be anywhere between thirty and fifty. He had the attitude of a young man but the sun-hardened complexion of a much older one.

"Ahoy!" he called, waving cheerfully. "I have your laundry!"

"Guys," Gemma yelled down the hatch. "Help Alberto unload, please."

The groggy crew filed out into the morning mist to lift

the laundry bundles onboard. Alberto had restocked his floating market with more fruits and vegetables, along with Fabuloso, Fanta, Pantene, Havana Club, and a large cooler, presumably containing ice.

"My cousin makes these," he said, holding up a collection of necklaces made from clay beads, shells, and sea glass. The items were simple and pretty, but clearly not a priority for Alberto. He displayed the jewelry out of obligation to some kin, and when Gemma showed no interest, he quickly tucked the display away. Without missing a beat, he launched into his next pitch.

"Come to shore with me! I'll take you on an island tour —my car's right here. We could hit the beach, go for a hike, see the city. You're in luck—it's Carnival weekend! The parade's coming up, and you'll need a guide to stay safe. Santiago's less than an hour away, and there's no better time to visit. Everyone's having a good time! My car is very nice—I'll pick you up. What time works for you?"

He rattled off the offer with the rapid-fire enthusiasm of an ADHD parakeet, his face lighting up at the prospect of landing a new gig with his customers.

A crackle of static from the VHF radio interrupted her thoughts. Crab leaned in to adjust the volume as the weather report came through.

This is a broadcast from the NOAA Weather Radio. Tropical Storm Baxter has intensified, with visible circular banding indicating the formation of a well-defined eyewall. Hurricane Hunter aircraft are scheduled to investigate the system within the next 24 hours. Tropical storm warnings are in effect for the Turks and Caicos Islands and the Bahamas.

Hurricane warnings have been issued for the U.S. Virgin Islands, Puerto Rico, Hispaniola, Cuba, and the Florida peninsula. Baxter is moving faster than average for a storm of this magnitude, and residents in the affected areas should prepare for rapidly deteriorating conditions. Stay tuned for regular updates on the development of this system on VHF Marine Radio channel 22. End transmission.

Gemma gestured for Alberto to hold on, as more urgent concerns demanded her focus.

"Guys, we've got a problem," she said. "A storm is forming. It's still a few days out, but it's heading toward us."

Crab frowned. "Does that mean we're stuck here?"

"It means we're not going anywhere until we know more," Gemma replied. "If a storm's coming, we'll have to wait it out."

Boon threw up his hands. "Great. Just what we needed. I'm about ready to lose my mind on this boat."

"Compañeros, this is not bad news at all! Mr. Baxter might force you to stay a little longer, but it's only because he wants you to see Carnival. It's a sign!" Alberto chimed in.

Gemma sighed, realizing they were all feeling the strain of their confinement and everything that had happened since leaving St. Columba. Cruz might have laid out a plan to rid themselves of Cowboi's burdens, but the crew was fraying at the edges. They needed a break.

"Alberto," she said, forcing a lighter tone. "Can you pick us up before the parade?"

Santiago de Cuba | 235

"My pleasure! My pleasure! Saturday, 9 a.m. My boat will be here!"

Alberto tapped his index finger on the side of his nose. The gesture startled Gemma. This signal could mean many things—cocaine, organized crime, or simply that he understood her request to avoid officials. Either way, it was a reminder that she couldn't trust anyone completely. Vigilance was key, and she needed to stay sharp, especially with shifting alliances lurking in every corner.

"Don't get too excited," Gemma cautioned. "We still need to keep a low profile. Alberto can guide us, and we'll stick together. But yeah, I think some R&R will do us some good."

"Fine by me," Boon said. "I'd do anything to get off this boat."

"Agreed," Crab said. "But storm prep comes first; fun comes second."

Gemma nodded. "Fair enough. I'll dive the anchor and throw out some more. Cruz, inventory our provisions. Boon, if you're dying to go to shore, grab whatever we might need for the storm. Do you want Alberto to take you, or do you want to take the dinghy?"

"I can handle it myself," Boon harrumphed, already retrieving the jerry cans from the locker for fuel.

"Alberto, we'll see you on Saturday," Gemma finished, hoping Alberto would take the hint.

As the crew dispersed to their tasks, Gemma lingered for a moment, staring out across their little bay. The storm was still days away, but its looming presence added to the tension hanging over them.

Alberto, still gripping the rail in his skiff, watched the crew scatter into action. "You're worried about the storm, eh?" he said with a knowing smile. "Baxter's still niño pequeño. But when he grows up, you don't want to be caught in his path."

"No, we don't," Gemma agreed. "We're staying here until it passes."

"Good choice, compañera. And Carnival will make the waiting easier. Trust me, Santiago will welcome you like family. We Cubans know how to weather storms, no matter what kind. And we know how to party."

Gemma gave him a half-smile, appreciating his optimism but wary of trusting it too much. "Thanks, Alberto. We'll see you soon."

He tipped his sun-bleached cap, started his outboard, and motored away, leaving a small wake in the still morning water. The scent of the bay lingered—faint, sulfuric fumes softened by the cool shadows of the mangroves.

The crew worked in silence, the hum of preparation taking on a rhythm of its own—the practiced choreography of survival. Gemma and Crab methodically readied additional lines and anchors, their movements synchronized after days at sea together. They worked the heavy chain and nylon through chafing gear, ensuring the *Mariposa* wouldn't break loose if Baxter's winds picked up.

Meanwhile, Cruz moved with his usual efficiency in the galley, inventorying their supplies with the same tactical alertness that seemed to underpin all his actions. His broad shoulders shifted fluidly as he counted canned goods, water jugs, and medical supplies. Apparently, he could turn on and off his alias like a switch, but Gemma couldn't forget so quickly.

Boon had taken the dinghy, and the putter of the returning boat broke the midday stillness. The metallic aroma of fuel wafted on the wind as he began hauling the cans aboard. Gemma scrutinized Boon. As if reading her thoughts, Cruz spoke up. "We'll be ready when it's time to move."

Gemma wasn't convinced that all the secrets had been told. The first whispers of storm wind danced across her skin—confused gusts that mirrored her scattered thoughts. These early signs reminded her of the uncertainty they still faced, the storm's path as unpredictable as their mission itself. The hurricane was coming, and with it, all the dangers that Cowboi Rivers had waiting for them.

23

CARNIVAL

On Saturday morning, Alberto showed up with enough enthusiasm to electrify the entire island. He had transformed himself from a boat boy into a rumba king in a red satin guarachera with ruffles cascading down the sleeves, a velvet vest, and white slacks. Even his skiff sparkled with a fresh coat of yellow paint, metallic streamers spiraling in the wind behind it as he approached.

"Ahoy! ¡Aquí!"

He held up armloads of colorful bead necklaces.

"I didn't know it was a costume party—let me change!" Gemma exclaimed when she saw how festive he was.

She dashed to her cabin and, from the bottom of a ditty bag, pulled out the slinky red dress with a slit up the thigh that she had bought at the club shop weeks ago. She quickly wrapped her hair in a silk scarf, rouged her lips and cheeks with quick strokes, and slipped on some cute flip-flops. In the mirror, a sexy young woman looked back at her. She had almost forgotten she was female, much less beautiful. She'd been living in shorts and T-shirts since they set sail.

Everyone loaded into either Alberto's skiff or the *Mariposa's* inflatable. In their party outfits, the group was as mismatched as a thrift store jigsaw puzzle—bright, chaotic, and missing some pieces. Cruz sported a tropical shirt and white pants that accentuated his mahogany skin; Nihir looked relaxed in linen pants, an open-collared shirt, and rows of Alberto's beads, while Boon and Crab looked as sailorly as always.

Despite everything hanging over them—the looming hurricane, their unexpected stop in Cuba, and the web of secrets that seemed to ensnare them all—there was an almost manic cheerfulness permeating the air.

Cruz's easy smile betrayed nothing of his CIA connections, a revelation that still stung fresh in Gemma's mind whenever their eyes met. Nihir maintained his serene demeanor, though she caught moments when his thoughts were clearly on the dangerous trap they were about to spring on Cowboi. Boon and Crab exchanged jokes that were a little too loud, their laughter a touch too forced, as if volume could drown out the reality of their situation. It was surreal—this moment of celebration balanced on a knife's edge.

Onshore, Alberto's car waited for them under a flamboyant tree on a wet patch of packed mud. The car itself looked like a missile pop—pale blue on top, white walls on the bottom, with a candy apple red interior. Alberto took the white ragtop down, and when he reached in to turn on the radio, the upbeat rhythm of Son-Cubano music filled the air, transforming the bleak shoreline into a lively, sun-soaked party. Horns, flutes, and rich, sonorous voices sang of secret romances, dances, and midnight swims.

"This is my little Rambler! You like her?" Alberto beamed with pride. Gemma knew it was a national pastime to care for these ancient vehicles, many of them nearing seventy-five years of age—relics of the era before the Cuban revolution, now lovingly preserved.

"I love her!" Gemma replied earnestly.

The car was a tight fit, but the party mood helped with the squeeze. Alberto handed around a handle of Havana Club and chatted happily as they drove through the countryside, his voice animated as he wove together a string of seemingly inconsequential stories about the locals and their daily lives.

They passed pastel cement structures, their once-bright paint faded under the relentless Caribbean sun. Windows without glass gaped like open mouths, revealing dim interiors sparsely furnished and cooled by battered fans. Each small house seemed to rest on a patch of hard-packed dirt or short, brittle grass, the ground scorched to shades of ochre and brown. Stray dogs roamed aimlessly, their ribs showing through patchy fur, their barks half-hearted as they lazily reacted to the passing car.

Every so often, a thatched hut broke the monotony, a reminder of older, simpler ways of life. Unlike the cement structures, these fantasy Hobbit homes featured gardens spilling over with vibrant foliage—cassava, plantains, and small plots of herbs—bringing a splash of green to an otherwise sun-bleached landscape.

Here and there, people strolled in bright, spandex fashions—floral leggings, neon crop tops, and glittery sneakers—sipping cold drinks, fanning themselves with folded newspapers or handmade paper fans. Some individuals chatted or sat silently on upturned buckets. Children chased each other barefoot, their laughter ringing out. Vendors lined the roadside, their makeshift carts piled with mangoes, pineapples, and bunches of bananas.

Alberto kept talking, his voice a steady stream of cheerful commentary. His hands gestured occasionally, leaving the wheel for brief moments as he pointed out a small church on the corner or a food stand he insisted had the best empanadas in town. It was impossible not to feel a twinge of admiration for his cheer against the worn and weary backdrop of the world outside.

"You know, it used to be nicer here—a paradise. I mean, I hardly notice, but I think maybe it's not so nice to see now," Alberto apologized, his voice tinged with nostalgia for a time before his birth.

"Alberto, please—it's lovely. Your car, the drive, the music—thank you," Gemma said, hoping to lift his spirits. "This is the break we needed." Alberto brightened at her reassurances.

"Now we go to Santiago: the jewel of Cuba. El Centro is beautiful," he promised with a proud smile.

Nihir leaned back in his seat, his arm around Gemma. "Thank you for this beautiful tour, Alberto. We can't wait for Carnival!" he said.

With that, Alberto cranked up the music, and the speakers filled the car with the pulsing rhythms of soca. The little Rambler bounced along the potholed road, the music blending with the sea breeze whipping through the open windows.

Alberto laughed. "You'll love it! Music, dancing, masks—everything! My friends, Carnival is magic!" He began to sing, grinning as he cast a playful look over his shoulder. "Juicy like a tomato. Shake that big potato!" It didn't take long for Gemma to recognize the song—it was the theme for this year's Carnival, a bawdy, upbeat anthem that seemed to be played on the radio every hour on the hour.

Gemma groaned, burying her face in her hands. "I swear, that song is going to haunt me forever."

Nihir chuckled. "It's catchy, though. Admit it."

"You don't really like it, do you?" Gemma asked, trying to suppress a smile.

But Alberto wasn't letting it go, his voice louder and more exaggerated as he gestured dramatically with one hand. "Tomato ripe, make it dance all night! Potato bounce, give me what I like!"

The little car skimmed across the landscape.

"You'll thank me when you're singing it at Carnival!" Alberto called.

He revved the motor. "'Tomato ripe, shake it all night!'"

When they arrived in Santiago, Gemma and the boys

Carnival | 243

got out at the edge of the packed crowd filling the public square. Alberto pointed to a café on the far side of El Centro, with a line of people waiting to get into a patio roped off in velvet.

"I'll meet you there, at Café Cubano, in half an hour. Parking's impossible, but I know a secret place. It's a bit of a walk, though," Alberto told them before scooting off in the Rambler.

Piles of discarded plastic cups and takeout containers teetered, spilling from gutters choked with garbage. Bodies pressed together in the chaotic surge, so tightly packed near the main stage that Gemma could barely push through. The air exploded with sound—shouted conversations, booming speakers, steady drumbeats. Paper-covered tables formed narrow corridors between vending booths, the smell of fried food and barbecue mixing with sweat.

At the cordoned-off Café Cubano, languages competed within the foreigners' enclave—English, French, German, Japanese—while Spanish lapped at its edges. Alberto returned from parking the car, and Gemma paid his cover before sending him to the bar. He returned with drinks on a tray and settled at their shaded outdoor table.

Outside the velvet ropes, the sun blazed down, baking the masses, but the fortunate foreigners inside the gated restaurant had ice clinking in rum glasses and ceiling fans spinning overhead. Gemma kicked off her shoes, letting the breeze play across her feet on the warm cobblestones.

Steel drum players struck up a staccato rhythm, sharp

notes ringing in unison. The hypnotic beat seemed to vibrate in Gemma's bones as the players swayed. The tempo quickened—horns blared, whistles screamed, harmonies soared, weaving into an irresistible tapestry. Hands clapped, feet stomped, hips rolled. Boundaries dissolved—performers and audience became one pulsing entity.

Shouts of excitement became calls of delight as showgirls emerged from shadowed alleys—impossibly tall figures with legs that stretched forever. Their skin shimmered with rhinestones, and their costumes were mere scraps of spandex. Towering headdresses crowned each head—bursts of ostrich feathers in blazing reds, electric blues, and dazzling yellows.

They moved with hypnotic precision—high kicks slicing through the air, every motion synced to the driving rhythm. Grace masked pure athleticism as they rolled their shoulders and twisted their torsos in serpentine waves. Gemma caught the intensity in their eyes—focus mixed with unfiltered joy. When the showgirls reached the parade route leaving El Centro, the music swelled. Drums pounded faster, horns soared higher, and the crowd merged to follow the dance troupes in a flowing river of bodies. One dancer spun, her costume refracting lights into scattered rainbows, and beckoned the way.

Gemma felt herself swept into the motion, her worries lifting in Carnival's raw, jubilant energy.

"It's starting! Let's go!" Alberto shouted.

They exited Café Cubano and joined the parade. A stranger linked arms with Gemma, pulling her into the tide. Disoriented but exhilarated, she scanned for her friends—Nihir and Cruz were right beside her, Crab and Alberto danced a few links down in the human chain. But Boon was nowhere to be seen.

Speakers on trucks blared as troupe leaders shouted through megaphones. Marching bands in intricate themes and colors moved in sync toward the hill's gentle rise. At the crest, Gemma saw the whole spectacle stretching below her. A low stone wall offered a reprieve. She pulled Alberto and Nihir into the shady rest with her, scanning the sea of bodies for Boon.

"What's wrong?" Alberto asked, sweaty and out of breath.

"Crab and Cruz are right there. I can see them, but I haven't seen Boon since the café. I wanted us to all stay together."

Gemma pointed toward Cruz. She could make him out, distressed and struggling in the throng of people half a block back. Her eyes darted through the mass of faces until she spotted Crab, but something strange caught her attention—a pinkish haze hovering over Cruz's head. *Was he vaping?* That seemed impossible in the crush of bodies. Before she could process what she thought she saw, Cruz's face disappeared, swallowed by the crowd as it surged around him.

"Alberto! Cruz is in trouble! He fell!"

Alberto charged into the sea of people with the forceful shove of a man called to duty. He cut through the pack. Without hesitation, Gemma and Nihir followed on his heels, pushing through as angry faces shouted and shoved back in frustration. Then Gemma heard a sound like a car backfiring—sharp and sudden. Chips of stone peppered her as a chunk of stucco crumbled from a nearby building.

Shots!

"Someone is shooting at us!" she screamed. "I think Cruz is hit! Get down!"

The threat of being trampled was as great as being hit by the sniper, but Gemma would rather take her chances among the knees and kicking feet of the crowd than be shot in the head.

"Crawl!" she yelled to Alberto ahead of her. "Cruz is just a few yards that way. I can see him on the ground. Crab's next to him."

When they finally pushed through, Gemma saw the contents of Cruz's head spilling down the hill. Revelers trod through the blood and bits of brain without noticing their source. Crab held Cruz's still body in his lap.

"It's Boon," Crab said.

"What do you mean it's Boon? Who shot Cruz? Are you saying Boon is shooting at us?"

The panic and fear in Crab's eyes confirmed what Gemma dreaded—Boon's betrayal was real. Nihir wrapped one arm protectively around her, his other hand resting gently on Cruz's lifeless shoulder. The weight of grief and shock pressed down on them all. Alberto sat motionless on the pavement, his head buried in his hands.

The five of them, one no longer breathing, had become an island amid the parade, a momentary disruption in the relentless flow of bodies and celebration.

Carnival | 247

But the procession didn't stop; it surged around them, unseeing in the chaos, the music and laughter clashing horribly with the reality of death in their midst.

Suddenly, another bullet whined through the air, ricocheting off the pavement with a sharp crack. Danger was still close, lurking above the frenzy.

"We have to move!" Gemma yelled. "Cruz is dead. Leave him. Crab, you go with Alberto. Get to the car. Nihir is with me. Now go!"

Gemma hated the thought of Cruz's body being carelessly shoved into the gutter, only to be claimed by the police after the parade had run its course. But if she wanted to keep the rest of her friends alive, she couldn't afford the luxury of reverence. They had to move—now. Alberto protested, but Gemma cut him short, shaking her head and pointing in two different directions. Without another word, Crab and Alberto disappeared back the way they had come. If they kept low and blended with the flow of people, they'd be nearly invisible to the gunman—to Boon.

Gemma leaned in, telling Nihir, "Follow me and keep out of sight."

She could feel Nihir's tension, but he nodded in understanding. They turned down an empty, barricaded alley that allowed them to cut back toward the square through backstreets. If Boon followed them, there wasn't much cover, but Gemma hoped that the split would confuse him.

She glanced over at Nihir. "We just need to keep moving." Nihir nodded, his eyes scanning for danger.

Gemma's heart pounded in her chest, each step fraught with the risk of discovery. From behind them came the cry, "Stop!" It was Boon.

"Run!" she yelled to Nihir.

They had a good lead, but Boon had a long-range rifle. "Faster," she added.

She could see El Centro, and if they could make it, the crowded Carnival Village would provide the cover they needed. It was their best chance. Without a second thought, Gemma sprinted at full speed.

The ping of bullets echoed behind her, time seeming to stretch out in a surreal haze. But in reality, it only took minutes to cover the distance. With one final push, Gemma dove into the sea of people. She gasped for breath as if she had just surfaced from a free dive. Only then did she dare to glance over her shoulder. Nihir was right next to her, his chest heaving, but he was safe.

24

BOON'S BETRAYAL

Gemma and Nihir watched from the shadows for Alberto's Rambler. When the pale blue hood appeared from behind Café Cubano's wall, Gemma spotted Crab slouched in the passenger seat. She and Nihir ducked low and moved swiftly.

Boon would expect this meeting spot—their only shared geographic reference. But if he tried to snipe them from a rooftop in Santiago's main square, he risked swift police action. Gemma doubted he was on a rooftop at all; more likely, he was moving to intercept them on the exit road.

"Go!" Gemma shouted from the back seat of the idling Rambler. She slammed her fist against the driver's seat. "Alberto, if you know any back roads to the marina, take them—now! Let's get the hell out of here!"

They had two options: return to the boat or disappear. Abandoning the *Mariposa* and the drugs would have been safer, but the thought of escaping with less than a hundred dollars made her sick. Where would they go? They certainly couldn't return to St. Columba like nothing happened.

"We're going back to the *Mariposa*," Gemma said.

Alberto drove in tense silence, dropping his mask of tourist-pleasing hospitality. He slumped over the wheel in his carnival costume like a sad clown. The landscape blurred past the speeding convertible. No cars followed.

"What if Boon's waiting at the boat?" Nihir asked.

Gemma's tone was resolute but edged with weariness. "All I have now is instinct, and it's telling me we need to get out—fast. Remember, we entered Cuba illegally, all except Crab. We can't waltz into an airport and buy tickets. And I'm not abandoning the *Mariposa* after everything we've been through."

She rubbed the back of her neck. "Look, Crab, you have legitimate papers. Alberto can take you to the airport. You can fly out without a problem."

Nihir wrapped an arm around her shoulders, showing unwavering solidarity. She was grateful for that.

Crab's tone was reluctant but honest. "You and Nihir can't sail that boat in bad weather without me. Baxter's a day away, at best. You'd be trying to outrun a hurricane. No offense, but Nihir has less than two weeks of sailing experience."

Gemma blew out a long breath, her mind racing—calculations, risks, worst-case scenarios. "Listen, I think Boon is still alone. The earliest he could have gotten a call out was when he went for fuel yesterday. That's probably when he called Cowboi and got orders to kill us. It takes at least a day or two to arrange a flight into Cuba, even for Cowboi Rivers—money and fame can only speed things up so much."

She paused. "Crab, you better tell us what you know."

Crab hesitated. When he finally spoke, his voice had dropped in volume. "I don't know much, but I do know Boon killed Vaughn."

Gemma's stomach tightened. "What? Boon killed Vaughn? That doesn't—" Her mind raced. "Are you kidding me?" She hadn't connected Vaughn's death to Boon until now, despite the visions in her dreams. She had felt the death blow but never saw the face of the killer.

Crab rubbed his mouth, exhaling hard. "Vaughn had your job, Gemma. Same setup—running drugs and girls. He wanted out. Thought he could outsmart Cowboi."

Gemma shook her head. "Vaughn was reckless, but he wasn't stupid."

"That's what he thought." Crab's voice tightened. "Thought he was clever. Planned to write a tell-all book. Had a publisher lined up, a fat advance. He didn't just want out—he wanted to blow the lid off Cowboi's whole operation."

Gemma felt cold, like she'd been dropped into shark-filled water. *A book*, she thought. The papers she'd been seeing in her dreams.

Crab let out a humorless laugh. "Vaughn even told Cowboi about it, like it was some funny joke. Said it'd be 'free publicity.' But he didn't get it. This business is a spiderweb of powerful people—politicians, celebrities, folks who'd burn the world to keep their secrets. What I didn't know until yesterday is that Cruz must have been feeding Vaughn classified CIA intel. It's how they operate sometimes—can't take someone down through official channels, so they leak enough to the public to force an inquiry. Vaughn must have thought a book was a win-win. Cruz gets his info out, and Vaughn gets a paycheck and some fame."

Gemma pressed her hand to her chest. "So, what did Cowboi do?"

"Sent Boon to talk to him." Crab exhaled through his nose, jaw tight. "Boon gave Vaughn plenty of warnings. Offered him money. Told him to drop the project and return the advance. But Vaughn wouldn't listen."

Her voice was hoarse. "And then?"

Crab hesitated, his gaze flicking away like he was looking for an escape route. "Boon killed him."

Silence stretched between them.

Gemma's breath was shallow. "How could Boon kill his friend like that?"

Crab's voice dropped. "He clubbed Vaughn over the head outside Paradise Burger. He did what Cowboi told him to do."

Every interaction Gemma had with Boon suddenly twisted in her memory, taking on a darker shape. "And now he's coming for us?"

Crab nodded grimly. "Cowboi ordered Boon to recruit you, Gemma. He wanted you in the organization to blackmail you."

Gemma clenched her teeth. "Why? What does he want from me?"

Crab let out a slow breath. "You're set to inherit the August Family Trust. Effectively, you'll control most of the beachfront at Sargasso Cove. Cowboi wanted to force you into a partnership. He framed it as an incredible opportunity—luxury marina, millions in development deals." He let out a bitter laugh. "Boon Dock would've been rebuilt into a mega-yacht emporium, with me and Boon as owners."

Gemma gripped the edge of the seat. "And now Boon's trying to kill me?"

Crab glanced away, jaw flexing.

"Why?"

"When you set up the deal in Florida, Cowboi saw it as betrayal. Worse than that—he'd lost control of the situation. Boon must've told him you set up a CIA sting. Once Cowboi knew that, you became a threat. And Boon—" Crab swallowed. "Boon's loyal to Cowboi. If Cowboi says you're a loose end, Boon's going to tie it up."

Gemma swallowed hard. "What about you, Crab? Would Boon kill you, too?"

Crab was quiet for a long time. Finally, he said, "I don't know what Boon's orders are. But we have to assume we're all in danger."

"Alberto," Gemma said. "I didn't want you involved, but I need you to do one more thing."

"I just want to go home, señora. All this murder—I don't want anything to do with it."

"Listen, I promise I'll keep you safe. Just get us back to

Boon's Betrayal | 255

the dock and act as a lookout. If you spot Boon, call the police. Tell them an armed American who entered the country illegally is on shore and shot someone at Carnival. They probably know about Cruz's death by now—maybe even found his badge. An APB has likely gone out. Do this, and I'll give you a kilo of cocaine. No strings. You'll be off the hook. We'll disappear, and you'll walk away with enough money to take care of your family."

"Señora, I'll make your call and keep watch, but I don't want your drugs. In Cuba, the maximum penalty for drug smuggling is death."

With mutual understanding, they left Alberto on shore to watch for Boon. Their Cuban friend waved a nervous goodbye. Back on the *Mariposa*, Gemma set Nihir and Crab to prepare for departure while she checked the weather forecast.

25

THE CHASE

They needed to sail now. The situation had reached its breaking point. Even if they confronted Boon while still at anchor, discovery by the Cuban authorities had already been set in motion. If Alberto made that call too soon, summoning officials before the *Mariposa* was safely away, the authorities would almost certainly investigate the solitary boat in an off-limits bay. But the alternative carried its own deadly risk. If Alberto waited too long to make that call, Boon might already be on the water, cutting through the waves in deadly pursuit.

"Nihir, you know what would be helpful? Take these binoculars and keep a close eye on what's happening near the public dock," Gemma said, her tone clipped with urgency.

"The dinghy is back on the davits, and we're ready to

cast off," Crab moved efficiently around the deck, doing the work of three men.

"Nihir, any sign of Boon?" Gemma asked more than once.

"No movement on shore. I can't even see Alberto," Nihir reported, scanning the horizon.

Crab started the windlass and pulled up the anchor. The machinery rattled and clanked while sticky mud and decomposed seaweed oozed from the spooling chain onto the deck. Crab dipped a bucket into the sea and washed down the hook. Black muck swirled along the toerails in small torrents, and tiny crabs scurried back to their watery homes through the chocks.

With no sign of Boon, Gemma started the engine and motored past the fortress, heading toward the channel that led to the Atlantic. Palms tossed their heads in the growing gusts on the craggy shore. She planned to round the point of Punta de Maisi and chart a straight course to Florida. She didn't like that a hurricane was bearing down on them, but at least it would give them some chaotic cover. The swell grew tall, but her hands were steady on the wheel.

Nihir scanned the harbor behind them. "Nothing yet," he said, his voice low but tense. "If Boon's coming, he's not making it easy to spot him."

Gemma's eyes fixed on the channel markers. "The less time he has to catch up, the better. Keep watching. He might try to cut us off."

The VHF crackled, and Gemma's stomach tightened as a static-filled voice broke through.

"Este es el control de radio de la Guarda Frontera. Por favor, identifíquese."

The words were calm and official, but Gemma felt the weight of the moment press down on her. Her mind raced. She shouted instructions for Crab to respond—he nodded, ran to the VHF, and pressed the transmit button, his voice steady.

"This is the *Mariposa*," he said. "We're en route to Guantánamo Bay for storm refuge. Over."

The reply didn't come immediately. The silence that followed pressed down like a weight. Then the radio crackled again.

"Espera un momento, por favor."

Gemma frowned. Not good. The border guards weren't buying it, and her ears caught a faint irregularity in the engine's hum. Barely noticeable, but there. The engine coughed again. She adjusted the throttle.

When the voice returned, it was in clear English this time.

"*Mariposa*, this is the Cuban Port Authority. Be advised: a hurricane warning has been issued for this region. The storm is expected to intensify to Category Three within twelve hours. For your safety, we strongly advise you to return to your anchorage. All outbound vessels are being advised to shelter in place. Over."

Crab glanced at Gemma. She gave a sharp nod and pointed to the ocean beyond the markers.

"*Mariposa* copies the advisory. However, our vessel is heading to a designated storm refuge in Guantánamo Bay, as issued by the U.S. Coast Guard. Special clearance. Over."

The pause this time felt longer.

"Would the Coast Guard even do that?" Gemma asked, impressed with Crab's quick thinking.

"No idea. I'm winging it," Crab said. "They probably don't know either."

Finally, the voice returned, more insistent now.

"*Mariposa*, the storm's projected path makes your intended course extremely dangerous. Do you understand the risks? Over."

Crab glanced at Gemma again.

"Confirmed. *Mariposa* assumes all risk. Requesting clearance to proceed. Over."

Another pause, then the voice returned.

"*Mariposa*, clearance granted. Proceed at your own risk. We will not respond to distress calls until Baxter has passed. Over."

"Copy that. *Mariposa* proceeding. Out."

Gemma gripped the wheel tighter. "Something's off with the engine." She pushed the throttle forward; the engine hiccupped, and the *Mariposa* surged ahead. Swells grew larger, lifting and dropping the boat in a steady rhythm. She tightened her jaw and narrowed her focus.

"We can't stop—not now." Gemma's knuckles were white on the wheel. "Something's wrong with the motor, but we need every bit of speed we can get. Four hours minimum to round the point, then another full day to reach Florida." She glanced at the darkening horizon. "And that's if we're lucky."

Crab scanned the water behind them. "Maybe we can take refuge on the north side near Baracoa. But the swell will be huge. Of course, it all depends on if Boon's chasing us and in what kind of boat," he said.

"Nihir, can you shoot a gun?" Gemma asked, cutting through the wind's rising howl.

"I have training, yes," Nihir responded.

Once again, Gemma admired the depth of Nihir's experience beyond the yoga studio.

Nihir lowered the binoculars suddenly. "Boon's on the water. I see him!"

"Shit! Really? What's he in?" Gemma asked, her pulse quickening.

"He's in Alberto's skiff. Bright yellow. I can see the streamers in the back. I hope Alberto's not hurt," Nihir said, concerned.

Gemma's heart sank. "Man, we're doing nearly ten knots, but that dinghy can do twenty. He'll catch up quickly."

She had to push aside her worry for Alberto and focus on her crew's survival. "Nihir, grab the rifle from the locker. Bring up the AK and the pistols, too."

Nihir scrambled below and quickly retrieved the guns. He set them on the cockpit bench and reclaimed the binoculars.

"Crab, give us a fast trim. We can't outrun Boon, but we can keep some distance until we're armed," Gemma barked.

"Boon's gaining, but not in range yet," Nihir shouted.

"Okay, when he's in range, aim for his engine. If you

have to hit him, go for his arm or leg, but focus on disabling the boat. I don't want to kill Boon, no matter what he's done," Gemma said, hoping Nihir's marksmanship was accurate.

Shots rang out. Boon was firing recklessly at the *Mariposa* while piloting his dinghy at top speed. The bullets flew erratically.

"He hit our jib," Crab cried.

The hole in the sail was tiny but quickly expanded with each gust of wind. Under normal conditions, this wouldn't be catastrophic, but with the fury of Baxter gathering, every flap of the sail made the damage worse. Smoke began billowing from the aft hatch.

"Shit! Can you tape the hole in the sail? What the fuck is going on with the engine?" Gemma shouted over the wind.

Crab yelled back, "Boon's getting closer!"

Gemma had to think fast. Dropping the sails and facing off with Boon might be an option, but the chaos of the maneuver in these conditions could spell disaster. Plus, she knew they were under surveillance by the guard on the point, although she doubted they could see what was transpiring in any detail or if they would send anyone if they did.

"Shoot him, Nihir!" Gemma yelled.

The crack of gunfire shattered the stillness of the waves as Nihir raised his weapon, his hands unsteady in the chop. He aimed at Boon, but the wild swell made precision impossible. The sound of the rifle echoed like thunder, a deafening reminder of how far they'd been pushed. Boon's skiff loomed closer, the man himself, a grim silhouette against the swirling opal storm clouds.

Boon returned fire; the sharp buzz sliced through the air. Gemma froze as the sickening slick of red ran along the rails. Crab stumbled, his body folding unnaturally before collapsing in a heap on the deck. Time seemed to slow, the world narrowing to the sound of heartbeats and the spreading pool of crimson under Crab's crumpled form.

"Crab!" she screamed.

The chaos around her made every movement feel impossibly slow. The yellow skiff scraped up along *Mariposa's* side, bringing Boon level with the deck. His face appeared twisted with shock and fury. For a moment, their eyes met, and the raw expression transformed from pain to hate. He had just killed his best friend.

Before Gemma could react, another wave, massive and unrelenting, reared up and crashed over the boats, throwing everyone off balance. *Mariposa* listed violently to starboard, the deck tilting sharply beneath her feet.

Nihir's gaze locked on Boon. When Boon aimed his weapon toward Gemma, Nihir squeezed the trigger. The report of the blast was overwhelming even amid the tempest's howl.

Boon's head snapped back, a fountain of red spraying into the air. His body went limp, slumping sideways and rolling out of the skiff. The sea claimed him instantly, swallowing him into its tempestuous depths.

For a moment, all that remained was the hollow ringing in Gemma's ears. She staggered to the rail, her legs

The Chase | 263

weak beneath her, and stared out at the heaving expanse of water where Boon had vanished. It was over, but the victory felt shallow.

Gemma rushed to Crab's side, her heart pounding, but he was already gone. Death hit her like a gut punch. They had survived, but at what cost? The storm still raged, and they were far from safe. Gemma looked at Nihir, who stood silent, gun in hand, his face like a mask.

26

HURRICANE BAXTER

Low hills stacked behind Guantánamo Bay. Onshore, coils of razor wire glinted steely bright, curling atop crumbling walls like tumbleweeds caught in the wind. The desolate prison loomed in the distance. Gemma's options were dwindling rapidly, each passing moment tightening the noose of her predicament. Who knew what chaos Boon had left behind him? They couldn't go back to Santiago Bay. There were murders behind them. The thought twisted in her gut like a knife.

Even if they decided to dump the drugs into the churning sea and sought refuge in Guantánamo, it was not a welcoming place. They could run for Baracoa, but Gemma's immediate concern was navigating through the growing storm with a smoking engine that sounded more asthmatic with each passing minute.

"Nihir, do you think you could adjust our course and bring in the jib? I'm going to see what I can do down below," she called out, her voice strained against the rising wind.

Trim would usually be Crab's job, and she momentarily forgot that Nihir was inexperienced in handling a boat. He'd learned a lot on their short passage, but his navigation and sail duties had been light, and his watches had been with a buddy or on autopilot.

"Let me look at the engine instead. I'm a decent mechanic," Nihir offered, his voice steady despite the chaos swirling around them.

In fair conditions and with plenty of time, Gemma could have taught Nihir to sail, but in a hurricane, the best she could hope for was moral support and, perhaps now, someone who was good with engines. Her eyes burned with exhaustion, and her shoulders sagged under the weight of despair. Florida was at least twenty hours away—but what was the alternative?

"Okay, go down below and see what you can do," Gemma said. The wind snatched at her words, but Nihir understood.

Gust, lull, gust, lull—the characteristic pattern of an approaching hurricane took shape. Dark clouds gathered on the windward side, churning with a malevolent energy, as if the storm itself were alive and hungry. She needed to decide soon—Baracoa or Florida. The thought of Miami or the Keys felt like a distant dream.

Minutes later, Nihir returned, his face ashen. "It's bad, Gemma."

She felt her stomach drop, a cold dread pooling in her gut. "How bad?"

He held up a paper sack, grains of white sugar spilling from a tear in the side, a stark contrast against the darkening sky. "Boon must've got to it before Carnival."

Boon's ruthlessness surprised and appalled Gemma, leaving her reeling. If the sugar was causing the motor to choke, it was too late. Sugar turned into thick, grinding sludge, clogging the fuel lines like a clot in an artery and damaging everything it touched. She'd run a good deal of the tainted fuel, and even if they could salvage the engine, there was nothing they could do about the sabotage while they were at sea. She turned off the key, and the hum of machinery cut out with a knock and a clunk.

"So that's it," she said, her voice flat. "We need to take care of Crab's body before the storm hits full force. Then we have to sail," Gemma said. The moment felt too big, too impossible.

The bloody body, stiffening in the cold, pressed into the rails with each violent lurch. Gemma took a deep breath, trying to steady her fraying nerves. Nihir took her hand in his, pulling her down to her knees. His eyes spoke of their shared sorrow, a bond forged in loss. Three men were dead. Four, including Vaughn. And maybe Alberto, too. The weight of grief pressed down, but they had little time for reverence.

"What should we say?" Gemma asked, feeling the inadequacy of words in the face of this latest death. The enormity of their situation loomed like an oppressive shroud.

"What was Crab's real name?" Nihir asked, his voice gentle yet firm.

Hurricane Baxter | 267

"Connor. Connor Rampling."

Gemma covered Crab with a sail bag, a makeshift shroud for a fallen comrade. Nihir closed his eyes and chanted in a deep, resonant harmony that seemed to fill the air with a solemn vibration—more a multitude and less a single person. It resonated with the grief that enveloped them.

"Aware that birth and death give way to each other, these states pass like waves on the sea. Connor has returned to the source. Understanding the impermanence of all things, Connor will take unity without constraint."

Nihir paused, then spoke in his normal voice, steady and full. "That one was for Connor. Here's a little one for us." He reentered his trance-like chant, his voice steady against the tempest.

"All my ancient, twisted karma—born of beginningless greed, hate, and delusion, through body, speech, and mind—I now fully avow."

Gemma unclipped the lifeline, her hands shaking. They rolled Crab's body and together slid him over the side of the boat. The sea took him, as it had taken millions before. Gemma stood at the railing for a moment longer, her throat tight, watching as Crab disappeared beneath the surface, her heart heavy with sorrow. She couldn't afford the time to grieve, not in the fury of the storm.

Gemma returned to the wheel, not knowing what else to do, her arms trembling from fatigue as the boat bucked and pitched. Every wave was heavier than the last, as if the sea itself conspired to drag her down. She almost wanted it to; it would be a relief.

"We don't have enough hands! Maybe we should get below and batten all the hatches. Ride it out," she shouted over the roar, her voice barely rising above the wind. Their options narrowed even further. Panic became paralysis. Gemma knew she should act but had lost the will to do so, her mind frozen with the gravity of their situation.

"Nihir, why did Boon do this?" Gemma asked in despair as she squinted into the lashing spray, fighting to hold on to her sanity.

The storm howled around them, waves crashing against the *Mariposa* as it fought to stay upright. Rain pelted the deck in relentless sheets, but Nihir's voice rang clear in her ears.

"Boon desired what Cowboi possessed," Nihir said, his gaze unwavering as he gripped the railing, his knuckles white. "But that path is a trap, Gemma. It always is."

Gemma tightened her grip on the wheel, her jaw clenching against the stinging spray of saltwater and rain that lashed at her. "I never wanted to end up in this mess, Nihir. But here we are." The anger she felt at herself mingled with something deeper, something harder to name. "Where does that leave me, Nihir? Where does it leave us?"

He held her gaze, his expression unyielding. "That's up to you, Gemma."

The wheel jerked in her hands as the boat pitched violently. She marveled at her capacity to feel regret when they were in mortal danger. What did being caught in Cowboi's web matter if they were both going to die? Was she taking a final moral inventory of her life, weighing her choices against the backdrop of impending doom?

But Nihir's words lingered. He had imparted this wisdom before, in many forms and at many times, but only now did the truth penetrate when it was too late to change course.

The storm closed in tighter, shrieking like a furious thing, the swells growing monstrous. *Mariposa* lurched violently, and the horizon disappeared behind a wall of water. The hurricane had them in its grip now, a merciless banshee.

Nihir looked up, his eyes finally wide with fear, a reflection of the chaos surrounding them. A massive wave crashed over the deck, sending him sprawling. The spar was coming down. Gemma saw a decisiveness flash across Nihir's face as he stood, determination etched into his features.

"Gemma! Help me!" he shouted as he released the lines on the davits and dropped the Zodiac dinghy into the churning sea on a trailing line. The red shape bucked violently behind the foundering *Mariposa*. He worked furiously against the storm, then disappeared down the hatch, leaving Gemma in a whirlwind of confusion and dread. Her chest seized with panic as she moved after him, fighting to keep her balance.

He hoisted up the oversized fiberglass case that contained the life raft first, then the black duffels began to emerge and slide across the tossing deck. They rammed into the gunwale, only to be kept onboard by the flimsy lifelines. Nihir climbed out after the last bale of cocaine and dragged them aft, tossing them overboard into the dinghy—a desperate act, but one filled with optimism.

"Nihir!" she yelled again, her voice barely audible over the storm, "Watch out!"

The mast crashed to the deck like a falling redwood, a catastrophic sound that reverberated through her bones. Rigging and steel divided the boat in half, separating Gemma from Nihir. Gear and debris tumbled over the water's surface. Gemma's senses overloaded, blinding her, but she saw the dinghy break free, and Nihir dive in after it, a figure swallowed by the tempest.

Had he been pulled under? Had he managed to get into the dinghy or—

Hurricane winds snatched the red, round shape like a cat's paw and quickly bore it out of sight. Nihir was gone, and it was all her fault, a crushing realization that settled like lead in her heart.

The *Mariposa* groaned beneath her feet, a death rattle that vibrated through the hull. Seawater poured through the open hatches in violent torrents, gushing up through the splintered hole in the deck where the mast had been—the cabin below filled with alarming speed, causing the vessel to list sharply to port. Gemma scrambled for purchase, her fingers raw and bleeding as she clawed at anything solid. The boat shuddered, then dropped suddenly as if the ocean had opened its mouth beneath her.

"No, no, no!" she screamed as the deck tilted nearly vertical. Her body slid helplessly toward the churning water, her legs already submerged in the freezing foam.

With one desperate lunge, she grabbed the life raft case, clutching it to her body as the *Mariposa* made its final descent. The suction of the sinking vessel pulled at her legs, threatening to drag her down into the depths. She kicked frantically, fighting the powerful undertow until her lungs burned and spots danced before her eyes.

Panic clawed at her chest as she pulled the deployment rip cord on the life raft. The two halves of the case split like a walnut, and the orange shape ballooned out with a sudden whoosh of compressed air. The howling wind threatened to tear the tiny craft out of her hands and into the sky, but Gemma held it down. Rain pelted her face as she clung to the slippery surface, her muscles trembling with the effort to maintain her grip on this fragile lifeline amid the storm's relentless assault.

Mariposa disappeared under a thirty-foot wave. Thousands of gallons swirled into the cabin, and in seconds, only a rail remained visible; that too blinked out of sight.

Struggling to crawl inside the expanding tent of the round rubber raft, she flattened herself on the bottom, her body trembling with trauma. She turned her gaze to the swirling vortex of clouds through the square openings in the canopy. Gemma found herself in a churning sea, but she was still here—clinging to life amid the wreckage of her life, her boat, and her plan.

PART III

27

ISLAND

The orange fabric of the life raft snapped and billowed in Hurricane Baxter's confused winds, each gust hammering against the rubberized walls like fists. The inflatable vessel plunged into valleys between mountainous swells that blocked out the world entirely. Through the plastic viewport—no larger than a dinner plate—Gemma glimpsed fragmented views. Shafts of ghostly light pierced the churning depths, illuminating silver flashes that darted and wheeled in their ancient choreography. Down there, in that alien realm of perpetual twilight, the ocean's inhabitants continued their daily rituals, blissfully indifferent to the human drama above. Schools of tuna moved like liquid mercury through the blue-black water, while deeper still, shapes too large and indistinct drifted past in shadows.

The storm had become both captor and salvation. Without Baxter, the current would have swept her toward

Haiti's treacherous reefs, or worse—dragged her south into the vast graveyard of the open Caribbean, where the nearest land lay hundreds of miles away. There, she would have become just another soul claimed by the sea. Instead, the departing hurricane pushed her from behind with long trailing fingers.

The life raft's survival kit sat wedged in the corner like a shrine: four-gallon jugs of fresh water, sealed packets of MREs, a first-aid kit, and a solar still that had proven useless in the storm's gloom. Gemma drank first from the makeshift catchment she'd rigged from the raft's rain cover, savoring every brackish drop Hurricane Baxter flung at her before sparingly drinking from the emergency rations.

She perfected the precarious ballet of relieving herself without contaminating her sanctuary by timing the swells and hanging partially through the zippered opening while praying no rogue wave would sweep her into the depths. The memory of Cuba's waters—of the bull shark's dead black eyes and sandpaper skin scraping against her leg—made swimming unthinkable.

Her body bore the accumulated toll. Every bruise from her escape, every abrasion from the raft's interior, felt raw. Her lips cracked with each grimace. Salt had crystallized in the corners of her eyes and the creases of her joints, creating a constant, burning reminder.

But she was alive. Against all odds, against the sea's relentless attempts to claim her, she was still breathing. She listened to the symphony: the wind's howl, the waves' percussion, and beneath it all, the steady rhythm of her pulse—a metronome counting down to either salvation or the sea's final victory.

Clouds thinned into a misty veil, and a green glow appeared along the eastern horizon—faint, almost imperceptible against the muted gray expanse. Was it a hallucination brought on by exhaustion? The humpbacked shape gradually took form as she drifted closer, its silhouette sharpening against the backdrop. Gemma squinted with cautious hope, afraid to believe she was heading directly toward land.

But it was not her imagination. The island's contours became more defined with each passing minute. Her raft surged forward as the current began to accelerate, as though the island itself were reaching out to claim her. Waves took the shape of the rising sea floor, their rhythm quickening in the shallows—a primal sound that both terrified and exhilarated.

But the danger wasn't over. The current pulled ferociously through an unseen reef looming just beneath the surface. Gemma unclipped the paddle from her raft. The threat of being dashed against the rocks so close to salvation filled her with fresh determination. The raft dipped and swayed, carried by chaotic energy. Getting to the island would demand every ounce of strength she had left.

As her target closed in, she studied the terrain. The reef had a classic crescent shape with a large break, perhaps three miles long, enclosing a shallow bay. The encircling hills looked cut away like slices from a cake, revealing pale cliffs and steep coves. A cluster of trees rose from the clifftops, their wind-blown canopies and twisted trunks suggesting years of battling the elements.

She pulled deep from her reserve to paddle toward safety. The island's current pulled harder, almost dragging her around to the eastern backside, but she resisted, gritting her teeth as she fought. Finally, she slipped into calm waters. The current and wind eased, and she could simply float.

Churning depths gave way to gray, then crystal blue over an undulating pattern of tarnished silver sand. Light refracted through the surface. Gemma paddled to where she could jump in and stand. Far from the actual beach, she marveled at the shallowness—less than five feet deep for hundreds of yards. Reef fish of all varieties darted around her ankles, and the distant trees were alive with the chatter of seabirds—like her, refugees from the storm.

She floated her raft behind her, guiding it to shore, and dragged it up the beach's incline. There, she collapsed onto wet sand, sighing as her muscles slowly loosened. Random, half-formed thoughts flitted through her mind.

Where is Nihir? Is he safe?

The need for shelter finally roused her from her stupor as the sun set. Her clothes were soaked, and she was getting cold. She scanned the treeline—a typical Caribbean forest: coconut palms and their stouter sisters, palmettos, lined the break between sand and jungle. Gumbo limbo, turpentine trees, and gris-gris covered the hillside.

A tall, spreading silk cotton tree was a much-needed friend. She dragged her raft to the base of the smooth-skinned tree. Its buttressed roots rippled like the skirt of a dancer, forming a protective shape. She brushed out the leaf litter between the roots until all that remained was a dirt floor and wedged the inflated boat between the root walls. It enclosed her in a tiny, sheltered room, just big enough for her to curl up like a small animal in its den. Rain pelted the tented canopy roof, and the wind whistled, but she was safe and dry. She fell into sleep, her consciousness slipping beneath layers of exhaustion until she crossed into the realm where borders dissolve.

In her dream, she stood on a beach that wasn't quite the one where her raft had landed. The sand beneath her feet glowed with an unnatural luminescence, each grain part of a flowing tapestry. The ocean before her rolled with indigo waves crested with silver, rhythmically advancing and retreating in impossible patterns.

"You made it."

Vaughn stood beside her, his form translucent yet more substantial than when she'd glimpsed him before. His blonde curls caught moonlight that existed nowhere in the physical world, and his eyes—clear now, not clouded by alcohol or regret—regarded her with something approaching pride.

"I didn't expect to," Gemma replied, surprised by how normal it felt to converse with a ghost. "Where's Nihir? Did he—"

"He's alive." Vaughn's words rippled through the dreamscape.

The dream sky darkened, clouds closing in with

supernatural speed. Vaughn's form began to fade, becoming more ghostly.

"What about Mari?" Gemma asked urgently. "Does she know where I am?"

"She feels you." Vaughn's shape was little more than a shimmer now. "There's more at stake than you understand. The land, Sargasso Cove, your heritage—"

"What about it?"

But Vaughn had dissolved completely.

The dream collapsed around her, and Gemma jolted awake, the taste of salt on her lips and Vaughn's message burning in her mind. She pushed open the roll tarp door and peered out. The rising sun lit the clouds. Pain racked her body as she climbed out to the loamy circle beneath the tree. Dirt streaked her limbs, bruises covered her body, and pain throbbed everywhere. Desperate to wash, she stripped off her muddy clothes and dove into the bay.

Vaughn's words gave her a flicker of hope about Nihir, but nothing more substantial. She had no way to reach Vaughn at will and no spiritual telephone to dial up the dead. The spectral presence seemed to manifest only in dreams, trance, or meditation, offering cryptic fragments rather than clear guidance.

Gemma sighed, floating on her back in a cradle of water. She was weightless, suspended. Finding Nihir would have to wait. She couldn't help anyone in her current state—dehydrated, injured, disoriented. First, she needed to tend to her survival and gather her strength. Only then could she hope to locate Nihir or make sense of whatever larger conspiracy Vaughn had hinted at.

From far out in the bay, she could survey the whole beach. More wreckage had washed ashore—broken bits and detritus from *Mariposa* dotted the sand. She recognized a blue bucket and something long and thin—a mystery. Curious, she swam to the beach. The object turned out to be a floating boathook. She walked the length of the bay, collecting anything useful and carrying it back to her camp at the silk cotton. Appraising her haul, she realized how famished she was. Panic rose within her again.

People starve on uninhabited islands, right?

But then she noticed the genips, hanging in clusters from dry wooden branches. She split one open with her fingers, peeling back its thin, leathery skin and slipping the tart-sweet fruit into her mouth. Its slippery flesh clung to a large seed, which she rolled with her tongue before spitting it away. She cracked another between her teeth, sucking out the juicy pulp and savoring the cool burst of flavor.

The bay teemed with fish, and coconut palms bore fallen nuts; hog plum and sea grape were all within sight. Rainwater trickled down gullies and through filtering rocks, and she had jugs to collect it. The desalination pump from the life raft kit would pull her through in a pinch. She would not starve or thirst, far from it.

Gathering her resolve, she ventured into the fringe of the jungle that bordered the beach, picking her way carefully, remembering Yaya Mari's lessons. Palm trunks curved gracefully. The familiar shapes of green, round coconuts loomed overhead. Fallen nuts littered the ground, heavy with water. She cracked one open on a rock, savoring the sweet liquid that spilled out.

The boathook proved indispensable. It became not just a tool for survival but an extension of her own body. She used it to harvest high-hanging fruit with a flick of the wrist that dislodged even the most stubborn prizes. With a sharpened stick inserted into its hollow end and a rope tied to the other, it transformed into a makeshift spear for fishing. She stood knee-deep on the reef's edge, balancing herself against the pull of the tide as she scanned for movement beneath the surface.

Her body stilled, every muscle attuned to the environment. Then she spotted a meal—a flicker darting among the coral—a fish, not too large but big enough, gliding just out of reach. She crouched low, gripping the boathook tightly, the improvised spear poised for action. With a swift motion, she thrust the spear downward, the tip slicing through the water with surprising precision. Resistance against the boathook told her she'd made contact. She pulled it back. The fish thrashed, its slick, shimmering body catching the sunlight. A surge of triumph coursed through her as she secured her catch, carefully prying it free and dropping it into the bucket she'd wedged into a crevice on the reef.

She thought of Yaya Mari with gratitude. The bushcraft her grandmother had taught her showed her what was safe to eat. Back on St. Columba, she had believed herself ignorant of foraging, but this proved unfounded. *I could live here*, she thought, feeling a mix of relief and unease.

The fish slapped against the side of the bucket, its struggles growing weaker with every passing moment. The tide pulled at her legs. Back at her silk cotton shelter, she gathered a small mound of grass and arranged branches around the tinder in a teepee. The waterproof matchbook from the life raft kit felt almost sacred in her hands. She struck a match against the box, the sulfur scent sharp in the cooling air. A catlike gust of wind pawed at the fluffs of grass and coconut husks, lifted the kindling ball, and batted it away. Frustrated over wasting a match, Gemma built a ring of beach stones to block the wind. She tried again. This time, she fed sticks into the flame until the fire took hold of the logs.

While the flames grew steady, she turned to her catch. She ran the blade along its belly and scooped out the innards. The scent of raw flesh mingled with the briny breeze, making her stomach clench in anticipation. She fashioned a spit using two forked branches and a sturdy green stick to hold the fish over the fire. As it roasted, its skin crisped and split, releasing the rich, smoky aroma of cooked meat. Fat dripped into the flames, sending up tiny sizzles of steam. She turned it carefully, watching as the edges blackened just enough to flake apart under her touch.

Sitting cross-legged by the fire, she peeled off a steaming piece of fish and popped it in her mouth. The first bite was bliss. It was hot, salty, and rich in a way that only true hunger could magnify. She chewed slowly, savoring the moment, the warmth spreading through her body. Stars winked on, and she felt at peace. The fire crackled beside her, a companion in solitude.

28

VAUGHN

Gemma burned fragrant barks and leaves in the evenings, their smoke keeping insects away. She scrubbed her skin with a mixture of sea salt and fine sand, feeling her body grow clean and strong. Each day unfolded with a sweet simplicity she had never known before, marked by small notches carved into the silk cotton tree.

A curious white-necked crow, intrigued by her store of fruit, landed near the wind chimes of coral and shells she hung from a tree branch to scare such thieves away. The bird tilted its head, studying her with an unsettling intelligence for a creature of its size, its obsidian eyes reflecting the afternoon as it assessed her every movement.

She ignored the bird at first, thinking it would lose interest and fly off. Instead, it hopped closer, its iridescent blue-black feathers gleaming. The creature paused every few seconds, as if calculating the distance between them, before darting forward another inch.

"Don't even think about it," she said. The crow cocked its head, as if considering her words.

Over the next few days, the bird became a regular fixture. It loitered near her shelter, hopping from rock to rock, watching her with unnerving focus.

"Are you part pirate?" Gemma asked as the new friend sat on a nearby branch, holding a hog plum in its beak. "Because you sure act like it. I should call you Seaman Beaky."

The crow squawked indignantly, dropping the fruit while it flapped its wings as if insulted.

"Fine. How about Captain Fairweather? Is that more fitting for your rank?"

The next day, Gemma tossed a piece of mango, which Captain Fairweather caught midair with the precision of an acrobat. It squawked approvingly, retreating to a nearby rock to peck at its spoils, the sound of its busy beak echoing faintly across the quiet beach.

Swimming washed away the sharper edges of her sorrow and anxiety. When she floated on her back, the soft roar of the current and the snaps of pistol shrimp clicked in her submerged ears. She felt impossibly far from everything that had once anchored her to civilization, yet as the waves rolled in and out—steady and unyielding—she realized she wasn't entirely alone; she had Captain Fairweather and Vaughn. Still, her thoughts drifted to Nihir and Yaya Mari. She missed them.

Knowing that her survival and locating Nihir

depended on her wits, Gemma devised a new plan. At dawn on the seventh day, she began the grueling ascent up the crumbling rocky slope. Scraggy vegetation clawed at her legs, and the loose ground betrayed her with every step, sending her skidding back nearly as much as she climbed. By the time she reached the summit, she had renewed her collection of cuts and bruises. She wiped her hands on her shorts—once white, now stained with dirt and sap.

From this vantage point, the world sprawled into unbroken solitude. The sight was both magnificent and terrifying. No sign of life. No boats. Just the wild, unrelenting ocean. The wind howled over the peak where she stood, cold and dry. With no sign of Nihir, she began the descent back to camp.

Back on her beach, Gemma stripped off her shorts and shirt, letting the wind slip over her bare skin. The sand, still warm from the day's heat, cradled her as she stretched out. After a while, she waded into the shallows and scrubbed her clothes with handfuls of sand, working out the dirt and sweat from the hike, then carried them back to drape over a low branch where the sun's last rays could dry them.

Leaning against a sun-baked boulder, she let its stored warmth seep into her, easing the ache in her muscles. The steady crash became a lullaby, each wave drawing her deeper into a quiet, drifting state. Her breathing slowed as she descended.

At first, Vaughn's presence entered her mind—a flicker at the edges of her consciousness. In her dream, the coinlike leaves of the sea grape tree shimmered in dappled sunlight.

"Vaughn," she called into the dream-space as she walked into the surf.

No answer. Her ability to reach her spirit guide remained maddeningly unpredictable.

In the crystalline waters of her sleeping mind, the tide whispered around her calves. A school of fish darted past, their movements forming a sacred geometry. The water transformed into fractal patterns blooming outward like living mandalas. Shapes folded and unfolded in impossible configurations. The very fabric of the dream-sea shifted into hypnotic spirals that mirrored the patterns she sometimes glimpsed behind her closed eyelids when exhaustion took hold—the tessellations that breathed and flowed, expanding into infinity before contracting into pinpoints.

A bolt of pain surged through her dream-foot, white-hot and searing, as if she had been stabbed. Through the water, she caught a glimpse of a lionfish—its delicate venom-tipped spines splayed like an elaborate feather fan of red and white, colors more saturated than any waking world could produce.

The pain wasn't static—it pulsed, deepened, and spread in waves that spasmed her body. Her breath hitched. She needed to reach shore before the paralyzing venom fully set in, though both beach and sea were dream constructs.

She collapsed onto sand that felt both real and unreal, as nausea swept through her. The dream-trees rippled, their leaves whispering in voices just beyond hearing—the language of spirits, of the in-between places where the living could touch the dead.

Vaughn spoke to her.

"You never learn, do you?"

"Oh, piss off, Vaughn," Dream-Gemma said as she took her injured foot in her hands. She knew this pain served a purpose—it was the price of genuine contact. A bridge.

She rolled onto her back, squinting at a sky that belonged neither to day nor night but to the timeless realm. Vaughn materialized beside her, looking more solid than he ever had, his form sharp and clear.

He appeared as he must have in his prime—a young, cocky sailor. His freckled nose carried the permanent kiss of sunburn, a badge of honor from countless hours on the water. The white polo shirt he wore contrasted with his deeply tanned arms, and his long khaki shorts hung loosely from narrow hips. He stretched out beside her on the dream-sand, propping himself up on one elbow like a man enjoying a lazy afternoon.

The jungle behind her breathed with ancient awareness, watching, waiting. Captain Fairweather perched on a branch that existed in both realms, real and dreaming, his head tilting as he crossed the thinning veil at will in the liminal space.

People of countless cultures knew this truth—birds were sacred messengers between worlds. In West African Yoruba tradition, the sankofa bird looks backward while moving forward, symbolizing the spirits of ancestors reaching through time to guide the living. Mari had once told Gemma that white-necked crows like Captain Fairweather were particularly potent vessels—creatures whose black and white coloring represented their ability to exist simultaneously in darkness and light, in life and death.

The ancient knowledge of birds as boundary-crossers was embedded in humanity's collective memory, passed down through generations in whispered stories and sacred rituals. Even those who claimed not to believe felt an instinctive shiver when a bird tapped at their window or circled overhead at significant moments, especially if it was a corvid.

Captain Fairweather cocked an eye toward Gemma, as if to acknowledge her newfound awareness of his true nature.

"Vaughn," she rasped, looking back to her dead companion. "I need to find Nihir. Please help me."

Another wave of dream-pain wracked her, and suddenly she could see Vaughn—blood in the water, sinking, his body eventually washing ashore on a deserted beach.

Dream-Gemma squeezed her eyes shut. "Not that. Tell me where Nihir is."

"He's here, on the other side of the island." Vaughn's voice carried the weight of absolute truth. He showed Gemma a vision of the rocky path to a hidden cove directly opposite her sanctuary.

"But before you find Nihir, I need to tell you where proof of everything Cowboi has done is hidden—my manuscript, all my notes, Cruz's hard drives. The evidence," Vaughn said, "is in Dream."

What? Gemma was confused. It's hidden in dreams? We are in a dream. That doesn't make sense. And then—Vaughn dissolved like foam on the waves.

The first part of the message was crystal clear—Nihir was here, a day's walk away. She also knew she had to stop Cowboi. But what had he meant about Dream? That mystery would have to wait.

29

NIHIR

Gemma felt inexorably pulled toward something waiting beyond the massive boulders that had seemed impassable before.

"Keep going, Gemma," Vaughn's voice whispered, carried on the salty breeze, yet somehow internal, resonating within her mind rather than in her ears.

She braced herself against the wind as each misstep sent a cascade of brittle fragments tumbling down the slope and into the sea below. As she edged closer to the bottom, the sapphire hole of the second bay emerged in fleeting glimpses through the breaks in the cliffs. The curving rock walls closed in protectively. The water winked in the sunlight, its surface shadowy and deep. Recesses hugged the edges where the sea lapped, swirling into caves or crevices beneath the cliffs. This was a stark contrast to the shallow, serene bay she had washed up in, but it felt just as protected from the open fury of the ocean. On the descent, she saw him—bare-chested, his linen pants torn, and his hair wild from exposure.

"Nihir!"

Her voice, buoyed by relief, echoed in the theater of rocks. He turned, startled, and the look of astonishment on his face mirrored her own. Scrambling down the last stretch of the jagged path, she stumbled onto the sand. Her knees buckled, but Nihir was there in an instant, steadying her before she collapsed completely.

"Gemma..." Nihir's voice wavered as he shook his head in disbelief. "I thought you went down with the *Mariposa*. All I saw was debris. The Zodiac was swept away, and the engine was dead! I... I thought you were gone."

She clutched his arms, her breath shaky. "I barely made it. The life raft you pulled on deck saved me."

For a moment, they both stood in silence, the weight of what they had survived pressing down on them.

"Boon sabotaged the outboard on the dinghy, too. I couldn't get it running in the middle of the storm. There's a current that runs like a river past the island, straight out to the open ocean. When I got close enough to the rocks, I jumped."

He shook his head to clear the traumatic memory. "The current caught the dinghy, and I was certain it would be swept around the island. But somehow, the water near the cliff pulled the boat into that sea cave instead." He paused, his hand trembling as he pointed. "I'm not much of a swimmer. If I'd stayed with the boat and gotten trapped in there..." His voice trailed off as his eyes met hers, the unspoken reality hanging between them. "I don't think I'd be alive."

Gemma wrapped him in her arms, so glad to be reunited.

"Thank God you're okay," she whispered. "I don't know what I would've done if..." She couldn't finish the thought. Their eyes held for a long moment, communicating what words couldn't express. She swallowed hard, trying to gather herself. "I just—I can't believe we made it."

After another moment of silence, she reluctantly released Nihir and shifted her focus to their more immediate concerns. "And the cargo?" Gemma asked softly. "Did any of it survive?"

"As far as I know, it's all in the cave," Nihir said, nodding toward the outcropping. "There's a toolkit and cans of fuel—I might be able to fix the engine if we can get the boat back to shore." He looked out at the churning water, his expression doubtful. "But the currents here are brutal, especially around those rocks."

Gemma's brows furrowed.

Nihir continued, "Oh! I almost forgot. I grabbed the ditch bag too. I had it around my neck. It's in my camp, under the tree."

Gemma blinked. "The ditch bag? Are you serious?"

"Yeah." He shrugged. "Figured we'd need that."

She stared at him for a beat, then let out a breath. "You're incredible! I was a panicked mess, but you grabbed money, our papers, and the cargo. Amazing!"

Nihir's lips curved into a smile. "Three grand in cash and our passports. Yep."

Gemma exhaled sharply, the weight of what he'd done settling over her. "Jesus, Nihir. That might save us."

"If we can get off this island," he reminded her.

For the first time in days, Gemma felt hope stirring—not just for herself, but for both of them. She looked at Nihir—really looked at him.

"Nihir, you're the best thing that's ever happened to me," she said, her voice softer now. "I'm so damn glad you're alive."

Nihir smiled. "You too, Gemma." He wrapped her in a sun-warmed hug.

Gemma felt Vaughn's presence stirring in her mind, stronger than ever, urging her to action. She closed her eyes, focusing. When she opened her eyes, Nihir had a concerned look on his face.

"Where did you just go?" Nihir asked.

"I have a lot to tell you," Gemma began, her voice tentative but determined. She paused, gathering her thoughts. "You know about Mariposa's End, the rites on the beach. I told you a little about my family, but I didn't tell you everything."

Nihir tilted his head, his expression open and curious. "Go on," he encouraged gently.

"I come from a line of Vodou priestesses," Gemma said, her words coming faster now, as if releasing a long-held secret. "My mom called them witches, but that's not right. They're holy women—herbalists, mediums, influencers of the fates from a long lineage. Each of these women, including me, has a guardian spirit. Mine is here with me now. He led me to you. He told me there is evidence that could put Cowboi away for life and that he can guide me to it." She hesitated, her voice softening as she added, "It's Vaughn. The one Boon killed."

Nihir's eyes widened for a moment before his face broke into a reassuring smile. "That's marvelous! We can use all the help we can get!" he exclaimed, his enthusiasm genuine.

Relief washed over Gemma. "That's not the reaction I expected," she whispered in his ear, her voice tinged with disbelief. Nihir loosened his arms, resting his hands gently on her shoulders, his gaze steady and encouraging.

"Sit. Tell me everything," he said, motioning to the sand. "How do you communicate with him? Maybe he can help us get out of here."

Gemma settled onto the warm sand, her body relaxing into the familiar texture, while Nihir sat across from her, his posture as composed and attentive as ever. She took a deep breath before beginning. "Vaughn can connect with me most easily when I dream," she explained. "Or when I'm in a trance. Meditation helps. In fact, your training has helped me more than any other technique, even the ones my grandmother showed me. I'm a woman of the world, I suppose." She smiled, pride lighting her face.

Nihir chuckled softly. "I feel honored. But wait—you said Vaughn, the man Boon killed? He's your guardian? Isn't that... unusual? I know a little about African magic, and my understanding is that the spirit guides are gods or at least ancestors."

Gemma's smile widened into a playful smirk. "As I said, I seem to be as multicultural as they come—African roots, Eastern methods, a dead white man for a guardian, a dream lionfish. Go figure."

Nihir laughed, his warmth dispelling any lingering tension. "Lionfish?"

"It's a long story and not important."

"You're a wonder, Gemma August," he said, his voice full of admiration.

He beamed at her and leaned in. Gemma could feel Nihir's warmth, the scent of the sea between them. She responded, placing her palms against his chest, feeling the steady rhythm of his heartbeat. She looked up into his eyes. There was no fear there—only love and gratitude. It was as if all the weight they had carried, the secrets unspoken, the risks taken, and the life-threatening chaos of the past few days had led them to this quiet moment.

"I don't know what happens next," she whispered, more to herself than to him.

"Neither do I," Nihir replied. "But we're here now."

Slowly, as if drawn by the unseen force that had brought them to this point, his fingers interlaced with hers, their foreheads resting together. Nihir's touch was gentle as he traced her spine up under her shirt, following each vertebra like a sacred path. Her skin prickled with anticipation, a cascade of goosebumps following his fingertips. She pulled back slightly, searching his eyes for any sign of hesitation, but all she saw was trust.

The wind shifted, blowing hot across the secluded beach, carrying with it the scent of frangipani. Gemma pressed her lips against Nihir's collarbone, tasting the salt on his skin and feeling the steady pulse beneath. She let go of the tension in her shoulders, the instinct to be constantly vigilant, to be strong and guarded. Here, in this hidden place, she didn't need to be anything but present, anything but herself.

Their movements became a conversation of bodies, wordless but deeply expressive—a way of grounding themselves in something real after days of danger and uncertainty. The soft brush of palms against skin spoke volumes that their voices couldn't articulate. They took their time, as if moving too quickly would break the spell that held them suspended between fear and hope.

Gemma's fingers traced the shape of Nihir's face, the curve of his jaw, the slight hollow beneath his cheekbone. He responded by kissing her lips with a tenderness that made her overflow with pleasure. Their bodies created shallow impressions in the warm sand that the tide would soon wash away. The world melted into the sound of the distant cry of seabirds circling overhead, their bodies entwined like driftwood. Gemma could feel the grains beneath her, pressing into her back and shoulders, the firm warmth of Nihir's weight holding her down, anchoring her to this moment, and the steady rise and fall of his chest against hers, their breathing gradually synchronizing.

Words seemed unnecessary, even intrusive, in this sanctuary they'd created. Nihir's fingers absentmindedly held her wrist. Gemma arched against him. Nihir's breath caught, then released in a soft exhale. Their movements were like waves—sometimes gentle, sometimes urgent.

For these precious moments, there was no danger, no spirits demanding attention, no past regrets or future uncertainties—only the present, only sensation, only connection. Gemma closed her eyes, surrendering completely to the feeling.

Afterward, they lay tangled together. Above them, clouds drifted across the deepening blue sky. Neither rushed to move, content to exist in this perfect pocket of time where nothing beyond this stretch of beach seemed to matter.

A sharp, curious sound broke through their reverie.

"Who's your friend?" Nihir asked, lifting himself onto one elbow.

Gemma turned. Captain Fairweather had followed her over the mountain. The crow sat on a nearby rock, hammering a nut with determined precision, his black and white feathers gleaming in the sunlight.

Gemma tilted her head, watching her crow friend with a fond smile. "That's Captain Fairweather."

Nihir studied the bird with curiosity. "Captain Fairweather, huh?"

"He found me," Gemma said with a laugh. "First, he was just a thief. He kept stealing my fruit. But he's persistent and surprisingly charming. That's how he earned the title of captain."

Nihir pushed up into a cross-legged seat and reached out to the crow, palm open. The bird cocked its head, considering the gesture. Thinking better of it, it let out a sharp squawk, then flapped its wings and flew off toward the cliffs. Nihir watched it go, shaking his head with amusement.

Nihir and Gemma sat for a long time, watching the tide creep higher and the sun sink toward the horizon. Neither felt the need to fill the space as they observed the day's surrender.

"The tide will be high soon," Nihir finally remarked, his voice soft as he gestured toward the water's advancing edge. Little by little, the sea was reclaiming the small beach where they'd spent these precious hours together. Gemma watched the water's methodical approach, mesmerized by its quiet persistence. "I hadn't noticed how fast it comes in," she whispered, reluctant to leave their comfortable nest in the sand.

"Come. I have a small camp set up in the trees. It's not much." Nihir led Gemma to a narrow path that wound through sea grapes and palms that rustled gently in the evening breeze.

"Here we are," Nihir said, pushing aside a branch to reveal a small clearing. A simple lean-to made of driftwood and palm fronds stood against the largest tree, with a tidy fire pit ringed by smooth stones nearby.

Gemma took in the modest camp with appreciation. "It's perfect," she said, suddenly aware of how exhausted she felt after her hike and the emotional day that followed.

They settled beside each other beneath the shelter. Despite the strangeness of their situation—shipwrecked on this isolated beach—Gemma felt an unexpected sense of peace wash over her.

"Sleep," Nihir murmured, his voice barely audible above the distant surf. "Tomorrow, we will make a plan."

As stars appeared in the darkening sky above, they drifted into sleep.

30

ESCAPE

Gemma climbed to a boulder high above the jagged maw of the whirling bay. Her bare feet tested each step, feeling the rough stone's radiant heat through her calloused soles. Beads of sweat formed along her hairline and trailed down her temples. She walked along the crescent rim, testing crumbling stones for footholds as small pebbles cascaded into the churning water far below.

At the precipice, the distance looked far greater, the water more violent. A smile crossed her lips as she steeled herself. She raised her arms above her head, fingers pointed skyward like a prayer. For a heartbeat, she was suspended between worlds—the scorching stone beneath her feet, blue sky above, and the wild sea below. Then she pushed off with explosive force, her body arcing through the air.

The wind screamed past her ears. Her form cut

through the surface with barely a splash—a blade slicing through silk. She was enveloped—the cold and fierce sea, shockingly alive. The impact drove breath from her lungs, but she didn't panic. Instead, she let herself sink into the blue, feeling the ocean's crushing embrace, its ancient weight pressing against her from all sides.

She surfaced with a gasp, water streaming from her face as she broke into the world of light. Powerful currents immediately seized her, pulling her toward the cave's yawning darkness with inexorable force. Her head dipped, and when she broke through again, she found herself at the line where sunlight gave way to shadow, the cave's mouth framing her in a gateway. Straining her eyes in the dim light, she scanned the darkness and caught sight of the familiar red shape bobbing in the surge.

A few strokes brought her alongside the dinghy. Placing her hands on the port tube, she swung herself into the boat with practiced ease. Standing inside, she took a mental inventory—black nylon duffels stacked, jerry cans of gas, and a tool kit in the console. Laughter escaped her, bouncing off the cave walls in sharp echoes. She nudged one of the bags with her foot. Still dry.

Until Nihir cleaned the sugar from the tank, the boat was useless. The cave pressed close around her, waves amplifying the rhythmic ping of the rubber hull against the rocks. Then, a flicker.

Vaughn's form wavered in the dimness. Below him, the India ink blackness of cave water swirled, sending a chill up her spine.

"Use the ropes," his voice wove into her thoughts.

She swallowed, nodding, and opened the locker at the bow, fingers closing around coiled lines nestled among life vests, just as Vaughn had suggested.

"Keep searching," he urged.

She rifled deeper into the console—her fingers closing on a handheld GPS. Hope sparked inside her. They had the essentials: a boat, an engine, gas, tools, and navigation.

Vaughn's form flickered again, less distinct this time.

Gemma exhaled. Timing was everything. With the tide reversed, she could tie the line to the dinghy, swim it out, and then she and Nihir could reel it in from the beach. But she had to act quickly.

Vaughn's voice became clearer in the quiet.

"You must return to St. Columba," he said. "Mariposa's End is in trouble. Cowboi's making his move, and he's putting the pieces in place."

The words prickled against her skin—a warning.

The tide was shifting, flow out. Gemma inhaled and dove back into the water, with the rope's free end tied around her waist. The current seized her immediately, a washing machine that threatened to dash her against jagged walls. The cave spat her back into open water with violent force. Her limbs burned with exertion, muscles screaming as she dug deep with each powerful stroke against the treacherous rip tide. The rope trailed behind her, its weight dragging at her waist and tangling her feet as she battled the ocean's relentless pull.

She knew the water's tricks. Swimming parallel to the shoreline, her body a diagonal slash against the current's grip. Only when she'd cleared the worst of the rip could she angle toward the beach, her lungs no longer heaving quite so desperately.

Nihir was already sprinting toward her across the sand.

"Gemma! You did it!" he called.

She staggered through the shallows with the rope tied around her. On the beach, she and Nihir braced themselves in the wet sand and wrapped the line around their hands.

"On three," Gemma called. "One... two... three!"

They leaned back, throwing their weight against the resistance. For a moment, nothing happened.

"Again!" Gemma shouted.

They heaved once more, but this time, they could pull in some slack. The boat was moving! Finally, after reeling in thirty feet of line, the dinghy's round nose appeared at the cave's shadowy mouth.

Nihir's face tightened with concentration. "I see it!"

The tide was growing stronger by the minute, or perhaps their muscles were tiring—both, Gemma guessed. If they lost the dinghy now, they might never recover it.

They gave another mighty pull, but the rope refused to give. Gemma's heart sank.

"It's caught on something," she said.

Nihir shaded his eyes, peering toward the cave. "It's the rocks just below the surface."

Gemma studied the situation, calculating their options. Every moment they waited, the sea threatened to claim their prize.

"We need to change angles," she decided. "Let's move down the beach."

They shuffled sideways, maintaining tension on the line. The new position altered the pull direction.

Nihir nodded grimly. They redoubled their efforts, straining, and the dinghy broke free. Each pull now brought it a few feet closer, but as it neared, Gemma could see that the rope was deteriorating. White strands had separated from the core. The submerged rock must have damaged it. A large wave crashed against the shore, and the dinghy pulled back like a stubborn mule.

"We're losing it! If the rope snaps—" Nihir shouted.

The fraying worsened. Gemma's mind raced, running through scenarios. Their window was closing.

"Keep pulling!" she commanded. "Steady pressure!"

Hope flashed across Nihir's face—only to vanish as the rope snapped with a sharp crack, the boat only feet from their grasp.

"No!" Gemma cried, watching the severed end whip through the water.

Without hesitation, she sprinted into the surf, her eyes fixed on the dinghy now drifting sideways. Behind her, Nihir shouted something, but the ocean swallowed his words. She lunged out; the dinghy was just beyond her fingertips, bobbing tantalizingly close. Her hand closed around the lifeline. Relief surged through her as Nihir came up behind her, and together, they hauled their salvation onto the beach, both trembling from the effort.

They collapsed onto the sand side by side. Gemma's quivering and Nihir flat on his back, eyes closed. Only the

Escape | 307

rhythmic rise and fall of his chest showed he was conscious.

"We did it," Gemma whispered, reaching for his hand. Their fingers intertwined, sand gritty between their palms.

After several minutes of silence broken only by the surf and their gradually slowing breaths, Nihir crawled toward the dinghy, examining it with a critical eye.

"It looks intact," he said, running his hands along the rubber sides. He moved to the outboard motor, tilting it to check the propeller. "No visible damage here either."

Nihir unscrewed the fuel cap. "Definitely sugar in there. The whole system needs to be flushed." He tapped the tank with his knuckles. "I'll need to drain it completely, clean the filter, check the fuel lines, and make sure none reached the carburetor."

"Can you fix it?" Gemma asked.

"Yes," he replied, determination hardening his features. He glanced at the toolkit she'd recovered. "At least we have these."

"I hate to poison the beach," Nihir muttered, "but I have to get rid of this fuel."

He fed the siphon tube into the tank, sucked at the end, and spat as the sugar-fouled gasoline gushed onto the sand. A metallic haze rose around them. Gemma turned away, her nose wrinkling against the acrid stench.

Nihir worked quickly, flushing the sugar as sparingly as possible with the jerry cans of fresh fuel, replacing plugs, and cleaning the carburetor on a makeshift workbench made from a flat rock. When he finished, they dragged the Zodiac waist-deep into the surf. He turned the key.

The engine whined, then roared. Gemma threw her arms around Nihir's neck, laughing and breathless. They climbed in, and she switched on the GPS, relieved when the green glow of the screen flickered to life. The Turks and Caicos were less than twenty-five miles away—under two hours' travel, well within the range of their fuel. She traced the map with her finger, pausing on icons for hotels, restaurants, and an airport—a place to regroup. It was only early afternoon, and though they were exhausted, Vaughn's warning gave Gemma a fresh jolt of urgency. They would leave now.

The squawk of a bird caught Gemma's attention. She looked up and smiled.

"Captain Fairweather!"

The crow circled overhead, his black-and-white wings flashing in the sunlight. The bird lit on the bow of the Zodiac.

"Well, Captain," she said softly, "I guess this is goodbye."

Nihir chuckled. "Looks like he doesn't want to let you go."

Gemma held out her hand, and the crow landed on her for the first time. "I'll miss you too," she said, her voice catching slightly.

As if understanding her words, Captain Fairweather let out a long, trilling call, then took off again, circling over the water, his wings skimming the surface before soaring away toward the cliffs.

Gemma opened the throttle, standing with knees bent to absorb the shock as the Zodiac leaped, throwing wings of spray into the air on the crests of the waves. The mist cooled her sun-warmed skin, and for the first time in weeks, the vast blue horizon stretched open before them. With the handheld GPS, they simply needed to set a course and follow it.

31

TURKS AND CAICOS

They were free from their island prison. And yet —ironically—Gemma felt a pull to turn around. The past month had been stripped down to survival, but in that simplicity, something had felt true. No obligations, no struggle for status, just the rhythms of nature. What if she and Nihir could recreate that kind of retreat for themselves and others? Gemma laughed at herself. What she was fantasizing about described a sort of combination of Royal Asana and Mariposa's End, the home she had all along.

Soon, a new low-lying smudge of land broke the horizon. Gemma felt her hope swell as the shoreline grew more defined with each passing minute. Her wide-open thoughts, which had floated freely across the open water, now condensed under the heavy weight of the inevitable confrontation with Cowboi Rivers. Brick by brick, her worries built a formidable wall in her mind. What would happen when they reached land? Would anyone believe their story? Could she find the evidence they needed as leverage?

Gemma glanced at Nihir, his profile chiseled against the blue. She tried to draw strength from his steady presence. But even his serenity couldn't fully quiet the storm building inside her.

At West Caicos, Gemma steered toward Providenciales. The pale crescent of Grace Bay stretched ahead, crowded with sunburned tourists sprawled on lounge chairs and wandering the shoreline with drinks in hand. The water near the resorts glittered with parasails, jet skis, and catamarans.

They needed a place close enough to slip unnoticed into the crowd but distant enough that no authority would bother them. To the west, the populated beach gave way to a lonely stretch of sand. There were no resorts, no lifeguard stands—just enough cover for them to work undisturbed.

"There," Nihir said, his voice low but certain. "Past the dunes. No one's watching. Tuck in there."

The engine hummed as they glided past anchored yachts and pleasure cruisers. In the shallows, they ran the boat aground and dragged it inland, past the waterline, to a cluster of trees.

Gemma turned to Nihir. "Let's move fast."

Working quickly, they dug into the loose sand to bury the black duffels and then dragged the Zodiac over the disturbed ground. Gemma stepped back to assess their work. Satisfied, she brushed the sand from her hands.

"It's not Fort Knox, but it will have to do. X marks the spot," Gemma swaggered up to Nihir, doing her best Jack Sparrow impression, and kissed him on the cheek. "At least if someone decides to steal the dinghy, they'll probably miss what's underneath it," she concluded.

Gemma grabbed the binoculars. In the fading afternoon, umbrella-covered vendors sat on plastic stools, braiding hair into cornrows or selling iced coconuts pierced with colorful straws to overheating sunbathers. With the money Nihir had saved from the sinking *Mariposa*, they could buy fresh clothes and anything else they needed to blend in with this tourist scene. Five Cays was within walking distance, and Gemma's mind raced as they approached the main street. They needed to contact Cowboi, but not to negotiate for their lives. This time, they would turn the game to their advantage.

The doughy smell of Johnny cakes frying reminded Gemma that she had only eaten fish and fruit for three weeks. Gemma's stomach growled in anticipation as she stepped toward the walk-up shack, its peeling wooden counter shaded by a sun-faded awning.

Nihir shot her a sideways glance. "That much grease after weeks of clean eating? You're asking for trouble."

She ignored him. "I'll take two," she told the woman behind the counter.

A moment later, the vendor handed over golden, piping-hot Johnny cakes wrapped in wax paper. The dough was crisp at the edges, pillowy at the center, glistening with oil. She passed one to Nihir and took a bite. The donut-like cake melted on her tongue, a combination of sweet and savory mingled with salt. She closed her eyes and moaned softly, then attacked the Johnny cake with abandon. The fried dough disappeared in four massive bites, leaving nothing but crumbs, which she chased with her fingertips, unwilling to waste even the tiniest morsel. She barely registered Nihir watching her with amusement as she licked the lingering traces of salt and fry oil from her hands.

After eating, they stepped into the brightly lit souvenir shop, thick with artificial piña colada smell. Nihir browsed racks of garish tourist t-shirts, each in neon hues and emblazoned with tacky sayings. *No Bad Days in Turks and Caicos.* Gemma gravitated toward the sundress rack, her fingers trailing over rows of lightweight rayon fabrics printed with palm leaves and hibiscus flowers in loud, clashing colors. She finally picked one with a gathered tube-top bodice and a sunset skirt.

Nihir went full-kitsch and selected a shirt with a cartoon crab waving its claws under the declaration: *Life's a Beach.* He paired it with nylon shorts covered in a pattern of tiny pineapples, the bright yellow shapes contrasting comically with the sky-blue fabric. They exchanged grins as they stepped out of the shop in their fast fashion. For a moment, they were as carefree as the travelers these clothes were truly made for.

They charged the phone from the ditch bag, and Gemma dialed Cowboi. She hadn't rehearsed what she would say, but she knew she couldn't show any weakness.

A voice answered on the other end.

"It's Gemma," she kept her voice steady. "I want to make a deal."

There was a brief silence. "I thought you were dead."

Gemma said flatly, "Clearly, I'm not."

The silence on the other end stretched longer this time. Finally, Cowboi spoke again.

"Where are you?"

"I know what you're planning, and I have evidence. Unless you want this to turn into a much bigger problem, I'd suggest you make a deal."

Her heart pounded, but she forced herself to stay calm. She had to be convincing. There was a pause, and the call clicked over to speakerphone.

"What do you propose?"

"Simple. The Beneteau is gone, sunk in Hurricane Baxter, but coke is all yours. I don't want anything to do with it. In exchange, Nihir and I want your guarantee that you'll leave Mariposa's End and us alone. Forever."

"That cocaine is spare change. The marina is a billion-dollar enterprise that will change the economy of a region. No deal," Cowboi said with finality.

There was a pause, and she could hear the faint murmur of voices in the background. Eventually, Cowboi's voice returned.

"Stay where you are. I'll send my jet. We'll talk when you get back here. Now, again, tell me where you are."

"Send the jet to Providenciales International Airport in the Turks and Caicos. We'll need a car for the cargo."

"Done," Cowboi concluded.

Gemma hung up, exhaling a shaky breath.

Nihir arched a brow. "I'm pretty sure we just told one of the most dangerous men in the world that we have evidence that we don't actually possess yet."

Gemma rubbed a hand over her face. "Vaughn's tried to tell me where the manuscript is. Cruz's CIA records, too. I didn't entirely understand the message, but I know what he told me is real. The files are hidden, and we can find them. He said they were in a dream."

"Which means, right now, you're bluffing. In a dream doesn't sound admissible in court," Nihir said, crossing his arms.

"It won't matter if we play this right. Cowboi can't risk those files being out there—of them getting leaked—that's what will keep him in check."

The jet wouldn't arrive until tomorrow. A hotel with a hot shower would have been bliss, but leaving the cocaine buried in the sand unguarded was out of the question, so they returned to the dinghy.

As the sun sank to meet the horizon, a new rhythm took over the beach. The scent of grilled snapper, conch fritters, and jerk chicken drifted on the breeze. Melodic steel drum melodies wove through the air, blending with the chatter and laughter of a crowd gathering nearby. Lanterns strung between the palm trees blinked on, their warm glow casting playful shadows over the growing crowd.

"Shall we?" Gemma asked. "We can keep an eye on our camp from the party."

"Sure!" Nihir replied.

They followed the foamy edge where waves kissed the

sand, drawn toward the evening's awakening celebration. Food vendors hurried to arrange their stalls—bowls of conch salad jeweled with lime and scotch bonnet peppers, plantains sizzling in oil that perfumed the salt air. Local artisans had claimed their spots along the makeshift promenade: silver bangles caught the last light, mahogany dolphins leaped, and hand-dyed sarongs snapped like prayer flags in the warm offshore breeze.

A stage had materialized while they'd been in town—rough planks elevated on cinder blocks transformed by string lights and the pulse of music. The lead singer rolled his shoulders to the drum's liquid rhythm, his shirt unbuttoned, his weathered Panama hat tilted at just the right angle of island cool. Around him, couples danced barefoot in the sand.

Gemma wandered toward the bar stalls, where local beers and rum punches flowed freely. A man with dreadlocks piled like a haystack atop his head poured a generous helping of rum into a Solo cup and topped it with a splash of fruit juice, handing it to her with a wink. She took a sip. The smoky warmth washed over her as she watched the dancing, the music pulling her into its irresistible rhythm.

Gemma turned to Nihir. "Come on," she said, setting her drink down on a nearby table. Nihir's eyes lit up, his smile widening as he held out a hand. "I thought you'd never ask," he replied smoothly, pulling her toward the stage.

As they reached the edge of the dancing crowd, Nihir spun Gemma into a graceful turn, catching her

Turks and Caicos | 317

effortlessly and pulling her close. His movements were fluid, each step confident and in perfect rhythm with the music. Gemma couldn't help but laugh, caught off guard by his skill.

"You've been holding out on me," she teased, trying to keep up as he led her through a series of quick, playful steps. Around them, the crowd moved in a joyous blur—children spinning in dizzying circles, tourist couples laughing as they stumbled through improvised dances, and old islanders executing sambas and rumbas with the grace of a lifetime of practice. Nihir's moves were among the most polished.

"You're full of surprises," Gemma said, her voice light and teasing. Nihir leaned in, his smile softening. "Just needed the right music."

Gemma felt herself relax, letting Nihir guide her, his energy and skill infectious. Her dress flared out as she spun, and when she came back into his arms, she was breathless from laughing.

32

COWBOI'S END

Gemma tried to get comfortable in the sand on an improvised bed of stolen hotel towels. Her stomach and head rebelled. It was 2 a.m., but a few diehard partiers still lingered on the beach, talking and laughing around the dying embers of the bonfires.

Nihir kissed the top of her head. She let the faint echo of laughter from the beach wrap around her like a blanket, coaxing her toward sleep, but her worries looped in her mind. Her body finally gave in. The weight of exhaustion defeated her stress, leaving only the faintest hum of unease as she tumbled through layers of consciousness, past the membrane separating waking from dreaming.

Colors swirled around her—indigo, violet, cobalt—until she found herself standing on the deck of an abandoned sailboat.

Vaughn materialized at the helm.

"Is this real?" Gemma asked, running her hand along the cabin top.

"Real enough." Vaughn's laugh sounded like water lapping against a hull. "You're getting better at this."

The boat rocked gently beneath her feet. Gemma could see the lights of Mariposa's End twinkling in the distance.

"Where are we?"

Vaughn moved toward the companionway. "You keep looking in the wrong place. Not in dreams—on Dream." He gestured below deck. "My manuscript. Cruz's CIA files. They're here, hidden here."

Gemma followed him down the ladder into the cabin.

"Under the V-berth, there's a compartment." Vaughn pointed to the forward cabin. "Behind the water tank. You'll need to remove this access panel."

Gemma climbed down and knelt, seeing the outline of the hidden space. "All this time, it was on your boat?"

Vaughn's form flickered. "The tide is changing. You're waking up."

The colors around her began to fade.

"Get the evidence. Protect yourself, save Mariposa's End, make Cowboi pay." Vaughn smiled sadly. "And Gemma? Trust what you know. It's all real."

The boat began dissolving around her, edges bleeding into darkness.

Gemma jolted awake, sand sticking to her cheek. It was still fully night, and beside her, Nihir slept peacefully. She lay still for a moment, heart pounding, the dream vivid in her mind. Dream—Vaughn's boat. It was anchored, swimming distance from the beach and Mariposa's End.

As the sun rose behind the trees, Gemma and Nihir slept for as long as they could, but at 6 a.m., they tidied up their camp and threaded their way between a few passed-out bodies still scattered across the waterfront. Gemma laughed in surprise when she noticed that the cleanup crew had raked the sand, creating elegant ripples around the passed-out revelers, like stones in an absurd Zen garden.

The morning streets of Provo were empty of tourists, but the Turks and Caicos locals moved with quiet purpose, tending to opening their shops and getting a jump on the day. A rhythm of normalcy and industry hummed through the town, in sharp contrast to the destruction and chaos of the last two months of Gemma's life.

Gemma ordered a coffee at a little ice cream counter nestled within four cement walls painted a vivid neon pink and plastered with weathered advertisements for sodas and popsicles. The tiny establishment was barely more than a hole in the wall, but it served strong coffee, bitter and rich, made with beans that had been roasted that morning.

Nihir and Gemma sat at a two-top table in the shade of the open door. Outside, the traffic on the street grew steadily as the weekend began in earnest. Gemma was watching the play of sunlight on the sidewalk when a large shadow filled in the dapples. She tilted her head up, squinting against the brightness as recognition dawned.

She offered a tentative smile as she met Aldo's familiar face.

"Come with me," he said. "I'm here to take you to the airport and help you with the bags. The jet is waiting."

"The bags are buried on the beach," Gemma said.

Aldo nodded. "Fine. Let's go."

Gemma led the way to where they had stashed the duffels, their footsteps crunching over dry seagrass and shells. At the edge of a secluded grove, Gemma scanned the area for any curious beachgoers. A few early sunbathers had laid out their towels, but they were far enough away to not notice the digging. Satisfied that they wouldn't draw attention, she nodded at Nihir and Aldo.

"That's it. Dig under the boat," she said.

Nihir dragged the Zodiac off to the side, grabbed a piece of driftwood, and began to excavate. Aldo took off his suit jacket and knelt to help. "Got one," Nihir said.

Together, Aldo, Nihir, and Gemma cleared the sand away. Nihir grunted as he heaved the bags from the damp, packed earth.

"I'll take those to the car," Aldo said.

Gemma hesitated, feeling a brief, irrational possessiveness—not for the cocaine, but for all she had been through to get it to this point. She watched Aldo load the bags into the trunk of a black Lincoln Town Car.

They drove down a nondescript road next to the main entry road at Providenciales International Airport, bypassing the commercial terminals entirely, and pulled up to a private hangar at the far edge of the tarmac. There were no security checkpoints or metal detectors. No one asked for passports. Here, the only currency that mattered was wealth and power.

Outside the tinted windows, the private jet gleamed in the morning sun. On the tarmac, two more of Cowboi's men loaded the duffel bags into the cargo hold. Gemma's stomach twisted as she watched—millions of dollars' worth of drugs vanishing into the belly of the aircraft.

Up the stairs and inside the jet, Gemma and Nihir settled into the beige leather seats. The hum of the engines vibrated through the floor as the plane taxied down the runway. As the aircraft lifted off, Gemma pressed her forehead against the cool glass of the window, watching as the sandy beaches, coral reefs, and the deep cerulean stretch disappeared beneath a low layer of clouds. Nihir's hand found hers.

"This is almost over," he murmured.

She nodded, but her mind was spinning. What was waiting for them on Easter Cay? More importantly, would she be able to get to Vaughn's boat before it was too late?

The jet bounced and skidded down the runway at St. Lucy Airport. Aldo led them to the familiar dock, and minutes later, Easter Cay loomed ahead. Unlike on party nights, no staff welcomed them. The boat eased up to the aluminum pilings, and a security guard pulled up in a truck to retrieve the cargo. Aldo took them up to the main house in a golf cart.

Dressed in a linen suit as crisp as fresh money, Cowboi Rivers answered the door himself. His custom ostrich leather cowboy boots clicked against the polished marble floor as he greeted them with the practiced charm of a man accustomed to making people feel both special and uncomfortable.

"Well, well, my favorite captain and her spiritual advisor," he drawled. "Come on in. Sorry about the minimal welcome party—I keep things discreet on delivery days."

The entrance foyer soared two stories high, crowned with a chandelier of blown glass resembling a school of tropical fish. They moved through a grand living area where floor-to-ceiling windows framed panoramic views of the turquoise Caribbean waters. White sofas and teak furniture created an atmosphere of casual luxury, though Gemma noted that nothing about the space felt lived-in. It was a stage set, designed to impress rather than to comfort.

"Most of my guests never venture past the pool deck and guest bungalows," Cowboi explained, leading them down a hallway lined with photographs—Cowboi with presidents, prime ministers, Hollywood stars. Each frame told a story of power and influence. "The girls stay in the east wing, of course. All the amenities they could want." His tone remained conversational, as if discussing hotel accommodations rather than what Gemma now recognized as a high-end prison.

They passed through a kitchen where staff avoided eye contact, busying themselves with preparations for what appeared to be lunches for the girls. The commercial-grade equipment gleamed under harsh lights, and Gemma noticed the windows were barred—decoratively, but barred nonetheless.

Nihir's fingers brushed against Gemma's wrist—a subtle gesture of reassurance that didn't escape Cowboi's notice. His smile tightened almost imperceptibly.

"Here's the business side of paradise," he continued, approaching a heavy wooden door secured with a keypad. He punched in a code, positioning his body to block their view of the numbers.

The door swung open to reveal a corridor that felt markedly different from the tropical minimalism of the main house. Here, the walls were paneled in dark wood, the lighting subdued, and the air noticeably cooler. Security cameras were mounted at regular intervals, their red lights blinking like predator eyes.

"I like to keep certain aspects of my operation... compartmentalized," Cowboi explained, his boots now silent on the thick carpet. "Helps maintain the fantasy for everyone involved."

They passed several closed doors before reaching the end of the hallway, where Cowboi used another keypad to unlock his private office. The room was impressive—a masculine space of leather, carved wood, and bronze, with windows overlooking a secluded cove. Through the glass, Gemma could see the *SV Freedom* anchored in the distance.

"This is where deals are made, fortunes change hands, and futures are decided," Cowboi said. A large desk dominated one end of the room, its surface nearly empty save for a laptop and a crystal decanter of amber liquid. Behind it hung a larger-than-life portrait of Cowboi himself, painted in an almost presidential style.

"Please, make yourselves comfortable," he said, gesturing to a seating area of butter-soft leather chairs arranged on either side of a glass table. "We have some important matters to discuss."

As they took their seats, Gemma noted the subtle details that spoke volumes—the multiple phones on the credenza and the small monitor displaying security feeds from around the property. This wasn't just an office; it was a command center for Cowboi's empire of exploitation.

"I've been thinking, Gemma. We could accomplish so much together," Cowboi said, pouring himself a drink. He didn't offer them any.

Cowboi leaned forward. "You're sitting on a gold mine. The End is prime real estate on St. Columba, and it's undeveloped. I've got the connections, the capital, and the vision to turn it into something spectacular: a luxury marina, high-end villas, private docks. Now that you're back from your little trip, you'll be my partner. Imagine that—wealth and power beyond your wildest dreams. No more scraping by. No more taking orders from anyone."

"No one except for you," Gemma replied, keeping her voice casual.

For a moment, Gemma couldn't help picturing the future he was describing—a world of yachts and glamour, of power and influence. But the images that came to mind weren't seductive. They were horrifying. She imagined Vaughn's body floating in the harbor, Boon's betrayal, Cruz crumpled in the street, Crab slipping beneath the waves. That marina would mean the destruction of Yaya Mari's way of life—a community and culture preserved for hundreds of years. Exploitation and fear were the foundations of Cowboi's empire.

"True, you would report to me," Cowboi said. "But you'd also be the public face of the marina, a hero on the island and beyond, an employer and woman of the people. In return, I'll take care of everything else: security, financing, development. I'm offering you a chance to be part of something great, Gemma. And trust me, if you don't take this opportunity, someone else will."

She took a deep breath, steeling herself. "You had Vaughn killed because he threatened your empire. How can I work for you? You're ruthless."

Cowboi remained unfazed. He denied nothing. Instead, he leaned back, his smile turning ice-cold. "At least you know the consequences of crossing me. Just like you said, people are dead."

Gemma felt a chill creep up her spine. Cowboi's confession hung between them, the truth finally laid bare.

"This was always a con," Gemma said, her voice hollow. "You don't want me as part of your organization. You just want my rights to the land you plan to develop. It has always been about Mariposa's End."

"Business, darlin'. Nothing personal." He gestured toward the crystal decanter. "Drink?"

"The land is in a trust," Gemma countered. "You can't touch it."

"You'd be surprised how many relatives of yours in your precious End are ready for change." He pulled out his phone, tapped up a photo, and slid it across the table. "See for yourself."

Cowboi's End | 327

The screen showed a conference room. Gemma recognized Senator-at-Large Jay August and her cousins Daryl and Remi sitting around a polished table, signing documents.

"They've been working for me," Cowboi said. "All I needed was the right pressure point. And with you presumed dead, I was moving the deal ahead by declaring Mari incompetent and transferring the trust to Jay. The problem with that is the whole thing would be tied up in legal battles and probate for years."

"But I'm not dead."

"Are you so sure of that?" Cowboi's smile turned menacing. "No one knows you're alive, Gemma. Your boat was lost at sea. But if you follow my lead, claim the trust, take the executive position on the marina board of directors, and move things along quickly, I can bring you back to life. A miraculous rescue."

Cowboi continued, "You just need to commit your grandmother to a care facility. Sign the papers, and everyone gets what they want."

Something stirred inside Gemma—not panic, but a deep, burning anger. She thought of Mari's weathered hands working healing magic, of the generations who had paid for Mariposa's End with blood.

"You don't understand who you're dealing with," she said softly.

Cowboi laughed. "Honey, I've done this before. I have proof of every illegal activity you've committed: drug and sex trafficking over international borders. A trail of bodies. Dead or not, I've got you cornered."

Gemma closed her eyes, feeling a tingle at the base of her skull. But instead of fighting it, she embraced it. She slowed her breath and listened.

I'm here. Vaughn's voice reassured her, clear as day. *We're all here.*

When she opened her eyes, Cowboi was staring at her, his smile faltering, his confidence slipping. "What's wrong with you?"

"You had Vaughn killed," she said, the truth crystallizing in her mind like ice. "He was investigating you for his book. The trafficking, the payoffs. The girls you brought to Easter Cay—many of whom never left. He knew everything, and you killed him for it."

Cowboi's face hardened, all pretense of charm vanishing. "That drunk was asking too many questions. Poking around where he didn't belong. No one will believe his delirious scribblings anyway."

Gemma rose from her seat, steadier than she'd felt in years. The certainty flooded through her like electricity. She held his gaze, refusing to flinch. "I'm not bluffing, Cowboi. I'll bring you down if you don't leave me and my people alone."

"You're in no position to make threats." Cowboi stood. "You're a small fish in very deep water."

"I have Vaughn's manuscript, yes. Perhaps the scribblings of a drunk. But better than that, I have records from the CIA operative who has been investigating you for over two years. Maybe the CIA's hands are tied, but I don't have the same limitation. I'm a free agent, and I have a full log of tracking data from nearly two hundred

Cowboi's End | 329

devices—everything backed up in multiple encrypted cloud vaults." She paused, watching his face change as he realized someone in his circle had been documenting everything. "In other words, everything goes to the FBI, Interpol, and every major news outlet if you don't do exactly what I say."

Cowboi took a long, slow drink of his bourbon.

"I'm talking irrefutable digital footprints," Gemma continued. "Politicians, celebrities, business moguls, even royalty—all tied to your island, along with a detailed narrative of what people do when they visit you. Your fans might enjoy the scandal, not that they'll keep buying your records; you'll be canceled. And your customers are not going to enjoy the news at all."

The silence stretched between them like an unplayed drumskin. Cowboi's face had gone pale beneath his tan.

"You're lying." Cowboi's eyes darted to the monitor showing security feeds, then back to her. For the first time since she'd known him, he looked genuinely afraid. "What do you want?"

"It's simple," Gemma said. "You leave Mariposa's End alone. Forever."

Cowboi laughed, but it sounded hollow. "You think you can just waltz in here and make demands?"

"I already have." Gemma's smile was as cold as winter. "The uploads will start automatically if I don't stop them—a dead man's switch, Cowboi. If anything happens to me, to Nihir, to Mari—everything goes public. Game over."

Cowboi stood, pushed a call button, and spoke into

the intercom. "Aldo, take our guests back to St. Columba. Our business is concluded."

Without saying anything more to Gemma or Nihir, Cowboi walked to the office door and clicked it shut behind him. Gemma felt something shift inside her chest —not relief, but a sense of completion. She had faced the monster and come out victorious.

Nihir's hand found hers. Mariposa's End was safe. Mari was safe. The trust would remain intact, the culture preserved, the land protected.

But more than that, Gemma had found herself—not a broken woman but a fierce protector. She had learned to trust what she knew, and what she knew was this: sometimes the only way out is through.

33

GREEN FLASH

The sun warmed Gemma's skin as tiny bananaquits darted between the sugar apple and calabash trees, their yellow breasts flashing like lemon drops. She walked the path that graduated from wild to cultivated, past towering ginger plants that stretched toward the sky. When she reached the gate, Yaya Mari was already waiting—thin and serene, framed by the vibrant greens of her Eden. The garden buzzed with bees from the apiary, and a huge, mangy rooster strutted between the rows of herbs like he owned the place.

"Come up, child," Yaya Mari called, her voice steady as granite.

Mari's eyes were sharp as ever, taking in Gemma with a knowing glance. It was one of the many things about her grandmother that was both comforting and unsettling—that penetrating gaze that seemed to see straight through to her soul. Mari turned without another word, leading her granddaughter toward the shaded porch.

"You've been away too long," Yaya Mari said, not unkindly, as she gestured for Gemma to sit. "But I knew you would return."

As Gemma sank into the woven vine chair on the shaded porch, the scent of freshly cut lemongrass drifted from the garden. Yaya Mari eased into her rocker opposite, her posture regal yet relaxed, as though the very air of Mariposa's End sustained her.

"The land welcomes you home," Mari said, pouring tea from a ceramic pot. Her tone was teasing but gentle. "Do you feel it too, or are you still too busy running from yourself to notice?"

Gemma accepted the criticism with a rueful smile. "I feel it, Yaya. More than I ever have."

Mari's weathered hands traced shimmering symbols in the air as she spoke in a low, steady voice. "This is the path of your bloodline. The spirits are watching. They know your fears, but they also recognize your strengths."

Her grandmother's eyes held knowledge that stretched beyond the physical world.

"I know about what happened with Cowboi," Mari said suddenly, her voice dropping to just above a whisper. "I know what he tried to do to you, child, and how you protected us. I know how you've kept him from devouring our lands with his plans. The ancestors are pleased with your resistance."

Gemma swallowed hard. "How do you know all that?"

"The spirits speak to me as they now speak to you. But

with me, it's an ongoing conversation, clear as the one I'm having with you." Mari's silver braids caught the sunlight as she shook her head. "Your training remains incomplete. The time has come for you to enter seclusion."

"For how long?" Gemma asked.

"A week. Not as our ancestors did for months, but enough." Her eyes softened. "This is not about abandoning your life, Gemma. Your Nihir understands more than you think. And your Vaughn—" she chuckled, "well, he will follow wherever you go. This ritual honors the old ways while acknowledging who you truly are—a modern woman."

Mari reached for a clay cup carved with intricate symbols that seemed to shift in the changing light. "The coal walk was just preparation. This is your transformation—from acolyte to priestess in your own right. You carry two worlds within you, child. Neither must be sacrificed for the other."

Gemma nodded, feeling something settle in her. Not quite peace—not yet—but acceptance. Perhaps even readiness.

Mari gently poured water infused with herbs over Gemma's head, the ritual cleansing cool against her scalp. It trickled down her face and soaked her clothes, each drop washing away another layer of resistance, another barrier between Gemma and the spiritual inheritance that had always been hers to claim.

The elders chanted softly as Mari led Gemma to the small hut where she would begin her seclusion. Vaughn's voice, quiet but firm, rose in her mind as she crossed the threshold. *This isn't just tradition, Gemma. Mari is preparing you for more fights ahead. Don't let the isolation fool you—it's where you'll find clarity.*

Inside, the world narrowed to the dim interior of the hut. A small altar had been prepared for her, its surface crowded with offerings: a bottle of rum, a handful of coins, a bundle of dried herbs, and a large ceramic bowl of water that reflected the flickering candlelight.

Gemma remained in this space, fasting and reflecting. The emptiness reminded her that she had been through far more harrowing rituals than this one, surrounded by friends and family just outside her walls.

By the second day, hunger sharpened her senses, and Vaughn's presence became a steady hum, his guidance keeping her grounded. The pangs in her belly transported her back to the uninhabited island, where survival had been a daily struggle rather than a spiritual exercise.

As she sat cross-legged on the earthen floor, Gemma's mind drifted to Captain Fairweather. She smiled, remembering how the bird had studied her with those black eyes that reflected intelligence beyond its small form. The way it had hopped closer each day, calculating its approach inch by inch, until it had finally landed on her open palm to say goodbye.

The island broke you down, Vaughn's voice drifted through her consciousness. *This ritual builds you up. Both are necessary.*

She nodded, understanding now why Mari had insisted on this traditional preparation. After experiencing the island's harsh lessons, this seclusion was not deprivation but refinement—not punishment but transformation.

The lionfish's sting in her dream had awakened something in her that could not be ignored or denied—a true conduit to the spirit world. Just as that pain had been the price of genuine contact with Vaughn, this hunger was the cost of spiritual clarity.

On the morning of the seventh day, Mari visited, her face impassive as stone. "You've endured the silence," she said, studying Gemma's face for signs of weakness or resistance. "Now you must endure the sound."

Gemma followed her grandmother back to the clearing, where the drummers awaited. Their hands hovered over taut skins, and at Mari's nod, the rhythm began—low and slow, building with each passing minute. The vibrations settled into Gemma's chest, syncing with her heartbeat. She swayed instinctively, her movements drawing her closer to the center of the circle.

As the drums quickened, Mari sprinkled a mixture of ash and crushed herbs around her, creating a sacred barrier between Gemma and the outside world. The rhythm pushed her deeper into herself, and soon, Vaughn's voice transformed from a whisper into a commanding presence in her mind. *This is it, Gemma. Don't resist. Let them in.*

The first possession hit her like a storm crashing over rocks. Her body jerked, her limbs moving in ways she couldn't control, guided by forces beyond her understanding. The spirit's presence enveloped her completely—ancient, vast, and knowing. The energy surged and ebbed, leaving her breathless yet strangely calm. The elders observed in reverent silence as Mari nodded her approval.

When the spirits released her, Gemma collapsed to her knees, trembling. Mari knelt beside her, brushing a damp strand of hair from her face. "You are not finished," she said softly. "But you are ready."

That night, as she sat by the dying fire, Vaughn materialized more clearly than ever before. "You have the power to protect Mariposa's End," he said. "But don't let power consume you. You have seen what it does to people."

Gemma nodded, her gaze fixed on the flames. "I won't. I have too much to lose now."

Vaughn smiled faintly, his form flickering like the embers. "Good. Because this isn't just about you—it's about everyone who came before and everyone who will come after."

In the morning light, Gemma faced the small crowd gathered in the sandy clearing near Yaya Mari's house. They had come because Mari had summoned them. It was time for Gemma to assume her rightful role, a position that had always belonged to her but had never been claimed by her heart until now. Mari, now in her 80s, was ready to pass the role down to her granddaughter. Gemma could feel Vaughn's presence beside her, his approval a subtle whisper in her ear.

"I won't let Cowboi or anyone else take our land from us," Gemma began, her voice carrying the weight of years spent denying her destiny. "Mariposa's End has belonged to us for generations. We've watched outsiders try to seize what doesn't belong to them, but we won't allow it anymore."

The elders' eyes held cautious hope. They had witnessed promises before. It was up to Gemma to prove she was different.

"I am stepping into my role as the leader of Mariposa's End," she continued. "Mari and the elders have granted this responsibility to me. We need decisive action and new ideas during this time of change. I intend to honor that role in a way that protects both our heritage and our future. We possess something that money can't buy—our history, our connection to this land, our way of life."

A murmur ran through the crowd. Some nodded, their faith in her growing, while others exchanged skeptical glances. Gemma met their eyes, steady and resolute.

Taking a deep breath, she felt the weight of what she was about to say. "Cowboi Rivers built his empire on the blood of the innocents. That empire is crumbling now, and justice will be served. But our work here isn't finished. There will be others like him—developers, politicians, anyone who sees our home as nothing more than profit waiting to be extracted."

The murmurs grew louder as more people nodded in approval. Gemma let her words sink in, feeling the shift in the air. She finished with a promise that rang like a bell. "I know there are doubts about whether I'm the right person to lead this fight. My blood is mixed; my path has been crooked. But I promise you—I won't rest until Sargasso

Cove and Mariposa's End are safe for our children and their children."

The people of the End exchanged glances, and one by one, they nodded. Yaya Mari spoke with quiet conviction. "The spirits are on our side."

The crowd filed down to the beach for the final ceremony, a procession of vibrant colors and expectant faces winding along the sandy path. This time, it wasn't just the joining of a woman with her community or with her guardian spirit, but the sacred union of wife and husband—a celebration of love amidst the ongoing struggle for their homeland. Gemma walked with Yaya Mari at her side. The old woman leaned on her carved staff, her movements slow yet deliberate, each footprint in the sand a testament to decades of protecting these shores.

As they approached the circle laid for the ceremony, a shimmer appeared in the golden evening light—subtle at first, then unmistakable. The ghostly form of William August materialized beside them, his vivid presence causing a hush to fall over the gathered witnesses. Gemma's breath caught in her throat as her father's spirit took shape, more solid than she had ever seen him, his warm smile exactly as she remembered from childhood. Though he had been taken from her when she was young, there was no mistaking him—he had her same determined jawline and expressive eyes.

William's spectral hand reached out to rest upon his daughter's shoulder, a touch she felt as a warm current running through her bones. His eyes, luminous and otherworldly, held both joy and pride as he gazed at the woman his little girl had become. Those close enough to see him gasped softly. Yaya Mari simply nodded in acknowledgment, as if she had expected his arrival all along.

"He's come to give away the bride," Mari whispered, her voice cracking with emotion. "The veil is thin today."

William moved to Gemma's side, opposite Mari, completing the family trio. Together, they continued toward Nihir, who waited at the circle's edge, his face reflecting wonder at the supernatural blessing that had descended upon their union. The ghost of Gemma's father would remain just long enough to place his daughter's hand in Nihir's before dissolving into the evening breeze, leaving behind only the faintest scent of jasmine.

Smoke from the ceremonial fires filled the air, and a stirring quickened within her as the spirits of her ancestors infused her with their strength and wisdom. She stepped onto the sand, raising her new staff—a gift from Mari, carved with protective symbols—in acknowledgment of her role. The drummers began, their steady rhythms echoing through the cove.

Gemma stood at the center of it all, her flowing white gown catching the breeze off the water. The fabric seemed to shimmer with its own inner light—white and electric blue that danced around her like captured lightning. Nihir joined her, their eyes locked, filled with an intensity that spoke of their shared struggles and unshakable bond. Together, they swayed to the ancient rhythm, enveloped in a whirlwind of spiritual power that connected them to lovers past and future.

Yaya Mari crossed Gemma's and Nihir's foreheads with symbols of joining. As the sun set, painting the sky in brilliant shades of orange and pink, the community erupted in dance, their movements a shared rhythm of joy and defiance. Children wove between the adults, their laughter ringing out over the sound of waves.

Gemma and Nihir stood hand in hand as husband and wife, as guardians of something precious and irreplaceable. The end radiated with joy and determination—a testament to their resilience and their refusal to surrender what was theirs. As the night deepened, stars cast a net upon the sea, and Gemma gazed out over the water that had carried her through so much darkness toward this moment of hope.

As the fire burned low, Gemma and Nihir settled in the warm sand, both watching the glowing embers pop and hiss.

"Tonight was beautiful," Gemma said softly, her head resting against his shoulder.

"You were beautiful," Nihir replied, pressing a kiss to the top of her head. "I've never seen you so... powerful. And so at peace."

The next morning, the beach was quiet. Gemma and Nihir had slept in a nest of handmade quilts that the community had wrapped around them. They were unwilling to break the spell of the previous night by returning to ordinary walls and ceilings.

Gemma inhaled deeply and closed her eyes, focusing

on Vaughn. He was always strongest in the quiet moments, and now she felt a genuine connection to him, able to call on his presence at will rather than waiting for him to appear unbidden.

"There you are, you old crust of bread," she laughed, her hands resting on her knees.

"I'm here," his voice came clearly. "*Dream* is yours now. She's a wreck, but I know you can restore her to her former glory."

"Your boat? You want me to fix her up?"

"She needs someone who understands what she's meant for. Someone who won't give up on her."

That afternoon, Gemma and Nihir motored out to where *Dream* sat at anchor. Once a beauty—a sleek bluewater cruiser built for crossing oceans—time had not been kind. The deck was delaminating, the mast was missing entirely, and the interior would have to be ripped out and completely rebuilt.

"Not as turnkey as the *Mariposa*," Nihir said with a wry smile, running his hand along the cracked gelcoat.

Gemma smirked. "Easy isn't always better."

Days passed in a blur of sandpaper, sawdust, and blistered hands. They applied gleaming coats of Awlgrip that brought out the graceful lines of her design. While the boatyard crew handled the re-rigging—installing a new mast and running fresh lines—Gemma focused on the interior. She reupholstered cushions and slowly brought *Dream* back to life. In the secret compartment lay Vaughn's legacy: the hard drives labeled "Easter Cay." This was what he had died for—the manuscript and the CIA records of every powerful person who had used Cowboi's services.

Nihir settled beside Gemma on the cushioned bench on the deck of *Dream*, watching the sun sink, its fiery orb hanging low over the water. Suddenly, a brilliant green flash pierced the sky as it disappeared below the horizon —a rare phenomenon lasting only a heartbeat but twinkling like an emerald jewel. Gemma gasped and clutched Nihir's hand, mesmerized by the otherworldly light.

"A good omen," Nihir said, filled with awe.

Gemma nodded, her heart swelling. It wasn't just a flash of light; it was a promise, a reminder that even in the face of darkness, brilliance could emerge. Together, they stood, ready to embrace whatever came next.

LETTER TO THE READER

I'd love to hear your thoughts! Please consider leaving a review on Amazon, Goodreads, or your favorite book review site. Every review, whether positive or critical, is deeply appreciated and helps other readers discover the book. Your feedback means the world to me.

ACKNOWLEDGMENTS

With gratitude to my husband, Kelly Turner, and my son, Buckaroo St. John, for their steadfast support; to Richard Ljoenes for his striking cover design; and to Jillian Mixon for her invaluable assistance. My thanks as well to the many friends, family, and mentors whose encouragement helped bring *Day Drinkers* to life.

ABOUT THE AUTHOR

Kitty Turner's circus and showgirl career spanned five years. Until 2017, she toured the Caribbean casino and resort circuit along the Antilles chain with her husband and a rotating cast of international circus performers aboard a 47 foot sailboat.

Before moving to the Caribbean in 2007, Kitty co-owned the award-winning nightclub 12 Galaxies in the Mission District of San Francisco. After hurricanes Irma and Maria destroyed her sailboat home, Kitty relocated to the Reno area and founded the book marketing company Daily House Media. Visit https://www.kittyturner.media/ for more.

ALSO BY KITTY TURNER

Zone Trip

Made in United States
Cleveland, OH
22 September 2025